EOLINE

OR

MAGNOLIA VALE

A DAY IN MAGNOLIA VALE.

EOLINE

OR

MAGNOLIA VALE

A NOVEL

By
Mrs. Caroline Lee (Whiting) Hentz

American Fiction Reprint Series

BOOKS FOR LIBRARIES PRESS
FREEPORT, NEW YORK
1971

First published in 1852
(Item #1157; Wright's AMERICAN FICTION 1851-1875)

Reprinted 1971 in *American Fiction Reprint Series*
from the T. B. Peterson edition

INTERNATIONAL STANDARD BOOK NUMBER:
0-8369-7041-1

LIBRARY OF CONGRESS CATALOG CARD NUMBER:
77-164564

PRINTED IN THE UNITED STATES OF AMERICA

EOLINE;

OR,

MAGNOLIA VALE.

BY MRS. CAROLINE LEE HENTZ

AUTHOR OF "LINDA," "RENA," "COURTSHIP AND MARRIAGE," "LOVE
AFTER MARRIAGE,," "THE BANISHED SON," ETC.

"His fair locks waved in sunny play
By a clear fountain's side,
Where jewel-colour'd pebbles lay
Beneath the flowing tide.
And if my heart had deem'd him fair,
When in the fountain glade,
A creature of the sky and air,
Almost on wings he play'd;
Oh! how much holier beauty now
Lit that young human being's brow!"—*Hemans.*

Philadelphia:
T. B. PETERSON, NO. 102 CHESTNUT STREET.

157400

Printed by T. K. & P. G. Collins.

THE FOLLOWING PAGES

ARE DEDICATED

TO

MRS. OCTAVIA W. LEVERT,

AS AN EXPRESSION OF THE

SINCERE FRIENDSHIP AND ADMIRATION

OF

THE AUTHOR.

EOLINE:

OR,

MAGNOLIA VALE.

CHAPTER I.

A cheerful fire burned on the hearth. An elegant sofa was wheeled directly in front of it, and an embroidered footstool placed ready for the feet of the expected occupant.

Mr. Glenmore, a portly and commanding looking man, in purple velvet slippers, and silver gray wadded silk wrapper, his evening costume, entered and took his accustomed seat.

A young girl was flitting from window to window, unfastening the curtains and arranging the folds, as they fell in rich volumes to the floor. After she had thus brought out the fire-light and lamp-light into brighter relief by the scarlet and orange colored drapery on which they flashed, she looked around with a smiling countenance, as if pleased with the air of home-born comfort and luxury that pervaded the room. Then she put a green shade over the lamp to soften its moonlight splendor, and drew a beautiful transparent screen before her father, so as to intercept the too glowing heat of the fire.

(5)

" And now," said she, seating herself at the piano and
running over the keys with sparkling fingers, " now for
your evening serenade, father."

She began to warble with the sweetness and volubility
of the mocking bird.

" That is a new song I have just learned. Is it not
charming?"

"I am not in a musical vein to-night, Eoline."

"Are you not? I am sorry, for I feel most particularly
melodious. I am sorry, too, my harp is unstrung—that
might please you better? (No.) Would you like the guitar?
(No, again.) Well I will not plague you with music. But
let me tell you the compliment that Mr. Leslie, the European traveller, paid me last evening. He said he wished
I were the daughter of a poor man, so that I might be
compelled to give my voice to the world; that nature never
bestowed such a treasure for the benefit of the domestic
and social circles alone. Think of that, father—a prima
donna! Would it not be magnificent? Well, if your
riches should take to themselves wings and fly away, I will
turn my breath into gold for you and me."

" There is not much danger of your being reduced to
such an alternative," said Mr. Glenmore, " especially at
the present moment."

"You don't feel musical to-night. Let me read to you;
I have a very interesting book here, whose leaves I have
just cut open."

Rising from the revolving-stool, on which she had been
making semi-circumvolutions, she opened a mahogany cabi-
net, inlaid with ivory, and took down a book, evidently
fresh from the press.

"Oh! how I love the fragrance of a new book!" she
cried, unfolding it and burying her face within the leaves.
" It is as sweet as a new-blown rose."

" Put up the book," said Mr. Glenmore, crossing his arms

majestically over his breast, and uttering an imposing hem.
" I am not in a literary humor."

"Indeed! then I will get the chess-board!"

" No, I am not in a mood for chess, either."

" A game of backgammon, perhaps," continued the
persevering Eoline, who seemed anxious to entertain her
father in any other way than conversation.   There was
something restless and excited about her, which she endeavored to conceal under an aspect of gay good humor.

" I am sorry I cannot amuse you sir," said she.   " If
you please, I will take my book and sit quietly and demurely in the corner, like a good little girl, without
disturbing your meditations."

" You are not so very little, Eoline—quite a full grown,
marriageable young lady."

" Don't call me marriageable, father ; I cannot bear that
expression—and whatever I may be to others, let me be
still a little girl to you."

Seating herself on the curving elbow of the sofa, she put
one 'arm caressingly round his neck, and laid her cheek
against his hair.

" Come, Eoline," said he, gravely kissing her, then taking
her hand and seating her on the sofa by his side—" this is
all very sweet and very pretty, but just now I want you
to be serious, and give your undivided attention to what I
have to say.   I have had a long interview with Mr. Cleveland."

Eoline started, but said nothing

" He thinks with me, that there is no use in delay.   Time
can make no difference in our intentions."

" Neither can it in mine," answered Eoline, with a low
voice and heightened color.

" I know of no intentions a young lady can have
in opposition to a parent's will," said Mr. Glenmore, with

great emphasis. "At least, I do not admit the possibility of their existence."

"They may, however, have as deep a life as if the admission were made," replied the daughter.

"I am not about to engage in a useless discussion," said Mr. Glenmore, uttering his words coldly and deliberately, giving each their due weight and accent; "my own mind is made up, and nothing can change its decision. When Horace was a little boy, and you a passive infant in your mother's arms, it was made up. When he was a youth in college, and you a child at school, it was confirmed. And now he is a young man, returned from abroad with a completed education and established character, and you in the bloom of young womanhood, it is fixed immutable as the decree of destiny. Mr. Cleveland has no more idea of change than I have. Horace has consented to obey his father, and I expect and require the same obedience from my own child."

"Consented to obey!" repeated Eoline, her cheeks burning with crimson—"consented to obey! And you would force your daughter on the acceptance of a young man who cares not for her—who even looks upon her with repugnance—whose consent to such an union is considered a noble sacrifice to filial obedience! Father! if you have so little family pride and dignity, so little regard for my delicacy and sensibility, I at least know what is due to my own character. I never will be a party in such a transaction."

"Eoline, have you done."

"No sir—nor will I ever cease, till you think as I think, till you feel as I feel. I pray I may not forget what is due to my father—but I must remember that I am a woman— a very young one, it is true, but no less sensitive on that account. Horace Cleveland loves me not. To me, he is ever cold, distant, reserved, and haughty. There is an expression in his eye, that makes me shrink into myself, whenever I meet him—I fear him. He dislikes me. There is a mutual repulsion, that never will be overcome. Obedience in such a case, instead of being a virtue is a sin. 'Tis sacrilege—and God will judge it so."

"Enough, enough!" interrupted Mr. Glenmore, impatiently; "I did not know that you could talk so finely. You are really quite an orator; but I tell you, Eoline, it is all stuff and nonsense. Horace Cleveland is a young man of fine principles, splendid talents, the heir of a large fortune, and the son of my earliest friend. There is not a more desirable match in the country. He is willing to marry you—and this is a sufficient proof of his love. He is no dandy or fop, no petty lady's man, I know; but he is made of better, sterner materials. If you expect the fooleries and raptures of which you read in novels, you may be disappointed, and deserve to be so. As for his being cold and haughty, you have made him so, by your own pride and reserve. It is you that freeze him into an iceberg, and then complain of his coldness."

"I do not complain," said Eoline, in a tone of the deepest dejection; "I care not for him or his coldness. I grieve to think that you are so anxious to rid yourself of me, as if I were a burden to your care. Ever since my mother's death," continued she—tears forcing themselves into her eyes, and glittering on their fringes, "I have tried to make your happiness my first care. I have never known a wish of yours that I have not endeavored to fulfill. Oh, my dear father, I know you do love me; I know you must want to make me happy. Let me be so," she cried, impulsively throwing her arms around him, and kneeling on the footstool in a most supplicating attitude, "let me remain with you, just as I am, and require not of me the only act of filial obedience, I would not gladly, unhesitatingly perform."

Mr. Glenmore seemed agitated, and struggled to free
himself from the soft arms that imprisoned him.

" You are right," said he, " I do love you—I do wish
your happiness ; and I know better than yourself, how to
secure it. You will thank me, one day, for the authority
I now exert. Eoline, you must obey me in this. You
must marry Horace Cleveland."

His voice assumed a tone of stern determination. " I
have said it," he added, "more than once—and did you
ever know me declare positively that a thing should be,
that I did not bring it to pass? Did you ever? Look me
in the face, Eoline, and tell me."

Eoline rose up, and shading back her hair with one hand,
looked him for a moment steadily in the face. There was
something in the expression of her now pale and resolute
countenance, that made him involuntarily rise also. The
dark shade of anger hung heavy on his brow.

" Well, young lady, do you see any symptom of weakness
or change ?"

" No, sir."

" Then policy, if not duty, must teach you submission."

" Father, I cannot marry Horace Cleveland !"

" Do you dare to tell me this, when it is my absolute
will that you should ?"

" I dare, when your will is contrary to a higher will."

Mr. Glenmore was a man who never could endure the
slightest contradiction, even in matters of the most trivial
import. He knew of no sovereign more absolute than his
own will, no rule of right or wrong but what he himself
established. What he had once *said*, must be, because he
had said it. That Eoline, so gentle, and yielding in all
minor things, so child-like and affectionate in her daily
demeanor, so attentive to all the sweet courtesies of life,
so anxious to please him in the minutest particular, so fearful of offending and inflicting pain, should now undauntedly

brave his authority, resist his will, and thwart the favorite plan he had been maturing from her infancy—he could not, would not believe. Yet there she stood before him, pale, calm, and self-possessed, with "*cannot*" on her lips, and "*will not*" in her clear, blue eye.

He actually trembled with passion. His under lip quivered like an aspen-leaf. The stamps of the horse-shoe grew deeper and deeper between his eyes.

"Mark my words," said he, in a husky voice, "if you persist in this rebellion, I will no longer consider you as my daughter. I will no longer be responsible for your support. The independence in which you glory, shall be your only inheritance. I will neither share my home, nor my fortune, with an ingrate who mocks at my authority, and resists my will. This is the alternative—choose this moment. On one side, wealth, talents, influence, friends. and favor—on the other, poverty, disgrace, and banishment."

"My choice is made, then," was the low, but distinct reply. "Be it poverty and banishment—it cannot be disgrace."

"Insufferable—insolent," exclaimed Mr. Glenmore, pushing back the sofa, till it rolled half across the room, and sweeping down the whole length of the apartment so rapidly, that his gray, silk robe seemed to shiver as he walked, "I never saw such a girl in my life. She is enough to drive one mad."

After working off in this way some of the superfluity of his passion, he suddenly stopped, and measuring her deliberately from head to foot, added:

"I should like you to tell me, Miss Eoline Glenmore, what you intend to do, when you launch out into the world—a prima donna, perhaps. That will be admirable. I dare say you will find some itinerant Italian to take charge of you, and give eclat to your debut?"

" Father, this is unworthy of you," said the young girl, with a dignity and spirit that gave fire to her eye, and elevation to her tone. " 'Tis an unmanly blow, and the hand that strikes it ought to burn with shame." Pausing, and trying to hold down her wounded and indignant feelings, she added with less warmth, but equal dignity, " with the education you have given me, and which you cannot withdraw, I shall have ample means of support. You will give me time to seek another home. You will not have it said that you turned your daughter from your own door before another was opened to receive her ?"

" I give you one month for reflection," said the father, in a calm tone, after a long pause, for though unmoved in his determination, he began to be ashamed of the violence he had betrayed. " Horace left home this morning to be absent that space of time. After giving you this long day of grace, if you persist in your obstinacy, on your own head be the consequences of your disobedience. I have done my duty as a father. I have spared no expense on your education. I have allowed you every luxury and indulgence, and made you the envy of your young companions. Every one knows that I have been an indulgent parent. Every one knows the character of Horace Cleveland. The world may judge between us. My conscience is clear. The shame and obloquy, whatever they be, will rest on you."

" But to be forced on a cold and reluctant bridegroom !" exclaimed Eoline, suddenly losing all her self-control, and bursting into a wild passion of tears—" to feel indifference and to fear hatred—oh—my dear father—you do not know what it is. It would kill me. Such a life would dry up my heart's blood. Have pity on me and give me back your love. Let me stay with you, and be to you all and ten thousand times more than I ever yet have been."

"Every thing depends on yourself, Eoline. You have a month of probation. Improve it well, for, remember, at its close, the door will be shut. You had better retire now, some one might enter and wonder at your agitation."

Eoline, still sobbing, took two or three steps towards the door, then lingered and returned.

"Will you not let me kiss you, father?" said she, gently. "I cannot sleep without your good-night blessing."

"Strange, incomprehensible girl that you are!" cried the more *strange* and *incomprehensible* father, kissing her moist cheek.

"Promise me one thing," she said. "Let us not speak of this subject till the month is past. Let every thing be as it has been before."

"Very well. I have no objection to such a compact. It is best upon the whole."

And the father and the daughter separated for the night.

The Cleveland and Glenmore estates were not only adjacent, but bore such an exact similitude to each other, that they seemed a twin-born pair. Nature had spread out two magnificent plains, side by side, and divided them by a line of forest trees so regularly, that the boundary seemed drawn by the hand of art. These rich plains sloped towards the rising sun, and its setting rays dyed with rosy gold the waters of a noble creek that flowed at an equal distance in the rear of the dwellings. From the centre of twin groves of oak, each stately tree the counterpart of the other, rose two granite houses, of the same imposing architecture. Massy rows of columns formed a colonnade to three sides of the mansions, which being elevated from the earth, were approached by a long flight of marble steps. The gardens and green houses were on the

71

same model; and as Dromio, in the play, could see by his
twin-brother that he was a "sweet faced youth," so Mr
Glenmore could behold his own magnificence reflected in
that of his friend, and Mr. Cleveland could admire his
own taste in the beautiful grounds of his neighbor. Thus
their mutual pride and vain glory were fed. They were
equally wealthy, equally prosperous, so they had no occasion to envy each other. When they purchased the two
lots so exactly corresponding to each other, they agreed to
put up habitations, neither more nor less grand, whose
beauty should be the admiration of the surrounding country. Even before the birth of their children they decided
upon the union which was to continue the fellowship of
interests through other generations. Unfortunately their
eldest children were both boys. It was not till the birth
of his third child, the Eoline of our story, that Mr. Glenmore saw a prospect of their mutual wishes being realized.
Horace was then between five and six years old, and when
carried by his father to see his little wife, he very ungal-
lantly declared that " he did not want a little wife, and he
wouldn't have her." Fortunately Eoline was not conscious of this slight to her infantine charms, and it did not
disturb the happiness of her baby heart. But the boy,
often forced into unwilling juxtaposition with the little
lady, sometimes compelled to sit on the carpet, with his
legs stretched out in a horizontal position, and hold his
miniature bride in his arms;—at others, which was a still
more awful infliction, condemned to the tortures of being
dressed in juvenile finery, and carried abroad with his baby
betrothal, to elicit the admiration of the whole neighborhood; learned to associate the idea of compulsion, restraint and weariness of sport with the innocent Eoline.
As they grew older, and met as school-children, in their
holiday amusements, he was constantly reminded that he
must take care of Eoline—if they walked, he was to be

her companion—if they danced, her partner. When he was in college, and she at a boarding school, and they again met in their vacations under their parents' roof, the sensitive and reserved youth avoided more and more the bright and beautiful girl, who laughed at his awkwardness, which formed indeed a striking contrast to her own remarkable grace. And when, after years of study and travel, he returned a deeply read and accomplished scholar, to his country and home, and found Eoline presiding with youthful dignity over her widowed father's household, his manners, though no longer awkward, were to her singularly cold and distant. The associations of his childhood, the coercion, the discipline in the graces he had endured on her account, were fresh in his recollection, and neutralized the effect of her blooming attractions. Eoline, already accustomed to spontaneous admiration, and beginning to feel it a natural consequence of her presence, was chilled by his indifference and stung by his avoidance During his absence, she had heard so much of his splendid talents, his extraordinary acquirements and improvement in all exterior accomplishments, that she was prepared to welcome him with the modest warmth peculiar to her character. She forgot the strange, shy, and ofttimes rude boy. Her imagination pictured the intellectual, cultivated and polished young man. She looked forward with interest and anxiety to a re-union on which so much depended, wishing most earnestly that duty and inclination might go hand in hand. It is no wonder that her feelings recoiled upon herself, repelled by his cold reserve and studied indifference. The gay, frank, and genial manners froze in his presence, like a sparkling fountain congealed by a sudden frost. Become as cold as himself, they created around each other an icy atmosphere in which no flower of feeling could bloom, no fragrance of sensibility be diffused. The parents, disappointed and vexed at a state of things so con trary to their wishes, resolved to hasten the marriage in spite of these inauspicious omens. The result of their conference has been seen in the conversation between Eoline and her father—but he withheld from her one clause of the consent of Horace. It was on the condition that Eoline *herself* desired the union, that he promised his own obedience. Acceptance or rejection was left in her hands. That her high spirit and warm heart should refuse their sanction to parental authority exerted for the consummation of this unnatural scheme—that her pride and delicacy, and self-respect should shrink with horror from their commanded sacrifice, can exite no wonder. But when a young girl, nurtured in the bosom of affluence and luxury, prefers the alternative of poverty, banishment, and self-support, to the immolation of her principles and her feelings, she exalts herself into a heroine, and as such her history is worthy to be recorded.

The month of probation was rapidly passing away. Eoline devoted herself, as usual, to her father's comfort and happiness. If possible, she was more assiduous, more solicitous to anticipate his slightest want. There were certain duties which she considered sacred, and which she would never allow a servant to perform; such as bringing him his evening wrapper, his slippers, which her own hand had embroidered, and arranging the lights and curtains, so as to produce that mellow illumination so pleasing to the eye. She wanted to make herself necessary to his happiness, to fill up with sweet and loving cares the void in his household and the loneliness of his heart, so that he might not bring a stranger under their roof, to occupy the place made vacant by Death. Her two elder brothers had died in infancy, but she had one younger than herself by eleven years, a beautiful boy of about six years old, to whom she bore the charming relation of young mother-sister. An excellent lady by the name of Howe, was the nominal

nurse as well as housekeeper at Glenmore, but Eoline made
the first office a sinecure as soon as she quitted school.
For two years he had been her pupil, brother, child. Lovely as a little Cupid, caressing, yet spirited and intelligent
beyond his age, Willie was the pet and darling of the
household, and the especial idol of Eoline. She always
went into the nursery at his bed-time, told him some childish story, listened to his bright little sayings, and heard his
innocent prayers.

One night, it was exactly at the end of the month, she
made her accustomed visit. Willie, the moment she
opened the door, sprang up, caught her round the neck,
and almost smothered her with kisses. He had been sitting
by the fire, till his cheeks were as glowing as roses. His
soft auburn hair fell curling to the edge of his white night-
dress, and his eyes sparkled like star-lit dew-drops. Eoline,
still holding him in her arms, sat down on a low seat near
the hearth, and bent her face down on the plump, white
shoulder, that peeped above the collar of his robe.

"What's the matter, sister Ela?" said the boy, nestling
closer to her, "you are making it rain on my neck."

"Never mind, Willie," cried she, trying to command
her voice, "it will soon be sunshine!"

"But what for makes you cry, Ela?" persisted the child,
feeling the warm drops falling thicker and faster on his
cheek and neck; "if anybody's hurt you," continued he, in
a louder tone, and clinching his fist bravely in her face,
"I'll fight them like a lion!"

"No Willie, it is not that," answered Eoline, wiping
the moisture from his soft skin with her handkerchief, and
then drying it still more with her kisses, "perhaps I shall
have to take a journey, and be gone a long time—and it
makes me very sad to think of leaving you behind."

"You shan't leave me behind!" exclaimed the boy,
jumping from her lap, and assuming a resolute attitude,—

"if you go, I'll go, too. I don't care how far off it is. If it is way off to Nova Zembla I'll keep tight hold of you, all the time. But where are you going, sister,—and how long are you going to stay?—and what for are you going at all?"

"I cannot answer all these questions at once, dear Willie, nor indeed any of them to-night. If I do go, you shall know all about it."

"To be sure I shall," cried Willie, positively, "for I shall go too."

And with the quick, changing feelings of childhood, he laughed triumphantly at the thought.

"Oh, that I could take you with me, my own darling Willie," cried she, with a burst of emotion she could not repress, and clasping him tightly to her bosom. "But father will not consent, and you must promise to be a good boy while I am gone, and love me as you now do even if— even if—"

Once more her face was buried on his neck, and he felt the rain-drops on its snow. Mrs. Howe, who was sitting on the opposite side of the room, busy with her needle, now lifted her kind, serious countenance, and gazed with sympathizing tenderness on the young mother-sister, thus bitterly weeping over the distressed and wondering boy.

There was another pair of big black eyes fixed upon her face, watching her every movement. Gatty, a negro girl, her own waiting-maid, who was sitting on the carpet by the side of Willie's bed, had observed, with affectionate interest and increasing curiosity, the thoughtful, abstracted, and ofttimes sad mood of her young mistress for weeks past. She dared not question her, for Eoline, though kind and gentle, had never indulged in familiarity with her servants.

"I hope, Miss Eoline," said Mrs. Howe, "that nothing

has happened to make you unhappy, and I trust that you are not going to leave us long."

"I cannot tell how long, Mrs. Howe! God only knows. But, for my sake, watch over this dear boy, and keep him if possible from evil. I would not have him associate with rude companions, and lose all his sweet and gentle, though brave and boyish ways, for ten thousand worlds. And one thing, my dear Mrs. Howe, never let him forget the prayers I have taught him. Yes, Willie, never, never close your eyes in sleep, without kneeling by your bedside and repeating to your God the prayers you have learned at your sister's knees."

Willie, who was awed by the sad and solemn tone of his sister, so different from her usual joyous accents, and who already felt the downy weight of slumber on his eyelids, whispered—

"Let me say them now, Ela."

Sinking on his knees, and folding his fair hands on her lap, Willie lifted his beautiful auburn eyes, in which the tears were still shining, and commencing with the simple, yet sublime adjuration—

"Our Father who art in heaven," went through the divine ritual of prayer, prescribed by our Saviour, with such devotional earnestness, that as the words issued from his cherub lips—"surely, surely," thought Eoline, "'Of such is the Kingdom of Heaven.'"

Leading him to his little couch, and covering him up for his night's slumber, she lingered, as if unwilling to leave him. Overcome with sleepiness, he half opened hi heavy eyelids, and murmured—

"You won't go to-night, sister Ela?"

"No—not to-night, my darling. Good-night—the holy angels guard you."

Then softly kissing him, she stole away from the bed, and approaching the fire, stood with her head leaning against the mantel-piece, lost in deep abstraction. She was startled by the voice of Mrs. Howe.

"I fear you are not well, Miss Eoline; can I do anything for you?"

"No—oh, no, I thank you; nothing can be done. To-morrow, Mrs. Howe, everything will be decided, and I will tell you all. I did not think I was so weak. My father must not see me in tears."

She bathed her face with water, brushed and arranged her hair, which Willie had loosened by his impassioned caresses, and smoothed the lace his hands had ruffled.

"There, Mrs. Howe, will that do?" she asked, trying to smile. "Father never likes to see a fold out of place, or a ringlet disordered."

"You look very nice and sweet, as you always do," replied she, with a deep sigh. She could not help sighing, for she saw there was something heavy on the heart of Eoline; and if it should involve her departure from home, it would press very heavily on her own.

Eoline descended with slow steps into the sitting-room, where her father sat, in his robe of silver gray, in front of the glowing hearth. He did not raise his head at her entrance, nor when she came and stood by the table, where the lamp, with its soft green shade, resembled the moon, glimmering through, or beneath a leafy canopy.

"Father," at length she said, in a low voice, "the month of my probation is expired."

He raised his head, and their eyes met. They looked at each other a moment, without speaking, reading steadily in that fixed gaze, the inflexible purpose of each other's soul. Her color changed, her limbs trembled, but still her eye quailed not before the severe and iron glance of his.

"Well, what is your decision?" said Mr. Glenmore. "You have had time enough given to recover your senses, and I trust you have profited by it."

"I did not ask for time, father, it could make no change in me."

"Nor in me, either, by Heaven?" exclaimed Mr. Glenmore, striking the arm of the sofa vehemently, with his closed hand. "Nor in me, either, as you will find to your cost."

"I have counted the cost," she replied, gathering courage and self-possession from his violence and severity. "I am willing to abide it. I know not what trials may be before me, but I can imagine nothing so dreadful as the loveless union you would force upon me. I have written to my friends, and secured through their influence, a respectable situation!"

"Respectable situation!" interrupted Mr. Glenmore, to hear my daughter talking of having secured a respectable situation! Never use such a phrase in my presence again!"

"A comfortable home, then, sir, if the expression offend you less."

"A comfortable Lunatic Asylum, you had better say," cried the father, walking about the room, and wiping his forehead elaborately with his handkerchief. "Really, the only thing I ought to do with you, is to put you in a straight-jacket, and feed you on bread and water. Respectable situation!—comfortable home! That I, Kingsly Glenmore, should live to hear a daughter of mine demean herself in this manner."

"When my father refuses me his protection and support," said Eoline, her lips curling with an expression she tried in vain to subdue, "what better can his daughter do? I should like to have you tell me, sir?"

"Obstinate fool!" muttered he. "Maniac, Idiot!"

"Permit me to tell you, sir, of my future destination," said Eoline, maintaining her calm demeanor. "I nave obtained the office of music teacher, since the word *situa*

tion displeases you, in Miss Manly's Classical Seminary
for Young Ladies, at Magnolia Vale, in Montebello. I trust
you will allow me to take my harp and guitar, as they
were both presents from my uncle, and they will be essen-
tials of my new existence."

"Yes, take them, take them, and every thing that belongs
to you," cried he passionately—"I want nothing left to
remind me of my disgrace."

Eoline heaved a deep sigh, and going towards her harp,
she began to draw the green covering over its gilded frame
and glittering wires. As she thus stood, with her head
slightly averted, and her arms raised in an unconsciously
graceful position, her father checked his angry steps and
gazed upon her with feelings of involuntary respect and
admiration, mingled with his wrath.

No one that looked upon the fair, sweet face, and girlish form of Eoline, would dream of the brave, undaunted
spirit, the firm self-reliance, and moral courage that formed
the deep under stratum of her character. Her gentleness,
modesty and sensibility were visible in her countenance
and *audible* in the tones of a voice, which, whether in
speaking or singing, discoursed the sweetest music. Her
complexion had the fairness of the magnolia blended with
the blush of the rose. Her hair, of a pale golden brown,
reminded one of the ripples of a sunlit lake by its soft
waves, giving beautiful alternations of light and shade, as
it flowed back from her face into the silver comb that confined its luxuriance. So naturally and gracefully was it
arranged, that it seemed as if the bright tresses meeting
with an impediment in their wild sport, formed themselves
into an eddy round the ornament that restrained them.
Her eyes, blue, soft and intense as the noonday sky in
June, had a kind of beseeching loving expression,—an expression that appealed for sympathy, protection, love,—
and her mouth had that winning contour, which suggests

the idea of a slumbering smile. Such was Eoline in repose, a fair, delicate, and lovely young girl, in appearance the tender and blue-eyed daughter of Dunthalmo, whose blushing face was turned from the sons of Morven; but in heart and spirit she was the fair-haired maid of Inis-huna, who, when the chiefs of Selma slept, went forth alone into the midnight, to warn the hero of the danger of Erin, and to urge him to deeds of renown. In moments of excitement she was transformed; heart and soul came up from their tranquil depths and illumined and dignified every feature.

Mr. Glenmore stood gazing upon her, as calmly and quietly she drew the yielding woolen over the sweeping curve of the instrument, whose chords gave a faint vibration under her touch.

"And shall this splendid young creature," thought he— pride and affection struggling with despotism in his bosom— "shall she be made a musical drudge, a hireling, a slave, perhaps, while I am rolling in affluence? What will the world say? What will Horace Cleveland say?" As that name came back to his recollection, his wrath rekindled. "It is her own fault. She is a fool, and deserves to suffer, and she shall suffer. It is for her to bend, not me. I have never broken my word, and I never will. I have said she *shall marry* Horace Cleveland, and she *shall* marry him, or be henceforth no daughter of mine. What if the world does talk? I care not. I have not driven her from me— it is she who plunges herself into banishment and degradation."

At the conclusion of these reflections he seated himself on the sofa, and folded his arms coldly on his breast. Looking steadfastly into the fire, he appeared to take no notice of the movements of his daughter, who also clothed her guitar in its comfortable travelling apparel, and placed it by the side of her harp. Then she came and stood at his side.

"May I sit down by you a few moments, father?"

She took the seat without waiting for permission, and they both sat in silence, looking into the fire, that emblem of all warm, household affections—alas! where were the warm household affections that might have made that fireside so happy and genial.

"Father!" at length said Eoline, her words stealing very soft and low on the silence—"I hope we will not part in anger. It is not without bitter struggles I have maintained this resolution. I believe I am doing right. If I am not, if I find myself mistaken, I trust I shall be forgiven for an error of judgment, pardonable, perhaps, in one so young."

She paused a little, but receiving no reply, continued, in a tone less firm—

"I shall go to-morrow—I am told the stage leaves early. I have been gradually preparing everything for my departure, for I have had no hope of your relenting. I know the inflexibility of your will, and I do not weakly seek to bend it. I have chosen my destiny—and whatever it prove, I will not murmur—but oh, my father," here she clasped her hands suddenly together, and turned toward him, tearfully, imploringly, "send me not out a stranger into the cold world, withering under your frown. I do not ask you to bless me, perhaps you cannot do it, but I do pray you to forgive me for all past neglect of duty, for all the pain I at this moment cause you. I cannot go without your forgiveness. I ask not for love. I ask not for favoring. I only ask, only pray—for forgiveness."

Eoline had slided down on her knees, and clasped her father's hands in both her own. He tried at first to free them, but she would not let him, she only imprisoned them the tighter in her throbbing palms. Tears fell in showers from her eyes. Never till this moment had she felt how strong was the ligament that bound her filial heart to her only parent. Now she felt it drawing and drawing, producing such an aching and anguish, that the thought of severing it was like death. And he, despotic, and self-willed and vain-glorious as he was, he felt the ligament drawing too, and though he writhed to break loose from it, he could not do it. Her arms were round him, her tears, her kisses on his cheeks and lips—he could not help it. He was weak as a child. Before he knew what he was doing, he was returning her embrace, and his eyelid was wet with a tear which was not hers.

"Bless you, father, bless you!" she whispered, " you do forgive me—you do love me. Must I go? Must I leave you? You cannot part from me. Oh!—I know you cannot."

"Then you consent to marry Horace Cleveland?" he cried. "I knew you would. I knew it would all be right at last!"

" Alas! sir—I cannot consent to be an unloved, unloving wife."

" Then go!" he exclaimed, breaking loose from her arms. " Go, and never let me see your face again. Go!" he continued, waving his hand imperiously towards the door— "this scene has been too long—I am weary of it."

Eoline bowed her head, folded her arms over her breast, and slowly withdrew. She went to her own room—closed the door, and threw herself on the bed, drawing the curtains over her face. She lay thus for more than half an hour— so still that had any one entered, they would have supposed she slept. And Mrs. Howe did enter, and went up to the bed, and stooping down, looked on her pale face and closed eyes, then not wishing to disturb her, she sighed and withdrew. Soon after, other footsteps were heard, and Gatty stood by her young mistress. Perceiving by the trembling motion of the eye-lashes, still heavy with moisture, that she was not asleep, she said—

" Does not Miss Eoline want something?"

"No, Gatty," replied she, sitting up and passing her hands over her brow. "I do not wish anything. And yet you may help me, for I have much to do to-night. I am going away early in the morning, Gatty."

"Well, sure enough, you will take me with you, to wait pon you," said the girl, anxiously.

"I must learn to wait upon myself, Gatty, and you know I like to do it, now."

"Yes, that is the truth, Miss Eoline—I never did see the like of you, for that. For all master's got such a heap of black folks, and there ain't one of 'em but what would be proud to do the leastest thing in the world for you. And, as for waiting on master, the way you've done it—is a caution."

"You must wait upon him now, Gatty, and fill my place as well as your own. You know how particular he is about light and shade, and about having everything in its right place. Be as thoughtful of his comfort as I have tried to be, and he will surely reward you."

"Goodness gracious! Miss Eoline, what makes you talk in that way for? How long, in the name of the Lord Harry, are you gontu stay away?"

"Gatty, you know I have told you not to speak in that way."

"Yes, I forgot. In the name, then, of the Lord Al—"

"Worse, Gatty, worse still—I wish I could break you of that bad habit. I fear you will learn Willie to speak in this manner. It would grieve me very much—you cannot think how the thought distresses me—and I know you would not willingly give me pain."

"For nothing in the world, Miss Eoline. You got pain in your heart now—I see it as plain as day. I'm nothing but a negro, and no business to ask questions—but it make me most sick to death, to see you cry and take on, and talk so about going off—and master all gumfligated sorter, making them two big wrinkles 'tween his eyes, he allos does when he mad."

"You must not speak disrespectfully of my father, Gatty; I cannot allow it."

"I no mean speak disrespectable of nobody," said the negro, folding her fingers across each other, and looking earnestly on the tear-dimmed face of Eoline ; "but I know something wrong, and I spect, I think—"

"No, no, Gatty," cried her young mistress, rising and opening a wardrobe, that stood at the foot of her bed— "you must not suspect, you must not think, you must not speak. It will do no good, and may do a great deal of harm. You must help me, for it is getting late. Fold up these dresses, and put them in my trunk. Pack up my work-box and toilet-case. Prepare me for a long stay. Put up everything as if I were going to be gone a year."

"Oh, dear! oh, dear!" murmured Gatty, as she followed the directions of Eoline, and one by one folded down her beautiful dresses into the large travelling-trunk, already opened to receive them.

"Master Horace come back to-night," said she suddenly, glancing at Eoline from the corner of her eye—(if a per· fect globe can be said to have a corner)—"Cæsar just tell me so. He say, too, he think there gontu be a wedding fore long."

Eoline did not speak, but the cunning Gatty marked the rising color of her cheek, and was sure this sudden journey had some connection with the return of the young master of Cleveland Villa.

"Cæsar say he mighty good young master," continued the girl, while she wrapped in nice folds of cotton the jewel-case, whose glittering contents had so often attracted her admiring gaze. "He mighty smart, too—know a heap, folks say—"

"That will do, Gatty," said Eoline ; "the dresses left

in the wardrobe shall be yours. Be faithful to my father—
be kind, and more than kind to Willie—and I will reward
you according to my means. And now, you may leave
me—but remember to awaken me by dawning light."

" Shan't I sleep in Miss Eoline's room, as I allos do ?"

" Certainly," she replied, faintly smiling at her own
abstraction, " but lie down and go to sleep, for I am very
weary, and would be silent."

Gatty rolled herself, head and ears, in her blankets, and
deposited herself on a low couch by the side of Eoline's
bed—but ever and anon she would roll one white eye-ball
over the covering, at her young mistress, who remained
standing where she had left her, in the centre of the room,
with her hands clasped together immovable as a statue.

" Now, don't she look like a heavenly serup, all cut out
on a tombstone?" said the negro to herself, " and oughtn't
master to shame hisself, if he cross and spite her, when she
so good to him. Well, if I was white folks, and rich folks,
I wouldn't make trouble, I know; it come fast enough hisself—nobody needn't run arter it. Oh, you go to sleep,
Gatty, and take care of yourself—it's none of your business, any how you can fix it."

And Gatty obeying herself literally, soon gave evidence
by her breathing that she had attended to her own commands.

Every thing seemed still in the house—every thing but
the heart of Eoline—that was beating wildly ; it was the
last night she might ever sleep under her father's roof—
and an unknown future hung darkly over her head. Like
another Phaeton, she had taken the reins from her father's
hand, and was about to guide, young and inexperienced as
she was, the chariot-wheels of destiny. What, if like her
rash prototype, she should rush through an ordeal of fire,
to a miserable doom !

" Better, a thousand times better," repeated she again

and again to herself, " than the doom from which I flee. Like the daughter of Jephthah, I could sacrifice my life, at a father's command; I could immolate my own happiness, but not the happiness of another. I have no right to entail wretchedness on *him*. He has spared me the humiliation of a refusal by *consenting to obey*, and for this I thank him. He is returned like a victim to the slaughter, never dreaming that a poor weak girl would have courage enough to resist an authority to which his stronger will has bowed. If he does not love, he shall at least respect me. Conscience does sustain me. I feel that I am acting right. All that an earthly father can claim of a child, I am ready to yield, but none but my Father in Heaven should have absolute sway over my heart, soul, and life. By the immeasurable capacities within me, never yet filled; by the deep sensibilities, never yet fathomed, I feel, I know that I am right."

And who does not feel that she was right—this noble young girl ! who refused to sell her birthright for a miserable mess of pottage ; and was willing to sacrifice wealth, luxury, and home, rather than barter her soul's independence, her heart's liberty, her life's good, in a traffic unsanctioned by God or man ! Had she loved another, and fled, to preserve her plighted vows inviolate, she could only have done what thousands of her sex have done before— but her heart was unawakened, her will was free. It was solely to preserve from legal desecration, the as yet lonely but pure inner temple of her spirit, that she was about to flee. It was to save herself from being thrust, by the hand of force, against a heart shut as with Bastile bars against her admission.

There is strength in thought—strength in a great purpose. Eoline grew strong in the contemplation of the responsibilities she had assumed. She could not go to look again on the sweet face of the slumbering Willie, lest it

72

should disarm her courage. But there was one farewell
visit she must pay—she must give a parting glance to the
flowers she had so fondly cherished. The green-house was
accessible by a winding passage that led from her chamber, and taking her lamp, she threaded it with stilly footsteps, so as not to disturb the slumbering inmates of the
house. As she opened the door, and the warm, fragrant
atmosphere mingled with her breath, she felt a sickness
an oppression, that made her lean against the frame for
support. The temperature was graduated by a stove, that
produced summer-heat day and night. This sultry air,
impregnated with the rich odors of tropic plants, and all
kinds of rare, flowering shrubs, seemed to the excited
senses of Eoline, fraught with a deadly languishing sweetness. Like a green pyramid, sprinkled with rainbows, the
flowers rose to the top of the crystal roof in gradually ascending beauty. Walking slowly through the alleys that
separated the floral families from each other, she gathered
leaf after leaf, and flower after flower, till her hand could
scarcely hold the odoriferous burthen.

It is too little to say that Eoline loved flowers—she ido-
lized them. She had often said if she had been born in a
heathen land, and worshiped any of God's works, it would
have been flowers. They were to her, living, breathing,
animated beings. They talked to her with their balmy
breath; as they bent their graceful stems and green leaves
in the wind, they seemed to woo her caresses, and she longed to fold them in her arms, and hold them against her
heart. She felt thus towards the flowers that sprang up by
the wayside—God's flowers, as she used to call them when
a child; then how much more precious were these, the
children of her care, the objects of her daily attention!

Casting a fond, lingering look on this, her own Eden,
blooming in the heart of winter, and cheating it of its
gloom, she could have exclaimed with the banished Eve,

"Must I then leave thee, Paradise? Thus leave
Thee, native soil?—these happy walks and shades,
Fit haunt of Gods?
                              Oh, flowers!
My early visitation, and my last
At even, which I bred up with tender hand
From the first opening bud, and gave ye names
Who now shall rear ye to the sun,
Or rank your tribes, and water from the ambrosial fount?"

Closing the door with a reluctant hand, she was about
to leave a place where her pure taste had erected an altar
and paid daily incense, when she found her dress was fastened in the door, and she must again unclose it. It seemed to her that the flowers she loved so much, were detaining her with blooming hands; and with a smile at her own
sweet fancies, she re-opened the door, and once more the
soft aroma of their breaths floated lovingly round her As
she ascended the winding stairs, she no longer felt lonely.
Every scented geranium leaf had something to say to her—
every rose petal whispered words of tenderness and love.

"These shall be my company in to-morrow's journey,"
said she, putting them in a crystal vase. "I will cherish
them, even when faded and dry. They shall serve me as
book-marks and perfumery. I must be content with wild
flowers after this—God's flowers—yes, my Father made
them all!"

When Eoline placed her flowers upon the bureau, she
saw a purse lying there, which was evidently laid upon it
during her absence. She took it up—it was heavy. Had
it been dropped by invisible hands? No! her father must
have heard her nocturnal visit to the green house, and taken advantage of her absence to leave in her chamber what
his pride would not permit him to offer as a gift. He
would not let his child go forth a beggar. That would
reflect too much disgrace on him. Eoline felt relieved
from her heaviest anxiety—she had enough in her own

purse to defray the expense of her journey, but she could not bear the thought of being pennyless after her arrival, and being compelled to ask for her salary in advance. Her father's purse had always been open to her, and she had but to ask to receive. She would have suffered rather than have asked any pecuniary favors after being discarded as a daughter, but she nevertheless rejoiced in receiving what might save her from deep humiliation. One thing, too, soothed her wounded affection. Her father had not slept. He could not rend her from his heart without a pang. She did not suffer alone!

No—she did not suffer alone. Mr. Glenmore never closed his eyes during that night—they turned and rolled restlessly in their hot sockets, but the lids would not shut over the heavy balls. He would have given worlds, if he had had them, to recall the last few weeks, but he could not give up his word. He would not bend his iron will. In a struggle for power, for a father to yield to a child was monstrous, unnatural; it was an outrage upon social regulations, an infringement of the Divine law. Thus he reasoned and justified himself, and cased himself in the panoply of his pride, but avenging Nature would lift up her voice and cry out, " Sleep no more! sleep no more!" through all the live-long night.

CHAPTER II.

The scene is changed. The high brick walls of Magnolia Vale Seminary rise above the evergreens that skirt the
ample yard. It is near the hour of sunset, the clear, mellow, Italian sunset of a Southern Winter's day. A little
army of young girls is arranged, in true warlike array, in
the enclosure, in two opposite lines, prepared to engage in
the royal game of Prisoner's Base, or Prison Bars, as it is
sometimes called. Royal indeed, it may be deemed, since
it was the favorite amusement of Napoleon, in the beautiful
shades of Malmaison. It was probably this circumstance
that induced Miss Manly, the most dignified of teachers,
and the strictest of disciplinarians, to allow her pupils to
indulge in this somewhat boyish but glorious exercise. It
was, indeed, a charming spectacle to see these wild, blooming girls, just loose from the restraints of school, buoyant
as skylarks, frolicsome as young colts, and graceful and
mischievous as kittens, running, bounding, and flying about,
and revelling in all the joy of motion, their locks of every
shade, from the faint, paly gold to the purplish or raven
black, flowing free as the wind;—their cheeks wearing
every tint, from the soft blush of the wild rose, to the rich
crimson of the damask, all glowing from exercise, and
every movement elastic and spontaneous as the deer of the
wild wood. There was one figure in this juvenile group,
which, though *with* them, seemed not *of* them. As the name
of Uncle Ben was ringing from mouth to mouth, as a kind of
slogan for the young belligerents, and as no other person
of the masculine sex was present, a stranger would have no
difficulty in fastening the familiar cognomen on the plea-
sant-looking, ruddy-faced, not very young nor very old
gentleman, who was frisking with extraordinary agility, in

(33)

the very heart of the light-footed community. To catch
Uncle Ben and make him prisoner under a noble-spreading
tree, the appointed base, seemed the sole ambition of one
party; to rescue him from his inglorious thraldom, the object of the other.   Surely Uncle Ben was an enviable
mortal, to be captivated and liberated almost every other
moment by these bands of fair warriors.   It must be acknowledged that he often pretended to stumble and knock
his foot against a stone, for the pleasure of being seized
upon by the triumphant captors; and not unfrequently
would he turn a voluntary somerset, which appeared perfectly natural, that he might hear the merry shout of
laughter reverberating on the air.   Uncle Ben, the real
uncle of Miss Manly, was the man of business, the secre-
tary, collector, major-domo, factotum of the establishment.
It was impossible to get along without him, or Miss Manly
would have done it—so much did his want of dignity shock
her august sense of propriety.   He *would* laugh, play, and
run with the girls, but as he made himself useful, indeed
indispensable to her, in a thousand ways, she was compelled
to submit to the evil for the sake of the good.   By his
perennial good nature and intense desire to oblige, he had
made himself the idol of the girls, though they delighted
in teasing and making sport of his peculiarities.   Even
now, as he was running, with his head extended, so that
his body lay almost horizontally on the air, a piece of
white paper in the form of a kite was pinned to his coat-
tail, that streamed behind him like a comet as he flew in
his eccentric orbit.   Unconscious of this addition to his
attractions, he joined in their vociferous mirth, and cut
many an impromtu antic for their especial amusement.
    At length two or three of the larger girls, weary and
panting, threw themselves on the ground at the foot of a
tree, sufficiently remote from the field of battle to avoid
the danger of being run over. While one replaced a truant

c.mb in her loosened tresses, another rebraided hers, and
a third gathered and smoothed her wind-blown ringlets,
they fell into earnest conversation.

"Do you think she will be here to-night?" asked Selma
Howard, she with the dark hair fastened with a silver
comb.

"I hope so," replied Annie Gray, whose

> "Soft brown hair was braided
> O'er a brow of snowy white."

"The Colonel said so, and what she says must be true."

"Oh, how I long to see her!" exclaimed Fanny Darling—or darling Fanny, as she was more often called—the
sweet girl with the wind-blown ringlets. "I do wonder
how she looks—whether she is pretty or ugly, dark or fair,
tall or short. I hope she will be gentle and good, and willing to let us love her. I cannot bear to have a teacher
whom I cannot love."

"Darling Fanny is made of nothing but love," said
Selma, twisting her fingers most lovingly in her fair blonde
curls. "Don't you love the Colonel? I'm sure *she's* lov-
able. Don't you wish the young lady who is coming may
resemble her?"

"Shocking!" exclaimed Annie Gray. "I should have
to speak for a new neck, for I have almost worn out the
one I have, stretching it up to look at her. She certainly
is six feet high."

"I have just found out the secret of Annie's long neck,"
said Selma, laughing. "My eyes feel as if they were
vanishing into my head, rolling them up so constantly. I
hope the new music teacher is low in stature, so that we
shall not have to strain our muscles to look her in the
face."

"I hope she will not rap our fingers as Miss Bates did,"
cried Fanny.

"Nor spat them with a piece of whale-bone like Mr. Devaux," added Annie.

Then the trio of lassies became very animated in describing the fancied appearance of the expected young lady. According to one she was freckled and had red hair; to another she was very pale, tall and slender; and to another very fat and ruddy. Gradually the wearied runners gathered round the reclining trio, and joined in the speculations on the appearance of the new comer, and Uncle Ben, with his comet-like appendage still adorning him, put his good-humored face over the shoulders of two blooming damsels to listen to their conjectures.

At this moment the stage was seen rapidly rolling along the road, and just as it stopped at the gate, the well-known bell, ringing within the walls summoned them to their respective apartments. Woe be to the delinquent who disregarded the sound of that warning bell. Though almost irresistible curiosity urged them to linger and watch the descending figure, with which their imaginations had been taking such unwarrantable liberties, they dared not so much as cast a glance behind them, as they flew with lapwing speed up the steps, through the folding doors, and then subduing their motions, and falling into a regular military march, they ascended, two and two, the long winding stairs which led to their dormitories. Quiet as dor-mice the young hoydens threaded the echoing passages of this baronial castle, for such it might be called, but some of them whispered with a suppressed titter, that "Uncle Ben, had gone to help the young lady out of the stage with the kite pinned to his coat tail."

"Oh! that I dared to open the door and get a peep at her," exclaimed Selma, as the commanding step of Miss Manly, accompanied by one of lighter, gentler tread, passed along the passage. But brave indeed must have been the hand that could have ventured upon such a deed,

in the face of the Colonel—the title with which her pupils honored Miss Manly *behind her back.*

The hour preceding supper seemed interminable to their
excited curiosity. They stood with their hands on the
latch of the door, ready to march forth at the first tinkling
of the bell, whose summons at this hour, was generally
obeyed with alacrity. The long double row of tables in
the dining-hall was lined with bright, eager faces, when
Miss Manly's towering form was seen emerging from the
arch which passed over the entrance, and walking by her
side, almost overshadowed by her immense height, appeared the fair and youthful Eoline. The tables were
brightly illuminated, and as she moved slowly between
them, keeping time as far as possible with the majestic
steps of her conductress, the pupils had a favorable opportunity of gazing on their new teacher. When they first
caught a glimpse of her, emerging from the shadow of the
arch, her cheek had the pale bloom of the eglantine, but
the color went on deepening and brightening, till, when
she reached the place assigned, it rivalled the depth and
brilliancy of the carnation.

The appointed seat was between Selma Howard and
darling Fanny, and they exchanged glances of delight as
the fair stranger glided in between them.

"Miss Glenmore, young ladies," said Miss Manly, with
a stately bow.

Eoline gently inclined her head, suffering her eye to
pass down the living line, meeting so many bashful smiles
and admiring glances, their warmth partially melted the
chill of Miss Manly's cold and formal greeting. She smiled
in return. Eoline had the sweetest smile in the world, and
it completed the conquest her beauty had begun. The
young Misses were not allowed to speak at table, unless
addressed by their teachers or Uncle Ben, but they had a
telegraphic mode of communication, peculiar to school-girls,

by which they interchanged ideas with astonishing rapidity
Before Uncle Ben had finished saying *grace*, the word
"angel" had run along at least a dozen pair of fingers,
concealed by the snowy damask of the table linen. Even
Uncle Ben, who stood more in awe of his dignified niece
than he was willing to acknowledge, had become expert in
the use of the deaf and dumb alphabet, and the emphasis
of sly winks and meaning glances. It was not long before
he had made all in his neighborhood aware of his exceeding admiration of the young music teacher. Miss Manly
alone preserved the same imperturbable demeanor. Like
the great pine of the forest, whose lofty crest is unruffled
by the breeze that agitates the tender shrubbery at its feet,
she seemed above the alternations of feeling in a higher
cooler stratum of the atmosphere.

She sat at the head of the table with erect brow and
folded hands, for she never ate herself till she had dismissed
her pupils to their dormitories, devoting her whole time to
the superintendence of their deportment, the preservation
of order, and the restraint of encroaching appetite. Her
eagle eye took in at a glance the whole length and breadth
of the hall and instantaneously detected the slightest breach
of propriety.

She was a remarkable looking woman. We have already
alluded to her extraordinary height, and as she was well
proportioned and erect, her figure was really commanding
and dignified. Her head was well formed, and her forehead decidedly intellectual, high, broad and prominent,
but her eyes had a peculiarity which gave a singular expression to her whole face. As much of the white was
visible above as below the pupil, which being very large
and black, had such an intensely wide-awake look, it was
impossible to conceive of her ever sleeping. The round,
quick-moving ball resembled an immense huckleberry
swimming in a saucer of cream. Firm and closely shutting

lips, a full and projecting chin, completed an assemblage
of features which were always shaded, morn, noon, and
night, by two long curls, drooping from her temples to her
shoulders.   No Parisian kid glove ever fitted with more
unwrinkled exactness, than her black silk dress.   No Parisian belle ever took more pride in her *chaussure* than Mis
Manly, whose long, slender foot always contrived to escape from the folds of her skirt, and assume a conspicuous
position.   She always commenced the discipline of the
table by a regular military drilling, which had probably
obtained for her the honorary title of Colonel, as Sergeant
would be immeasurably below her merits.

"Young ladies," said she, in a clear, decided tone of
voice, "heads up—chins down—shoulders back—backs in—
elbows close—and toes out. Very well. Now beware of
opening your mouths too wide while you are eating—it imparts an appearance of greediness, as unladylike as it is
unbecoming.   In moving your elbows, avoid making a
sharp angle, but form the curved line of grace in every
motion.   In masticating your food, be careful of making
any audible manifestation of the process in which you are
engaged—in quenching your thirst, allow no gurgling sound
to be heard in the throat. Young ladies," repeated she in
a tone still more elevated, observing their glances wandering from her to the smiling countenance of Eoline, (for in
spite of all her efforts to repress it, a smile would play
around her lips,) "it is exceedingly rude to indulge in a
prolonged stare, and doubly rude, when addressed by a
person to whom you owe the utmost politeness, respect
and attention."

The blushing girls dropped their eyes upon their plates,
and some of them in their confusion, were guilty of putting their knives into their mouths, which elicited a fresh
lecture on the graces of eating, from their high-bred in
structress

"Miss Glenmore," continued Miss Manly, addressing her so suddenly, that her blood gave a sudden bound in her veins, "you will perceive that my object is the improvement of my pupils, in school and out of school, in whatever situation they may be placed. Whatever they do, I wish that it should be done with grace and propriety. Too much attention cannot be paid to manners and deportment, and I wish all my teachers to assist me in this most difficult and exceedingly important, not to say, much neglected, branch of female education. "Miss More," said she, glancing towards a pale, delicate, pensive young lady, who sat with veiled lids nearly opposite Eoline, "Miss More is my auxiliary in the dormitories. I shall expect your assistance in the same department. The table, where the manners and graces of a lady are revealed to the greatest advantage, I make my own peculiar charge. I require no coadjutor," added she, with an exalted motion of the head, "and I desire none. You are very young, Miss Glenmore," continued she, in a more condescending tone, "and have probably seen very little of the world. You will find me ready to overlook any little deficiency, provided I find a desire to please, and an earnest attention to the duties that devolve upon you."

"I will endeavor not to tax your forbearance too much, madam, notwithstanding my inexperience," replied Eoline, the blood rushing even to her temples, at the patronizing, humbling manner of Miss Manly. She was not aware how much pride there was in her look and accent, but Miss Manly was—and remembered it, too.

"And now, Miss Selma," cried the principal, "we will commence the intellectual banquet that we always mingle with the grosser elements which are necessary for the sustenance of the material frame. Can you tell me the subject of conversation selected for this evening?"

"I think it was Peter the Great," replied Selma.

"You are right. It is a *great* subject, and I hope it will be discussed in a manner worthy of its merits."

Then commencing with the young Miss on her right, she was required to mention some fact connected with the illustrious individual in question. As they were obliged to prepare themselves for the occasion, and a black mark in the Doomsday Book, as the culprits named the weekly report, was the inevitable punishment of silence and ignorance, they gave, one by one, an outline of the life and character of one of the greatest heroes of modern times. It was an instructive exercise, and might have been made delightful, had Miss Manly permitted anything like a spontaneous remark, a flash of wit and humor. But she measured even the time of their answers with the rule and plummet. "Thus far shalt thou go, and no farther," was the language of her lips, eyes and gestures. But Canute might as well have attempted to restrain the rolling billows of the main, as human will bring to an uniform level the wild elements of the juvenile mind. They must be wisely directed—not too forcibly repressed. Like the growing tree, springing up by the side of a resisting wall, the branches denied room on one side, will only shoot out with more wanton luxuriance on the other.

When Eoline's turn came, in regular succession, the bird-like eyes of Miss Manly paused upon her face.

"I think Peter the greatest of all great heroes," she said, modestly, "because he overcame the greatest natural defects—he had the strongest will."

"I see very plainly," said Miss Manly to herself, perusing the lineaments of her beautiful and intellectual countenance, "that this girl has a will of her own, as powerful as Peter the Great's. But there is but one will at the Magnolia Vale Seminary, as she will know by-and-bye."

Uncle Ben's remark was the climax of the entertainment. There was a general leaning forward when he opened his lips; for, thinking that a sufficient quantum of wisdom and historic lore had preceded him, he always wound up with a jest or conundrum, so as to be regaled with a little silvery laughter, as he rose from the table.

"Peter was a great man," said he, gravely passing his hand over the top of his head, and bringing his hair up in thin spokes into a focus, "a very great man, but I know a greater Peter still."

"Who, Uncle Ben?" whispered a bright little creature near him.

"Peter Piper," he exclaimed, and a stifled chorus of laughter rolled round the room. A loud laugh was not permitted in Miss Manly's presence—and as Uncle Ben's witticisms were not always of the most brilliant kind, the effort of repression was not so unnatural as it might have been. Miss Manly rang a little bell, the signal for order, and repeated in a clear, sonorous voice, "*Neapolian,*" (she was fond of heroes.) He was the subject for the next day's lesson. The meal was now closed, and the young ladies permitted to retire in military file.

"I will join you in the parlor in a short time, Miss Glenmore," said Miss Manly, "where I shall enjoy an opportunity of judging by auricular demonstration of your musical talents. As I flatter myself, that I have a correct taste and delicate ear, I can decide upon a single specimen."

"I trust you will excuse me to-night, madam," replied Eoline, "as I feel too much fatigued from my journey to do myself justice, or you pleasure. To-morrow I shall be most happy to oblige you."

"I only ask one song," said Miss Manly, "so slight an effort cannot add to your fatigue, I am sure. I will promise to dismiss you after having gratified me thus far."

"Dismiss me!" thought Eoline, her high spirit chafing

against the offending words. "I certainly shall not give her the opportunity." "Indeed, madam," she said, respectfully, but decidedly, "you must excuse me. It is not possible for me to sing to-night, since my reputation must depend upon the effort. You will have the goodness to permit me to retire."

"*Must* and *will!*" repeated Miss Manly to herself, as Eoline with a graceful salutation left the dining hall. "We do not allow but one person to use those words here. Really, my young lady deports herself most royally."

Uncle Ben, who was lingering near the stairs, to light Eoline's ascending steps, waited upon her with an assiduous politeness, that would fain make amends for the cold hauteur of his niece.

"You must be tired," said he, kindly taking her hand, and leading her along as if she were a child. "I know your poor little soul must be nearly jolted out of your body, rattling over the rough roads in a hard stage. You don't look as if you were used to such things. I know you can sing like a nightingale, but they shan't make you sing to-night. Bless your sweet face, they shan't."

They had now reached the platform where the stairs diverged.

"Good-night, my child," said he, giving her the candle, which he had been holding at arm's length above his head, "Go to bed and sleep like a good girl, and to-morrow you will be as gay as a lark."

"Thank you, sir, for your kind wishes," replied she holding out her hand, with a grateful smile. "I see I shall have one friend at least."

"That you shall," cried he, energetically, "that you shall. God bless you."

The blessing of the affectionate old bachelor, cheered Eoline, as she passed on to her lonely chamber. Placing her candle on a little table covered with green paize, the livery of the establishment, and seating herself in a dark green windsor chair, with a high, perpendicular back, she carried her eyes slowly round the apartment, and closed the survey with a feeling of inexpressible drowsiness. She did feel very weary from the rough jolting of the stage, so different from the easy motion of her father's carriage, and it would have been a soothing indulgence to repose on one of her own soft lounges, or rock in a soft-cushioned chair. The room was small, and a large portion of it was occupied by an immense wardrobe of black walnut, whose tall columns and severe outlines reminded her of Miss Manly. Narrow green curtains covered the windows, a dark counterpane was spread over the bed, and a piece of dark colored carpeting laid in front of the fire. Every article of furniture looked dark and forbidding. There was nothing to relieve the eye and gladden it with a sense of beauty. Yes—there were the flowers which Eoline had gathered in her green-house, and having surrounded them with wet cotton, whose moisture she renewed on her journey, they were still fresh and fair, and filled the chamber with their redolence.

"Oh, sweet flowers," was the language of poor Eoline's sighing heart, "are ye all that are left of the blossoms of my young life? Have I scattered all behind me, but your frail petals and fading leaves, that to-morrow will be withered and pale? Ah, me, this is rather a joyless commencement of my new career. I have offended the supreme majesty of Magnolia Vale already, but I cannot help it. An independent spirit is now my only inheritance, and after having thrown off the chains of parental despotism, with a mighty struggle, I certainly cannot willingly submit to any other. I hoped to have found in Miss Manly the guardianship of a mother, and the tenderness of a friend.

Tenderness! I wonder if she ever felt—if she ever can feel? Good Heavens!—what a woman!"

With a sudden conviction that such reflections were as unprofitable as they were unpleasing, and that she had voluntarily imposed upon herself the stern discipline whose smart she was just beginning to feel, she resolved to employ herself in some way, before retiring, so as to escape from her own haunting thoughts. She opened her trunks, hung her dresses in the solemn-looking wardrobe, arranged her work-box and toilet-case on the little green table, then putting on her white night-wrapper, began to loosen and comb her soft, abundant hair. This soothing occupation brought back thoughts of home and home luxuries, of her darling Willie, who delighted in hiding, as he called it, in her mantling tresses; and the tears again gathered in her eyes.

A gentle knock at the door was heard, and two smiling faces peeped in.

" Miss More has sent you a rocking-chair," said Fanny Darling, drawing in a low, comfortable-looking one, and placing it in the corner.

Selma stood holding the door in her hand, gazing with vivid admiration on Eoline, in her white robe and flowing locks.

" Come in," said Eoline, making room for them both at her fireside. " Miss More is very kind, but I fear she is depriving herself of a comfort, which she requires more than myself. She looks very pale and delicate."

" She is sickly," replied Fanny, " but she never thinks of herself. She would give up her bed, and sleep on the floor, to oblige even a servant any time."

" Is she so self-sacrificing?" cried, Eoline—" then how dearly you must love her?"

" We do love her," said Selma, " but we pity her very much, too."

73

"Is she unhappy?" asked Eoline, the shadow of her own destiny falling over her spirit.

"She is so good that every one imposes on her," replied Selma. "She works from morning till bedtime, as hard as a slave, and because she never complains, people forget all about it."

"And yet," added Fanny, earnestly, "she says she is never so happy as when doing something for others. According to her own principle, she must be the happiest person in the world."

Eoline was becoming deeply interested in the remarks of her young companions. The character of Miss More grew on her imagination. There was a charm in the recollection of her pallid cheeks and drooping eyelashes— associated as they now were, with patient endurance and self-renunciation.

"How are you pleased with the Colonel?" inquired Selma, with a mischievous smile.

"He seems a very kind-hearted, affectionate old gentleman," replied Eoline. "I think I shall like him very much."

Here, to her astonishment, both girls burst into a merry fit of laughter.

"Whom do you think we mean by the Colonel?" they asked, as soon as they could speak.

"The gentleman whom you call Uncle Ben, of course— I saw no other."

"Oh, no—it's Miss Manly. Every body calls her so."

Eoline could not help smiling at the appropriateness of he title, though she felt it was not right to encourage the pupils in speaking in a disrespectful manner of their teacher.

"She seems a remarkable disciplinarian," she said, with as much gravity as she could assume

The girls looked at each other.

" We shall get a black mark," they said, " if we are out
of our room too long."

Eoline rose, and took them both by the hand.

" You must come and see me often," she said, " I shall
be very lonely at times."

" You are so young," said Fanny, laying her cheek lovingly on the white hand that held hers. " Oh, what beautiful hair !" she added, running her fingers through the
golden filaments—" how long and silky !"

" Darling Fanny is dying to tell you how sweet and
lovely you are," cried Selma, taking one of the *long, silky*
tresses, and twining it round her neck, "and so we all are,
but we dare not say so."

" You must not spoil me by your flatteries," replied Eoline, putting her arms caressingly round them, and feeling
that some heart-flowers might bloom for her, even in the
wintry atmosphere of Miss Manly. The considerate offer
of the rocking chair ; the visit of the light-hearted girls ;
their frank, affectionate manners, and winning expressions,
dispelled, in a great measure, the dreariness of the apartment. The chilled heart of the stranger grew warm, and
notwithstanding the hard bed and ugly counterpane, and
grim wardrobe, she slept soundly and sweetly till the
dawning of morning, when she was aroused by a blast,
so loud and dread, she started upon her feet in dismay.
Miss Manly, who was original in all her regulations, finding that, accustomed to the ringing of the bell throughout
the day, her pupils did not always attend to its awakening peal, had substituted a horn in its stead, which, being
blown by a stout negro the whole length and breadth of
the long passage which divided the dormitories, made a
volume of sound that might call the wind-gods from their
subterranean caves. When her door opened, Eoline half
expected to see the dogs of the chase rushing after then

prey, but it was only a negro girl, sent to kindle her fire, who explained to her the mystery of the winding horn.

At the breakfast-table, to which she was summoned at a very early hour, after receiving the greeting smiles of her two young friends, and acknowledging the imperial nod of Miss Manly, she contemplated with growing interest the pensive features of her *vis à vis*—Miss More;—and there she read her whole character. Patient sweetness, perfect resignation, and chastened sensibility, were all written there in gentle lines. Once she raised her meek, gray eyes, and meeting the fixed and serious gaze of Eoline, they were instantaneously lowered, and a deep blush suffused her whole face. She did not seem more than twenty years of age, though the drooping neck, and listless fall of the arms, did not harmonize with the springing grace of youth. There was nothing which could be called attractive about her, but Eoline felt the influence of that moral charm, to her more irresistible than beauty, and her heart was drawn toward this lowly and self-forgetting being.

"Attention, young ladies," cried Miss Manly, her long side-curls waving like the ambrosial locks of Jupiter. "Let us commence the morning's exercise."

This was a text from Scripture, recited by each pupil, in regular progression. The recitation proceeded very gracefully, till a little sly-looking creature was called upon in her turn. She hung her head, pulled the frock of her nearest companion, and at length stammered out—

" The Lord is my Shepherd—I shall not want."

" Repeat," said Miss Manly,—" I cannot hear."

The child began again, in a sharp, frightened tone—

" The Lord is my Shepherd—I shall not want."

" Failure, and a black mark," cried Miss Manly " You repeated the same yesterday morning. You must commit two verses to-morrow, as a penalty."

Eoline looked with compassion on the little delinquent, whose flushed cheek and swelling bosom told the struggle of anger and shame. What associations would be hereafter connected with that hallowed volume! How much better would it have been to have allowed her to have repeated a second time those beautiful words, which could bear ten thousand repetitions. Nor was this all. At the close of the exercise, Miss Manly again turned to the child, on whose cheek the glow was just subsiding, and said,

" Bessie Bell, upon reflection, your offence is worse than inattention. You endeavored to deceive me. Miss More, under the column of Premeditated Misconduct, you must put the name of Bessie Bell."

At this public disgrace, in the presence of the new teacher, little Bessie burst into a passion of tears, and hastily moving back her chair, was about to escape from the hall.

" Go to your room, and make your breakfast on bread and water," cried Miss Manly, without changing her voice or manner.

" I don't want any breakfast," sobbed Bessie.

" Your dinner, too."

" I don't care," cried the exasperated child, " if you starve me."

" Your supper likewise, Miss Bessie Bell."

By this time the child was heard flying up the stairs, with a step that showed that every fierce passion was raging in her young bosom. The children looked at each other in silence ; but there was a world of expression in their meeting glances. Miss More seemed distressed, Eoline shocked. As for Uncle Ben, he could not restrain his excited feelings—

" I declare, niece, you are too severe," said he laying down and taking up his knife and fork, between every

word—"the child meant no harm—she forgot, as who
doesn't sometimes ?"

"Uncle, I cannot allow you to encourage my pupils in
disobedience and disrespect. *You* forget yourself, sir, I am
sure. I hope you will recall your judgment and recollection.
Young misses," continued she, addressing them, collectively,
"you were, some of you, deficient in your geography yesterday. So as not to encroach on the time allotted to other
lessons, you must now atone for past remissness. Miss
Fanny, you will tell me something of the statistics of Russia.
It is my constant aim," she added, looking imposingly at
Eoline, "to combine instruction with every act of existence. My object is to show the triumph of mind over
matter, the predominance of the intellectual over the animal nature. I consider every meal at the Magnolia Vale
Seminary as a banquet of the soul, a feast of the mind."

"Ah! but the heart," thought Eoline, "what do you do
with the heart ? Is not that sent starving away ?"

Eoline was not aware that this sentiment was written as
if with sunbeams on her face. Miss Manly read it, while
she pursued her geographical investigation. It was rather
a laborious task for the poor girls to travel over the civi-
lized globe, climb its mountains, traverse its oceans, and
wade through its burning deserts, while swallowing their
coffee and disposing of their muffins. It is not strange that
Franklin's excellent rule, to rise from the table with an
unsatiated appetite, should be obeyed through necessity, if
not choice, under circumstances like these.

As Miss Manly never would commence any thing on
Friday, Eoline was not required to assume her duties till
the following Monday,—but in the evening, with the
pupils arranged in perfect order around the walls of the
music room, Miss Manly seated on the right of the piano,
and Uncle Ben on the left, she had to pass through the fiery
ordeal of criticism. The little culprit of the morning had

humbled herself before her offended teacher, and obtained permission to be present. She had slided between the knees of Uncle Ben, whose kind heart was ready to weep at the sight of her pale cheeks, and heavy and swollen lids.

" Can you sing that?" said Miss Manly, pointing to stiff, old-fashioned song. " That is one of my favorites."

" I do not play it," answered Eoline, and fearful of a selection she knew would be in variance with her own taste, she began one of those sweet and touching airs which penetrate the soul, like the fragrance of flowers that are so sweet the " sense aches at them."

No Italian Prima Donna ever had a more clear, brilliant, powerful voice than Eoline,—no mountain lassie one more wildly warbling,—no nightingale one more mellow and pathetic. Mr. Leslie had said truly, that she would make her fortune on the stage. As an operatic singer, she would have witched the world with thrilling melody. Though Miss Manly had no ear for music, and could hardly tell one note from another, she felt through every fibre the *majesty of the loveliness* of Eoline's music. Eoline had indeed achieved a great triumph. She had made Miss Manly feel and forget herself so far, as to look pleased. As for Uncle Ben, who was an impassioned lover of music, his ecstacy was beyond words. He sat with his mouth open, tears gathering into his eyes, which were fixed steadfastly on the rosy lips from which such heavenly strains were flowing.

" You sing very well, Miss Glenmore," said Miss Manly drawing a long breath. " I am satisfied that you are qualified to teach. If you have as much patience and perseverance as you have natural talent, you certainly will succeed."

" No, she don't sing *well!*" cried Uncle Ben, striking the piano. " It is a shame to say that. She sings like an angel, like a choir of angels. She has almost sung my soul out of my body. What are you crying for, Bessy ?" asked he, of the child now cradled in his lap, and whose face was all bathed in tears.

"It is so sweet it makes me feel sad," was the low reply, Eoline heard it, and gave her a smile as sweet as her song.

"I should like now to hear you perform upon the harp," said Miss Manly. "I am glad to see you have restrung it for the occasion. The harp is a sacred instrument. It is immortalized by the holy Psalms of David, which were sung in unison with this beautiful accompaniment. It is a classical one, and associated with the poetry of ancient bards. The heroines of Ossian inspired the souls of heroes to deeds of renown by sweeping the sounding lyre. The very ghosts came forth in the moonlight to hear the echoing strains. In short," said she, looking round with an air of self-complacency, as if conscious she had made a beautiful harangue, "I feel much gratified that I can introduce into my seminary a branch of music so noble and ennobling."

"Let us applaud the Colonel's speech," whispered Selma.

But Fanny, who felt the Divinity stirred within her, shook her head with a soft—

"Hush."

In the mean time, Eoline had uncovered the harp, and drawing it towards her, ran her fingers over the wires.

"That's it. Come, little David," cried Uncle Ben, clapping his hands. "Come, little Ossian. The piano is nothing to this, I know."

Uncle Ben had never heard a harp, and with his nerves still vibrating from the divine breath that had floated over them, it is no wonder he sat like one entranced, watching the white fingers of Eoline gleaming among the glittering chords and producing the most ravishing harmony.

"I should like a sacred theme," said Miss Manly.

Eoline immediately commenced the beautiful strains of "I know that my Redeemer liveth." Eoline, with her fair hair, and celestial blue eyes bending over the harp, and breathing those holy words, really seemed "little lower than the angels," and an aureola of purity and piety appeared to beam around her brow.

Miss Manly, who had thought her far too young and superfluously lovely for her vocation, began to think of the *eclat* she would give to her concerts, and the advantage such extraordinary musical talents would be to her seminary. She had long been, in vain, seeking a teacher who could not only play upon, but supply this elegant instrument, and she could not but think herself singularly fortunate in having secured this young girl. If it were not for the independent spirit that sometimes flashed from the deep and serene blue eyes, she would have felicitated herself still more.

When Eoline paused, after giving that full sweep to the chord which announces the finale, Uncle Ben cleared his throat several times, and exclaimed—

"I don't want to go to Heaven, while I can hear such music as that on earth. Young lady," said he, in a low, reverent voice—for Uncle Ben had a great deal of reverence, in spite of his levity—"you ought to thank God for giving you such a glorious gift. *I* thank Him for sending you here."

"I am very much pleased with your performance, Miss Glenmore," said Miss Manly, with unwonted condescension. "You have had great advantages—been taught by eminent masters. You were probably educated for a music teacher."

"No, madam," answered Eoline, a brilliant color flashing into her face.

"Family misfortunes, I presume?"

"Yes, Madam," she replied, with a deep sigh.

"Surely," she added to herself, "there can be no greater misfortune, than the estrangement of a parent from his child—death itself were less cruel."

The children had listened with rapt and smiling attention to their future teacher. Like Uncle Ben, very few of them had seen a harp, and the charm of novelty was added to its other fascinations. The poetry of Eoline's appearance, the elegance and fashion of her dress, the graceful self-possession of her manners, added to the matchless sweetness of her voice, and her exquisite and brilliant execution, formed a combination of attractions that completely captivated their young imaginations.

Thus triumphantly did Eoline pass this dreaded ordeal. Monday was her inauguration day, and Miss Manly attended to the rites with due solemnity.

CHAPTER III.

Eoline commenced her new duties with feelings of awkwardness and repugnance, known only to herself, but she became gradually interested in the progress of her pupils, whose enthusiastic attachment and admiration imparted brightness and beauty to her daily tasks. Constant employment gave wings to the hours, which at first dragged so weariedly, and the all-exacting Miss Manly seemed satisfied with her attention to her classes.

At night, when retired to her little room, she welcomed its quietude and rest, notwithstanding the absence of all those elegancies and luxuries to which she had been accustomed in her father's mansion. It was sweet to repose after a day of toil, and it was sweet to hold communion with a heart as pure and a mind as enlightened as Louisa More's After the nine o'clock bell had rung, and the young misses retired to their beds, this young lady generally sat an hour with Eoline, who called this her *balm hour*, for her spirit seemed bathed with holy unction, after the evening intercourse. Strangers who visited the seminary, beheld in Louisa More only a pale, delicate, shrinking young woman, a faithful and hard-working teacher; but those who knew her, as Eoline now did, who had lifted the veil that shrouded the temple of her heart, saw glimpses of the Shekinah, whose glory was concealed by a curtain so thick, the rays burned within, with a radiance more intense and consuming. She was the daughter of a New England minister, who, after languishing for years on a sick bed, died, leaving a wife in feeble health, and a young and helpless family—Louisa being the eldest of the children, felt as if the burden of their support devolved upon herself. Though only sixteen, she commenced a small school in her native town, but its profits were very inadequate to their wants. About two years previous, she had an offer from the South, which she gladly accepted, for she already felt symptoms of that fatal malady which had numbered her father among its victims, and physicians told her she might find health, as well as wealth, in the genial latitude to which her hopes were now turned.

"How much more exalted are your motives than mine!" exclaimed Eoline, after listening to Louisa's simple and touching history; "I feel, since I have known you, as if my life had been one tissue of selfishness. Yet I dared to glorify myself as a martyr, when I gave up wealth and home to avoid the immolation of my own happiness. I have gloried too in my independence, and exalted it into magnanimity. And yet your Christian meekness, your lowly resignation, how much more lovely. There are moments when I doubt even the rectitude of my conduct—when I feel as if, like the Prodigal Son, I could arise and go to my father, and casting myself upon his neck, exclaim—'I am not worthy to be called your child.'"

"You do yourself great injustice," replied Louisa, to whom Eoline had confided the story of her banishment; "I consider your conduct far more magnanimous and really self-sacrificing, than mine. The happiness of another, as well as your own, was at stake, and that you had no right to destroy. Hundreds, nay, thousands, dear Eoline, have done and are doing what I now do—urged by necessity, that stern and relentless taskmaster. But where is there one, young, beautiful and affluent like yourself, would gird themselves with hempen chords, as it were, unmindful of their roughness, and walk unshrinking in a path where thorns, i know, start up on every side to pierce your bleeding feet, rather than barter their integrity and truth."

"How charmingly you reconcile me to myself," cried Eoline, "and how I thank you for the generous warmth with which you defend me from my own aspersions. Yes! I have met with some thorns, but your friendship is a balm for all the wounds they have made. Had I not come to this place, I never should have known you, and now I wonder how I ever lived without you. Then there is Darling Fanny and Selma, and little Bessy—such charming girls, whom I love so dearly, and good Uncle Ben. They are all treasures, which I have found, when I sought them not."

"And Miss Manly," said Louisa, with a smile that beautifully illuminated her pensive face.

"I should be sorry not to have known Miss Manly, for she is a character such as the world seldom sees. She really has a powerful mind, and is a female Napoleon in her line—but she seems that strange anomaly, a woman without a heart."

"I think you are mistaken," said Louisa, "she is capable of feeling. In sickness she is very kind, and I am told she is very charitable to the poor. There are few characters without some redeeming excellencies. I should not wonder if she had her weaknesses, too."

"Do you think she was ever in love?" asked Eoline, laughing. "That must be a strange passion," added she after a pause, "and I do not think I shall ever experience its power—and yet, when I have read of devoted, self-sacrificing attachment, of love stronger than death, deeper than the grave, I have felt as if I could thus love, thus die for the beloved object. But Louisa, it seems to me, to love, I must be loved, devotedly, passionately, exclusively, loved as a woman never yet was loved. Nay, even love would not satisfy my heart's boundless cravings. It must be worship, adoration. It must be something I never shall find in this world and therefore l shall never love—

unless," exclaimed she, changing the impassioned tone in which she had been speaking to one of merriment, " unless it be Uncle Ben, for I verily believe he worships me."

" You seem created for such worship," said Louisa, gaz-ing on the lovely face of Eoline, now glowing with the warmth of latent passion, " and I tremble to think of the trials that may yet await you. It is a mystery that is inexplicable to me, that Horace Cleveland, who has known you from your childhood, has not thus adored you."

" It is for that very reason he cares not for me. Edu-cated to consider me as his own property, as something he must take *nolens volens*, his pride rebelled against coercion and guarded every avenue to his heart. I really honor him for his coldness. I wonder what he thinks of me now, the banished fugitive, the self-willed, indomitable girl," said Eoline, looking thoughtfully into the dying embers.

" He *must* admire you now," replied Louisa, impressing on her warm cheek the kiss which sealed their parting moment.

Not many days after this conversation, Eoline was summoned from the music-room to the parlor, where she was told a gentleman wished to see her. The image of a relenting father came to bear her back to a home too lonely, uncheered by her filial love, rose before her glis-tening eyes.

" Oh! I knew he could not live without me," repeated she to herself as she flew down stairs, leaving the messen-ger far behind her. " I have done injustice to his affection. I have thought him cold and inexorable, cruel and unkind. Oh! dear father, with what rejoicing gratitude will I throw myself into your arms, and never, never leave them more."

Arrived at the door, she stopped and turned pale. Her hand trembled on the latch. Perhaps it was not her father after all—if it were he might only have come to upbraid

her and renew the conflict which had so lately rent her
heart. Summoning her failing resolution, she entered
and beheld, instead of the portly master of Glenmore,
the figure of a tall young man, standing with his back
towards the door, examining a picture that hung over the
mantel-piece. He turned around at her entrance, and she
found herself face to face with the dreaded Horace Cleveland.

It was a moment of intense mutual embarrassment. The
revulsion of feeling which Eoline experienced was so great,
that every drop of blood forsook her face, leaving her as
colorless as alabaster. The fear that her father was sick
or dead annihilated every other thought. She could not
speak, but making a motion to a chair, she sunk into one
herself, unable to stand.

" I fear you must look upon me as an intruder," said
the young man, scarcely less agitated than herself. " Indeed, it must have been a very powerful motive that
could have induced me to brave your displeasure."

" Has my father sent for me ?" she asked, intent on one
thought.

" Your father does not know of my being here. I saw
him a few evenings since in his usual health."

Eoline breathed more freely, but the embarrassment of
her situation pressed more painfully upon her. Why had
Horace sought her? On what mission had he come?

" And Willie, my darling Willie ?" she asked. " Have
you seen him, too ?"

" Yes, and he talked of nothing but Ela. He told me
to come and bring sister Ela back, for he could not live
without her."

" Dear little fellow !" exclaimed Eoline, tears rushing
to her eyes. " What would I give to see him!"

There was silence for a few moments. Young Cleve
land, the deep student, the bookworm, the dweller of libra

ries, the inhabitant of the world of thought, so little versed in social etiquette, so diffident and reserved in the presence of woman would have met with less dread the gleam of a thousand tomahawks, than the glance of Eoline's tearful eye. Notwithstanding his repugnance to a compulsory union, he had looked upon it as inevitable, never dreaming of the brave, resisting spirit enshrined in the fair yet slight form of his young betrothed. When he learned of her flight and banishment, her noble self-reliance, to avoid a hated wedlock, though the object of hatred was himself, he felt a thrill of admiration, such as the history of heroic deeds inspires. He had seen her a beautiful and accomplished girl, but he deemed it a matter of course that all young ladies must be beautiful and accomplished, and it excited in him no especial emotion. He had seen her surrounded by admirers in her father's drawing-room exchanging with them those sportive sallies which give grace and piquancy to the passing hour, and he had thought her frivolous, as he took it for granted that all young ladies were. His life having been one of intense study, he knew nothing of the world, but little of mankind, and still less of himself. Great thoughts were always rolling through his mind, like chariot wheels, crushing the wild flowers of feeling that bloomed by the wayside. Hitherto he had been all intellect, but there never was a great intellect without a corresponding heart, though the possessor may live and die without feeling its awakened energies.

To follow Eoline and entreat her to return, to promise to exile himself from country and home, if necessary to her happiness, was due not only to her but to his own honor and sense of justice.

An unacknowledged curiosity to see once more a girl capable of such heroic conduct, and whose perfections he

had so strangely slighted, added strength to the impulse
that urged him to Magnolia Vale.

"If I am the cause of your exile," said he, making a
strong effort to speak with composure—"let me be also the
means of your restoration. Believe me, I am very unhappy to see you an alien from your father and home on my
account. There is no sacrifice I would not make to insure
your return. If I had known the unconquerable repugnance
you felt for the union our fathers desired, I never would
have returned to my native land. I would rather have
died on a foreign shore."

He spoke with earnestness, and Eoline raised her eyes
to see if it were indeed the cold, unimpressible Horace
Cleveland that thus addressed her. His own eyes were
fixed upon her face, and instead of the haughty self-concentration, she had thought their prevailing expression,
there was truth, dignity, even sensibility in their beams.
For the first time she felt as if she might value him as a
friend, however she might shun him as a lover. Her embarrassment subsided before his tone of manly sincerity.
She could think with calmness—she could speak with confidence.

"You have no cause of self-reproach," she said. "The
repugnance you have manifested has been no more under
your control than mine. I have never resented it. I felt
that it sprang from the same source as my own—a coerced
will. It was for your sake, even more than my own, that
I have taken the extraordinary step which has freed me
from parental authority. My own happiness I might have
relinquished, but I had no right to involve yours in the
sacrifice. You must give me credit for some disinterestedness," added she, with a smile and a slight blush.

"You impute feelings to me," he replied, wondering he
had never observed before the intellectual beauty and spiri
tuality of Eoline's countenance,—"feelings I am not con-

74

scious of displaying. I plead guilty to the most unpardonable rudeness and neglect, but not to dislike. I disliked the position in which I was placed, and believed myself an object of ridicule and avoidance to yourself, but you have misunderstood my character."

"I am very glad if I have," said she, with animation. "I am sure I have. The past cannot be recalled, nor its consequences, but the future may be made happier by our cherishing for each other kindness and good will. I shall like you very much as a friend, you are so true and sincere. Our parents have erred very much in judgment in trying to make us more, but we must forgive them, as they must have meant our happiness. We are friends, then, are we not?" she exclaimed, holding out her hand, with a gay smile, for she felt released from an awful restraint, and her spirits rose with spontaneous lightness.

As Horace took the fair hand so gracefully extended, he smiled, too, at the oddness of their position, and it was astonishing what a magic effect that smile had on his countenance. Those who have naturally a grave and thoughtful expression, when they do smile, seem to be illuminated, especially if they have a fine set of teeth, as Horace had. She had never seen him smile so before, for the true reason that he never had so smiled.

"But will you return to your father?" said he. "You must not remain here. What a place for the daughter of Mr. Glenmore!"

"I shall never return till my father recalls me, and I know too well his inexorable will to expect such a summons. I again repeat, you are not to blame, nor should you suffer one moment's unhappiness on my account. I am very far from being miserable. I reign like a Queen among my young subjects. I have found here a friend, who is dear to me as my own soul, and a dear old Uncle Ben, who would walk over burning ploughshares, if it would give me any pleasure. I have learned, too, the pleasure of being useful."

"Are you really contented and happy?"

"1 cannot say that I am—but I am *resigned*, and I have not time to be heart-sick."

"Do you think your father can be happy without you?"

"He has banished me—it was his own act."

"Can I ever be happy, who am the cause of all?"

"Yes, for you are innocent. Let us leave misery to guilt—we have no right to feel it."

A kind of rushing sound overhead, indicated that the school was dismissed, and Horace rose to depart.

"I cannot bear to leave you here," said he.

"Stay and take dinner with us. Miss Manly will welcome you with characteristic dignity to one of the intellectual banquets of Magnolia Vale."

"No, I am not equal to such an honor just now. I could rush into the field of battle with far less effort than encounter a formidable band of school girls."

"Return in the evening, then, when I shall be at liberty, and the 'formidable band' engaged in study."

"Do you really wish it, or do you ask from politeness?"

"I really wish it," said she, laughing, "and I think it polite to ask, besides."

"And I shall find you alone?"

"Oh, no—not entirely alone—I want to introduce you to my particular friend, Colonel Manly, to my sweet friend, Miss More, and my nonpareil of an uncle."

"You intimidate me, but perhaps I will come," said he, as they passed through the door together.

Miss Manly's towering form was seen standing on the platform of the stairway, just above them.

Young Cleveland bowed hastily to Eoline, and hurried

away, as if that majestic being were indeed the military chief whose honors she wore.

Eoline saw at one glance that she was not pleased. The white rim of her eye was enlarged, an unfailing sign.

"You have had a long call, Miss Glenmore," said she, with stately mien.

"From an old acquaintance," replied Eoline.

"Your pupils have been idle in the meantime."

"I will give them their lessons after dinner," said Eoline, with rising color.

"It will be impossible—every moment will be occupied by others."

"I did not expect to be considered such a slave to hours, Miss Manly, as not to have the privilege of greeting an old friend."

"I never leave school myself during recitation hours, Miss Glenmore, and I expect all my teachers to follow my example. But as you were perhaps not aware of my rule, we will overlook it this time. In future, ask your friends to call in the evening. At any rate, such very long visits from very young gentlemen are not consistent with my views of propriety."

Eoline was about to reply as her high spirit prompted, when she felt a gentle touch on her arm, and the soft gray eyes of Louisa More, looked beseechingly into hers. Without uttering one word, they clasped each other's hands, and ascended the stairs, while Miss Manly swept by them towards the dining hall.

"Oh, thou smoothing oil to the troubled waves of passion!" exclaimed Eoline, laughing in spite of her anger, at the recollection of Miss Manly's preposterous sense of propriety, "why cannot I be as gentle and lowly-minded as thou art? Do you know, I think there are boiling springs in my veins, they come bubbling up to my cheeks so often. Just feel how hot they are," putting Louisa's

hand first to one and then the other of her crimson cheeks.
"But who do you think has been here ? Horace Cleveland—and would you believe it ? we are the best friends
in the world ! We talked about our mutual repugnance,
laughed about it, and concluded to bury the tomahawk
and smoke the calumet of peace in the good old Indian
style. He is coming here to-night. I long to have you
see him."

"I did see him as he passed out, and certainly discovered no reason for personal dislike. He seemed a fine
looking young man, with a very gentleman-like bearing."

"Do you think so ? It seems to me that we have been
looking at each other through a glass darkly, for I liked
his looks better this morning than I have ever done before,
and notwithstanding my prejudices, I really thought him
agreeable. I want him to see you and fall in love with
you, for if I mistake not, you are just the person to interest
him."

"Do not talk in this foolish manner, dear Eoline. Such
a jest does not seem natural on your lips."

"I am not jesting—I never was more serious !"

"I never expect to inspire love in any one," said Louisa,
pressing her hand against her aching side, "and least of
all, in one who has been proof against your attractions.
I know that I am doomed, and that an early death will
save me from the oft dreaded title of *old maid*, and I sometimes rejoice in the thought, for I would not like to pass
the years of a long life, unloving and unloved."

"Unloved !" repeated Eoline, putting her arm fondly
round her, "who could know you and not love you ?"

"I am an ungrateful being !" cried Louisa, returning
Eoline's warm caress, and unworthy of the praise you bestow upon me ; for, oh! Eoline, there are times when I
envy you—you, so full of health, and life, and beauty—
you who seem born for love and happiness. There are

moments when I forget the countless blessings my God
has given, and pine for those he has withheld; when I
dare to ask why he has given me this pallid cheek, and
feeble frame, and weary step, instead of your radiant
bloom, elastic form, and buoyant spirit. Eoline, you ought
to be happy—you know not what bounteous gifts Heaven
has showered upon you."

"I would give them all, Louisa, for your meek, Christian
spirit."

The thoughts which Louisa had suggested were sad and
chastening. Was it, indeed, true that she was doomed
to an early grave!—and was not she, and every human
being, hastening to the same dark bourne? Were they not
all shadows, hurrying along one after another, with unrest-
ing speed, coming and going every moment,—coming
from one abyss, and plunging into another? Even Miss
Manly, iron-framed and iron-hearted Miss Manly, must
meet the common doom—she, too, would be hurried away.
No! *She* would not hurry—she would move majestically
onward to meet the King of Terrors himself, as if marching of her own accord. She held up her own hand, and
looked at the rosy palm, beneath which the life-blood was
brightly flowing, and wondered if that warm hand would,
indeed, be cold and stiff, incapable of the grasp of friendship, or the pressure of love. She shuddered.

"Of what are you thinking so deeply," asked Louisa.

"Of death!—and oh, what wild thoughts have been
running through my brain! Can we command our thoughts?"

"We are told to do so, and nothing is required of us
beyond our strength."

The ringing of the dinner-bell interrupted their conversation. Eoline met Miss Manly at table with a serene
countenance—the contemplation of their common doom
had subdued all her resentment.

She welcomed Horace Cleveland, when he made his even-

ing visit, without embarrassment. Their morning interview had removed the painful constraint she had always
felt in his presence. It was the first time since his manhood that she had ever spoken with him frankly and
unreservedly, and a feeling of liberation, of expansion,
swelled high above the broken chains of her former bondage.

"I thought you did not care about music," said she,
while she fluttered the leaves of a music-book, for the song
he had asked her to play, "I always avoided my instru-
ments when you were near, for fear of disturbing you."

"Do not punish me for past obtuseness," he replied, "or
rather for past awkwardness and silence. I do love music
intensely, but I cannot speak of it. It stirs an under current that never flows up to the surface."

"I am glad you love music; but I see plainly I know
nothing of your tastes. I do not like to play to deaf ears,
like Uncle Ben's, for instance."

"Do hear the little witch!" cried Uncle Ben, patting
her affectionately on the cheek, "she sets me half-crazy
with her singing, makes a complete fool of me, and then
pretends I don't hear her!"

Horace did not turn the leaves of the music-book for
Eoline, as she played. He never thought of that, or that
Uncle Ben, who stood with his hand hovering above the
leaves, eagerly following the motion of her eyes, to know
when to whisk them over, was doing what he had not the
gallantry to offer. He sat leaning against the piano, shading
his eyes, feeling, as the sweet voice of Eoline stole around
him and glided within him, as if he were reclining on
some green bank, swept over by long, swaying boughs,
through which the summer sunshine shot a golden glance
here and there, while a silver stream ran murmuring and
gurgling and rippling, diffusing a kind of haziness over the
soul, like the delicious languor of a dream. Then, again,

his spirit seemed a moonlit lake, curling and undulating, as the breath of music floated over it, then swelling high under a full breeze of melody. Thus Horace felt, but he said nothing. He forgot the songstress in the emotions she inspired. He lost sight of beauty in his deep sense of the beautiful. He never thought of thanking her, or of praising her, any more than of praising the stars for their lustre, or the flowers for their fragrance. He felt like praising God, not her. Could Eoline have looked down into his mind and read all its deep and glowing thoughts, she would have felt more complimented by his expressive silence than by Uncle Ben's rapturous applause, but she had been accustomed to think him cold, and she thought him so still.

As it was Friday evening, several of the elder pupils were allowed to sit in the parlor, so that they might become accustomed to society. Darling Fanny, Selma Howard, and Annie Gray, sat on a low sofa in the back part of the room, amusing themselves by watching Miss Manly's shadow on the wall. Anxious to impress on the mind of the young man, not only her taste for music, but her knowledge of it, as a science, she kept the most elaborate time, bowing her head, waving her long curls, and opening and shutting her eyes between each note.

"She looks as if she were purring," whispered Selma.

"She seems pleased at any rate, and that's a comfort," said Annie.

"I wish he would ask her to sing," Fanny said upon her fingers. "But she could not see the keys, they would be so far below her."

Eoline moved from the piano, and there was a slight pause. Miss Manly cleared her throat in order to utter some brilliant remark, when Horace suddenly turned to Eoline, and said,

"I have not had the pleasure of seeing Colonel Manly yet. I think you spoke of introducing me this morning."

This unexpected remark acted as a match to the smothered mirth of the mischief-loving girls, and they exploded at once into a burst of laughter. Miss Manly's face turned a violent red.

"Go to your room, young ladies," said she, commandingly, "if you cannot preserve your decorum in society better than that, we will dispense with your presence."

The young trio, with their handkerchiefs to their faces, left the room with demure steps, but the moment they had closed the door, another merry peal was rung and kept ringing all the way, as they flew up stairs.

Horace looked very much confused, for Eoline began to look earnestly for something on the carpet, instead of answering him—and Uncle Ben, with his mouth drawn up like a purse and his eyes brimming with laughter, took out his handkerchief and dusted his boots most laboriously.

"I thank you, Miss Glenmore, for the compliment you have paid me," cried Miss Manly, with freezing dignity. "I have given you credit for some good-breeding, but I find I am mistaken. I pity the young lady who is reduced to so low an ebb of enjoyment as to ridicule her friends and superiors in the presence of strangers."

"I plead guilty to the offence, madam," cried Eoline, as meekly as Louisa More, herself, for she was unaffectedly penitent, and grieved to have wounded Miss Manly's feelings, however unwittingly, "and sincerely beg your forgiveness. I little thought what I said so thoughtlessly and sportively to Mr. Cleveland, would be understood seriously. I forgot—"

"You forgot that he was not aware of the respectful soubriquet you have been pleased to honor me with."

"Indeed madam," cried Horace, vexed with himself for his unfortunate remark, "you must excuse Miss Glenmore. They told me at the hotel that Colonel Manly resided here. so whatever may be said of the title, she certainly has not the honor of inventing it. I hope, likewise, you will acquit me of all intentional disrespect."

" The truth is," exclaimed Uncle Ben, who seemed sa-tisfied of the purity of his boots, " my niece ought to feel flattered with the compliment the public have conferred upon her. She is a wonderful disciplinarian, and as she conducts her school with true military order, and as she has, as you see, a commanding appearance, they call her the Colonel. As for little David here, I am sorry she seems so crest fallen. She meant no harm, no more than a crow-ing baby—bless her sweet singing tongue. Come niece, tell her you forgive her, for I am sure it is not worth being angry about."

" I cannot forgive myself," said Eoline, ingenuously. " I have always felt respect for Miss Manly, and intended no-thing but a light jest, a very foolish one, I ackowledge."

" I accept your apology, Miss Glenmore," said Miss Man-ly, with unexpected graciousness; then turning to Horace, she added, " We, who are placed in elevated situations, and have taken a lofty stand before the world, are conspicuous targets for the shafts of envy and the arrows of wit. Few young ladies have acquired the reputation I have attained as an instructress of youth. I say it with modesty, sir; and I suffer the usual consequences of brilliant success. There is a striking adage, that Envy, like the sun, shines hottest on the highest ground. I feel the truth of this time-honored aphorism."

Horace bowed respectfully at the close of this harangue. It was all he could do. He felt uncomfortable and rose to depart. Eoline followed him into the passage, which was illuminated by the lamps in the upper gallery.

" You will see my father," she said. "Bear to him, from me, a daughter's fondest love—and Willie, my own dear Willie, tell him I send him a thousand kisses, and yearn more than tongue can speak for one of his dear caresses."

"Can nothing prevail upon you to return? There is no sacrifice I would not make, nothing I would not do to see you restored to the home from which I have been so unfortunate as to have driven you. You cannot be happy here. It is impossible. Your life must be a continual martyrdom."

"Nay, not so," she answered, gratified that he seemed roused to some interest in her welfare. "I need the discipline I am passing through. You have not seen the sunny side of my life. I am sorry for the little cloud that arose to-night."

"And I, as usual, sad blunderer, was the cause," said Horace. "Really, Eoline, you have reason to hate me. I am a cold, dark wall between you and sunshine. I could bless the tempest that laid me low, so that the barrier to your happiness might be removed."

"You wrong yourself to speak or think in this manner," cried Eoline, with earnestness. "It is thus I have felt with regard to you, and I would be willing to meet far greater privations than I now endure, for the joyful consciousness that I have broken the chains that galled you, and restored you to freedom of choice and action. It is your right, and may you enjoy it, as freely, as gloriously, as God intended you should. Forgive me if I have thought you unfeeling. I see you can feel, and nobly, too."

He did not answer immediately, but stood with his arms folded and his eyes bent upon the floor.

"If you know what injustice I have done your character," he said, "you would never ask forgiveness of me. I thought all young girls were mere flowers to bloom in a drawing-room. I did not know they could breast the wind and wrestle with the storm."

He spoke with energy, and his serious, dark eye lightened.

"My mother," he added, "is in feeble health, and physicians have recommended the mild climate of Cuba. She
wishes me to accompany her; and we may not return for
many months. If, by leaving my home permanently, I
can secure your restoration to yours, most willingly, gladly
will I exile myself. It is this I came to say—it is this I
must again and again repeat."

"It would make no difference in the conditions my
father has imposed." she replied, with a heightened color,
"I know his terms, and they would not be affected by any
sacrifice of yours. Perhaps, however," continued she,
with a bright smile, "should you bring back a beautiful
bride from a foreign land, and he saw the impossibility of
his wishes being fulfilled, he might relent, he might perhaps forgive, and take the wanderer to his arms again.
I shall live in hope of such an event, and of such a
result."

"I do not think it likely I shall oblige you in that way,"
said he, with a vexed look, and turning coldly towards the
door, "though I thank you for the suggestion."

With a distant bow, that reminded her very much of
the Horace of old, he was about to leave her, when, moving between him and the door, she said, playfully,

"You are not angry with me, Horace. I little thought
of making you so. We must not forget our compact, and
friends do not part thus coldly."

"I am conscious that I am rude in manners," said he,
taking the hand, with which she impeded his egress, and
giving it a cordial pressure, "and this very consciousness
makes me ruder still. I know nothing of the little courtesies and gallantries which are the current coins of society, and I often offend when I most wish to please. There
are but two places where I feel perfectly at home, in a
great library and in the wild green woods. There, waves
of deep and solemn thought, roll in upon my soul and

drown the petty feelings born of the world. But they are silent homes. The secret of expression is not found in their dim aisles and solemn shade. I have not learned to *talk!*"

"Then your knowledge comes by inspiration," said she, laughing, "for you do talk very well. One of these days I shall like to visit your two magnificent homes, with you, and see the waves as they flow grandly along. Perhaps I can turn one little one out of its course towards the thirsty void of my spirit. I think it will feel very dry and sandy after being here six months longer."

"You *must* not remain here six months. I *must* find you at Glenmore."

Eoline smiled, shook her head, and after a few more kind and friendly words they parted. She immediately sought Louisa, who, complaining of indisposition, had remained in her own room.

"He is gone, Louisa," she said, thoughtfully—"and now his coming and going seems a dream."

"Perhaps you will yet be willing to obey your father's commands. Your prejudices already seem yielding."

"You are mistaken, Louisa. I acknowledge that I have not done him justice, and that he has noble qualities of whose existence I had not dreamed. I may esteem him. I do even now—but as for love—it is a feeling he never could awaken. I may have very romantic ideas on the subject, but they were born with me, and I cannot separate them from my being. Love, with me, will be the lightning's flash. A moment will decide my destiny. No, no—I never shall love Horace Cleveland. There are no electric wires running along to bridge the abysmal distance between our hearts. I wish you could have seen him to-night, Louisa, when I was singing the song he said he loved best of all. He said he loved music, too; oh, so much! He sat cold and unmoved as a rock, though my own voice was full of tears—so sweet and pathetic were the words."

"He might have felt, notwithstanding."

"He might have said one little word, for courtesy's sweet sake—but that is a mere matter of taste after all. He manifested real and just feeling on the subject of my alienation from home. I did not expect so much. He is magnanimous too—and there is a world of thought in those unfathomable eyes."

"I think there is a world of *feeling* too, if I am any judge of physiognomy," said Louisa, " though I had only a glimpse of his countenance. But describe to me, Eoline, if you can, the ideal being who is to come with the lightning's bolt, and electrify that now insensible heart.

"I can feel what he must be," cried Eoline, her blue eyes darkening as the vision passed before them—"but I fear I cannot describe. I speak not of him personally, for I shall see his face and form in his mind and heart. He must be a pillar of strength on which I can lean and cling round in the storms of life. He must be the eagle in ambition, and the eyrie of his soul near the sun; and the dove in tenderness, whose nest shall be lowly as my heart. Then the love he bears me must be illimitable as the Heavens, and boundless as the air. It must be firm as the mountains, and unfathomable as the ocean. You smile, Louisa—as if I were only making a fine speech, *á-la-Manly*, but they are the words of truth and soberness. Bear with me a little longer, and I shall have done. Round this marble pillar of strength the wild-vine of sensibility must twine, the eagle must bear the myrtle in its talons, and the dove carry the laurel to its downy nest. So must all great and tender, and kind and glorious things blend together, ennobling and softening each other, and forming a perfect whole. No—not quite perfect. He must have some weaknesses, to sympathize with my poor humanity.

And last of all, he must love me, not for beauty, not for
talent, not for goodness,—for he might imagine them all—
but just because I am Eoline. Good-night. Your mild—
sad eyes seem to say—'Poor girl! how I pity her. Doomed to see her wild dreams turn to life's cold realities.' "

Such indeed was the language of Louisa's chastened
houghts. She believed truly, that there was but one Being
capable of filling the boundlessness of the human heart,
but one pillar on which human weakness could lean se-
curely, and that was the Rock of Ages.

CHAPTER IV.

Gradually the mild, Southern winter melted away into vernal softness and bloom. So gradually, that the morning twilight of spring brightened into its risen day before the eye was conscious of the transition from leafless boughs and a barren soil, to the wreathing foliage and the springing grass. In no place in the world is awakening nature hailed with such rapture, as in a female boarding school. In the occasional freedom of the open air, in the midst of sunlight and flowers, the young prisoners forget the bondage of in-door restraints, and indulge in the natural enjoyments of childhood and youth.

As the first of May approached, the pupils of Magnolia Vale Seminary pleaded eloquently for permission to select a Queen, whose coronation rites should be celebrated by the three immortal Graces,—Poetry, Music and Youth. There was the loveliest spot in the universe, not very far from the seminary, irrigated by a beautiful creek, where the regal Magnolia bloomed, itself a Mayday Queen, wearing its pearly crown of glory, and the wild flowers revelled in wanton luxuriance. There they could erect a coronation bower, and usher in that joyous month which has long worn the blooming honors of the year.

But Miss Manly shook her head with a majestic negation. She could not listen to such a useless proposition. It was a wretched waste of time, an innovation on her strict established rules. It would be an unpardonable interruption to their studies, and retard their preparation for a public examination.

" Besides," she exclaimed, " my republican principles will not permit me to sanction these royal rites. I cannot

allow the daughters of our free-born land to ape the manners and customs of the poor vassals of European tyranny.
The Magnolia Vale Seminary is a democratic Institution,
and the germs of monarchy shall never be nurtured in its
bosom.

The Colonel spoke with patriotic energy, but the young
democrats still sighed for their Queen. At length, moved
by the united pleadings of Uncle Ben, Eoline, and Miss
More, she condescended to give them a holiday, with permission to pass it in the beautiful spot they had chosen for
the coronation. The children were wild with delight at
the prospect of a gala day, though disappointed in their
original plan.

The morning dawned without a cloud, though the sun
had set in darkness, and every one was sure it would rain,
for it always *did* rain when any out-door enjoyment was
anticipated. But the May sun shone bright and cheeringly
on the ungrateful little creatures, and they were soon ri-
fling the garden of its roses, and filling their baskets, to
make garlands and bouquets in the woods. The baskets
were not entirely filled with roses, for their dinners were
in the bottom, but not a trace of the food was visible
through the flowery covering. A more ample provision still
was deposited in a small hand-carriage, drawn by a negro
girl, who delighted in being made a participator of the
holiday sport. Uncle Ben was to take charge of the juvenile band. We verily believe he would have wept, had
any thing occurred to detain him at home, he was such a
pure lover of Nature and children. Eoline entered into
the spirit of the day with all the sweet enthusiasm of
youth, and even Louisa's pale face was lighted with the
glow of anticipation.

The pupils assembled on the green in front of the aca
demy, where Miss Manly, arranged them in military
file, and gave them a thousand instructions about march-

ing, of preserving an erect carriage, and a lady-like deportment.

" Come with us, Miss Manly," cried the children, smiling to think how funny Miss Manly would look running
about in the woods, and sitting under the Magnolia boughs.
The idea seemed as preposterous as for Jupiter to lay aside
his thunder-bolts and dance a polka with the Muses.

She waved her head with a superior smile, and giving
the signal for their departure, they commenced their march
with due dignity and deliberation, through the long, grand
alley, and continued it down the road, that is, as long as
they were within reach of the telescopic eye of Miss
Manly; but the moment they turned into the greenwood
path, the path through the tall, odorous pine trees, the little
soldiers began to desert their ranks, and fly about, as
wild as a flock of pigeons. It was a royal avenue through
which they were winding, so cool, so breezy and shady,
that they ran with their sun-bonnets swinging in their
hands, under the tall, green umbrellas rustling over their
heads. Uncle Ben frolicked and capered like a big boy
just let loose from school, and the girls stole his hat and
hid it in the little hand-wagon, making the negro girl
show her white teeth all round her head. Eoline, who
felt the bounding pulses of eighteen in all her veins, would
gladly have run on and shared in their frolics, but she would
not leave her feebler companion, whose flagging steps
showed the weariness her lips concealed.

" I cannot bear to have you fettered by me," said Louisa,
gratefully, " you who are so tireless and buoyant. It is
as bad as chaining a bird to a snail."

" I shall have time enough to fly after we reach there,"
said Eoline, putting her arm round Louisa's slender waist.
" I wish you were well and strong for your own sake, but
I should not love you as well. The plant that we nurse
is the plant that we love. But look, we are almost there.

See that beautiful opening. And hark, the roar of the mill-dam mingles with the shouts of the children."

A few moments brought them to the vale from which the seminary derived its name—the Magnolia Vale—and a peculiar and intense odor proclaimed the presence of this magnificent tree of the South. With its long, deep green, lustrous leaves, and large, splendid white blossoms, white as marble, yet yielding and impressible as wax, it stood the representative of the floral beauty and grandeur of a South-ern latitude. And on the margin of the water, wading in it up to their immense knees, the Tupeloes bowed their spreading branches and looked at each other in the clear, blue stream. This stream, which flowed just above over a rocky channel that partially impeded its current, here expanded into a kind of lake, vulgarly called a mill-pond, because the utilitarians had made the babbling waters work for their living, and erected a dam near the bed of rocks, and a mill on the opposite bank. The vale was carpeted with grass, and embroidered with wild flowers, and under almost every tree there were low ottomans, made by Nature herself, and covered with green velvet, woven by the same great manufacturer.

Eoline led Louisa to one of these velvet ottomans, and reclined on the grass at her feet.—And now there were mysterious groups, with heads put close together in grave consultation, and then a dispersion and a gathering again. They made Eoline turn her back to a certain natural arbor, and promise not to look behind her till a given signal.

" Remember Lot's wife," said Fanny.

" And the fate of Orpheus," cried Selma.

" Or the wife of Bluebeard," exclaimed Annie; as they retreated, carrying off Uncle Ben captive. For nearly an hour, Eoline, obedient to her promise, sat at the feet of Louisa, with her arm upon her lap, and her affectionate, confiding eyes lifted to her face, listening to her gentle

words, when sly footsteps stole behind, and a mischievous
pair of hands bandaged her eyes.

"Come with us," cried half-a-dozen voices, "and when
we seat you again we will restore you to sight."

Yielding with graceful willingness to her laughing guides,
Eoline was led over the soft grass to a slight elevation.
She knew it was under a tree, for she could hear the branches
rustling overhead.

"Now bow your head, lady fair, just a little," cried her
conductors, gently seating her; "and now," added they,
slipping the bandage from her eyes, "hail to your flowery
throne!"

Eoline found herself in an arbor, within an arbor, formed
of freshly-gathered boughs, and festooned with garlands of
wild flowers. A cluster of large magnolia blossoms was
placed just over her head, and golden wreaths of yellow
jessamine, fastened near that central crown, and extending
to the edge of the lightly woven roof, formed the brilliant
radi of the lattice-work. The young girls, who all wore
simple, white dresses, the Sunday Summer uniform of the
seminary, (as it was a holiday, they were permitted to
wear it,) had garlands of flowers round their heads, arranged
with a wild grace that was bewitching. Fanny, whose
ringlets were playing holiday with the breeze, held in her
hand a crown of white rose buds, with which she encircled
the brow of Eoline. Selma threw a garland of roses round
her neck, and little Bessie Bell, kneeling at her feet, stuck
flowers all round the binding of her shoes, while half-a-
dozen little creatures pelted her with roses.

"We *will* have a Queen of May!" they cried. "You
shall be our Queen! This is your throne, and we are your
subjects, and Uncle Ben is, too. He helped us build our
bower, and we promised him that our Queen should sing
for him, as soon as she mounted her throne."

"*Shall* is a strange word to use to a Queen," said the

laughing, blushing Eoline, almost crushed with her blooming honors, " but as you have given me no sceptre, I suppose I must not claim absolute command."

Away ran one of the girls, and catching with a jump a
drooping bough, twisted round it the flowering jessamine,
and presented it to her Floral Majesty. Eoline did, indeed, look like the royal bride of Spring, in her white rai-
ment and regal blossoms, while sweeter and fairer than
these regal blossoms were the roses of youth and health,
made brighter by excitement, that bloomed upon her
cheeks. She could not help feeling happy, thus loved and
honored. Existence itself was a joy on such a day as this.
Had she been alone on that charming spot—alone, with
all that loveliness, she would have felt happy, and thanked
her God for making her the denizen of so fair a world.
But the beautiful, loving children and fair young girls that
surrounded her, gave such life and enchantment to the
scene, that her soul was ready to gush forth in the melody
for which they were pleading. Just as she opened her
lips, she cast her eyes towards the spot she had quitted
blindfold, and there Louisa sat, her head leaning on her
hand, forgotten in the bright and jubilant scene.

"Poor, dear Louisa!" exclaimed Eoline, " we have left
her alone. How sorry I am we did not think of her
sooner!"

Forsaking her vernal throne, she flew to her neglected
friend, and insisted that she should share her honors.
Louisa turned away her tearful eyes, but she did not resist the arm that encircled hers. She could not mar the
happiness that beamed in the blue eyes of Eoline. She
had felt, for a moment, the demon of Envy breathing its
venom into her heart, but an invisible angel came and
strengthened her, and she met with smiles the children
who had unconsciously forsaken her. They loved her,
but they did not associate her in thought with the

flowers of Spring, as they did the bright and beautifu.
Eoline.

"Oh, that I were a boy!" cried Uncle Ben, who was
sitting on the ground in the midst of the children. They
had made a crown of magnolia leaves, and put it on his
head, and pinned a tremendous bouquet in front of his
vest. "Oh, that I were a little boy—a pretty little school
boy again—instead of being a musty old bachelor!"

"What's the reason you never married, Uncle Ben?"
asked little Bessie, looking slyly in his face.

"What's the reason?" repeated he, smelling his huge
bouquet. "Why, I loved every body so much, I could
not make up my mind to love but one at a time; and then
I thought I should keep young as long as I lived, and that
there was no use in being in a hurry, when, one morning,
would you believe it, pussies, I waked up and found myself an old man!"

"Oh, no, you are not an old man, Uncle Ben, you can
run so fast and spring so light. You are the youngest of
all of us."

"So I am!" exclaimed he, jumping up and crossing
his feet twice in the air, "who says l am old? It's no
such thing—I am nothing but a boy, after all!"

Eoline's warbling voice brought the *boy* back to his
grassy seat. She felt inspired by the influences surrounding her, and never sung so wild, so sweet a strain. The
very mill-dam seemed to hush its roaring, for no one heard
it while she was singing. She was not afraid to give full
scope to her voice, with such a sounding-board above her
as that blue arch, and the notes went up, and still up, till
the ear feared to follow them, lest the clear, crystal sounds
should break and shiver like glass; then, gliding, floating
lower and lower, with the softness of down, they died
away among the flowers.

All at once, changing her key, she struck into a gay,

flute-like warble, that set the children dancing round her,
like magic. Fanny Darling had a long garland twined
round a grape-vine, which she skipped as she danced, and
a lovelier looking fairy never flitted over the green.

At this moment, a beautiful dog ran in their midst, and
seizing one of the wicker baskets in his teeth, was about
to carry off his prey, when a young man, who appeared to
be his master, emerged from a cluster of trees, at a little
distance, and approaching the bower, motioned the dog to
return the stolen treasure. Eoline ceased her warbling,
the dancers stood still, and Uncle Ben sprang from the
ground, and removed from his head its Bacchus-like ornament.

"Do not let me disturb you," said the young man,
lifting his hat from his head, with a low and graceful bow,
" I trust you will pardon my intrusion. I would apologize
for the rudeness of my dog, and for my own too," added
he, looking towards Eoline, "in pausing beneath those
trees to listen to strains which left me no power to pass
on. The temptation was too irresistible. Am I forgiven ?"
cried he, again looking at Eoline, who, conscious of the
strange picturesqueness of her appearance, blushed amid
her roses, while she involuntarily bowed her head before
his appealing glance. Then turning to the children, with
another, though less reverent bow, he smilingly repeated,
" Am I forgiven ?"

" Yes, sir," said Bessie Bell, who was nearest to him,
and on whom his eye happened to rest, " yes, sir," making
the prettiest little curtsy in the world. The girls laughed a
her demure answer, and the stranger was thus put perfectly
at his ease. Indeed, he did not appear embarrassed from
the first, but probably thought he had as much right to
enjoy the beauties of nature as they had. He was singularly engaging in appearance. His dark hair flowed back
with a graceful wave from his white forehead, and poetry

and enthusiasm flashed from his large, dark, romantic-beaming eye.

Uncle Ben, who was the politest man in the universe, and who was charmed with the countenance of the young stranger, assured him that it was no intrusion at all, and that he was very happy to see him. He even offered him the ground to sit down upon, as courteously as if it were a chair. But there was something in the countenance of Eoline, the Fairy Queen of the scene, that forbade the young man to take advantage of Uncle Ben's cordiality. She knew too well Miss Manly's strict rules of propriety, to encourage even by a look, the continuance of a stranger's presence in the midst of her pupils. She regretted the syren notes which had lured him to their retreat, and looking gravely down, avoided meeting a second time the lustrous glance that had rested so admiringly upon her.

"Fido," said the young man, calling to his dog that was sticking its nose rather too familiarly into the dinner-basket—"let us go, before you destroy your master's reputation for honesty. We are indeed intruders in this charming group. Once more, I trust, my impassioned love of music will plead my apology."

Again the young man bowed with lowly grace, and smiling on little Bessie, who had so heartily promised him forgiveness, passed under the shadow of the magnolia trees into the path that led to the mill-dam.

This was an adventure, and it put a check for a time to their unrestrained merriment. They all felt curious to know who the young stranger was, and the children were loud in his praises. As Eoline would not sing any more, and they could not dance, they became suddenly conscious of being very hungry—and Netty, the black girl, who had never left her carriage for a moment, was called into immediate service. A nice table-cloth was spread upon the grass, and cakes and pies, cold ham and pickles, all garnished with flowers, soon covered its surface.

"We ought to have asked that young gentleman to dine with us," said little Bessie, "and his dog too. It seems to me, it was rude to let him go."

"So it does to me," cried Uncle Ben, slapping a pie, as was the first thing he came in contact with—"little Bess is right—I did mean to ask him, but young Madam Queen looked so grave, I was afraid of offending her majesty."

"It would have displeased Miss Manly," said Eoline, regretting herself their apparent inhospitality.

"Oh, the Colonel—I had forgotten—" exclaimed Uncle Ben.

The company around the grassy board became very merry, and the tongues so silent at the long table of Magnolia Vale Seminary, revelled in freedom in Magnolia Vale. No matter what was said, a laugh was sure to break forth.

At length Darling Fanny, who had stolen Eoline's comb, and tucked up all her hair, excepting two long curls, which she left dangling at the sides, like Miss Manly, suddenly elevated her head with a dignified motion, and exclaimed—

"Young ladies, Charlemagne."

The mimicry was perfect, and the effect electrical. Uncle Ben actually threw himself back and rolled on the grass—and even Louisa could not help laughing.

"Order!" exclaimed Fanny, with much gravity. "Miss Selma, what can you tell me of Charlemagne?"

"Charlemagne means great Charles," replied Selma.

"I don't like Charlemagne, because he made his daughters work so hard," said Annie. "If I were a princess, I would not spin or weave. Let us talk of William the Conqueror."

"I don't like William the Conqueror," said another, "Because he kept a Doomsday Book, like Miss Manly's."

" And he made folks go to bed before they were sleepy, at the ringing of a bell, as we have to do," cried a young creature, always wakeful with mischief.

"I like Alfred the Great the best," said a fat, laughing girl, who dispatched the pies with wonderful celerity, "because he knew how to bake nice cakes."

"I like Uncle Ben the Great, the best," exclaimed little Bessie, who sat next to him, "because he *gives* me nice cakes."

This was received with acclamation. Uncle Ben of course was expected to contribute his mite to the reservoir of juvenile wit.

" Why am I like Priam of old?" said he. "Do you give it up? He was father to fifty sons, and I am uncle to fifty daughters?"

" Hush," cried Eoline, laying her hand suddenly on his shoulder. A deep mellow voice came floating in music, across the mill-dam. Rising in rich, manly tones, it was borne over the water with the winding sweetness of the bugle. It was one of the airs Eoline had been singing, and she knew the singer must be the stranger who had just addressed them. A thrill of delight penetrated her spirit at the sound of those exquisite notes, that seemed so much like the echo of her own.

" Oh! how sweet," she exclaimed, when they melted into silence, after a low flute-like *cadénza*, "how more than sweet!"

Louisa smiled, and whispered to her,

"Do you feel the lightning's flash?"

" No," said Eoline, drawing a long inspiration, "but I feel the breath of Heaven on my soul."

There was silence for a few moments. That voice, like " the far-off, exquisite music of a dream," proceeding from an invisible minstrel, and thus having the charm of mystery added to its melody, created a feeling of sadness. It belonged less to earth than Heaven—and Heaven with all its glories is a subject of sadness to the young and glowing heart. It knows that the path to Heaven leads through the grave, and shrinks from the coldness and darkness and gloom of the passage. But there are shadows in life darker than death, deeper than the grave—and when they are folded round the spirit, it passes on untrembling, protected by the clouds that envelop it. This is a sad reflection—in the midst of all these flowers and vernal beauty. But it seemed that there *was* a shadow lingering, ready to roll down upon them.

A cloud, a very small cloud began to float near the horizon. First it was white as snow, and no larger than the wing of a bird, then its base became a faint slate-color, then it suddenly enlarged and darkened, and rose up like a tall castle, with giant pillars and leaning turrets. Then it expanded into the giant's causeway itself, and dark figures seemed hurrying near its base.

"It will rain," said Eoline, looking anxiously at the darkening horizon, " we must hasten our departure. Louisa must not get wet."

The children were sure it would not rain, it was nothing but a cloud such as they saw every evening; but even Uncle Ben, who was not remarkable for foresight, insisted upon their hastening homeward. As they had but few preparations to make, and Miss Manly was not there to put them into military array, they were soon on the wing, Netty following with the fragments of the feast, and a castaway garland on her woolly head. The prospect of being caught in the rain was perfectly delightful to the children, and Eoline cared not for herself. It was for the frail and delicate Louisa she trembled—who hurried on as much as her strength would allow, though her flushed cheek and panting breath showed it was nearly exhausted.

They had hardly reached the beautiful pillared aisles of the pine wood, before big drops came splashing down faster and faster, till they suddenly fell in sheeted rain. There was no shelter near but the pine trees, whose lofty plumes were a far better protection from the sun than the shower. The children shouted and ran, and bared their flower-bound ringlets, and tossed out their arms as if to embrace the rain, which wrapped them as if with a mantle. Their white dresses were drenched and soiled—their flowers crushed and torn—their hair dripping and straight. A few who had green parasols, as useless as a magnolia leaf would have been, were discolored with green stains that not only mottled their white frocks but rosy cheeks. Netty toiled on after them, manfully pulling the little carriage, though the remnant pies and cakes were reduced to a mass of jelly by the deluge.

"Oh, if that carriage was only big enough to put you in, dear Louisa!" cried Eoline, as Louisa sunk down upon a bank by the way-side, declaring that she could go no farther.

"I will carry you in my arms," said Uncle Ben, "I am strong enough to carry you all."

"No, no, leave me here, I ought not to have come—to be such an incumbrance. When the rain is over I can follow."

"Here is an umbrella, if it will be of any service," cried a mellow voice near them.

And turning round, they beheld the young stranger, with his silky-haired dog. As the rain was pursuing them they had not looked behind, and were not aware of his approach. He was panting from haste, and his face glowing with exercise and excitement.

"Thank you," said Eoline, to whom the stranger evidently addressed himself. "If you will shelter my friend,

I shall indeed be grateful. As to the rest of us, it is nothing but pastime."

Eoline looked at this moment as if she were born to make pastime of the most warring elements of nature. One of the girls, as we said before, had stolen her comb, while they were at their rural dinner, and her hair, wet and darkened with the rain, floated wildly over her shoulders. The floral diadem still encircled her brow, and partially confined her wandering locks; as it was formed of evergreen, and half-unfolded buds, it was not rent and defaced by the shower, as the more carelessly arranged chaplets of the children were. Eoline was fair and beautiful in repose, but in moments of excitement she was splendidly so. She was kneeling on one knee, her arm supporting her half-fainting friend, and her eyes were raised eagerly to the stranger's face. She looked, through the falling rain, like a flower enshrined in crystal.

" It will cover you both," said the young man, going behind them, and kneeling so as to bring the umbrella nearer to them, as a shelter. As he thus held it over their heads, exposing his own to the elements, they formed a romantic looking group.

" I cannot suffer this," said Louisa, raising her head from Eoline's shoulder. "I feel better, stronger. I can walk on alone, now."

"If you *can* walk," said the young man, assisting her at the same time to rise, " you will be in far less danger, than on the wet ground. There is no house nearer than the mill, which you have left behind."

The violence of the shower had subsided, so that Louisa found less difficulty in forcing a path through it. The young man walked by their side, holding the umbrella, and he even took off his hat, and held it before Eoline's face, in spite of her laughing remonstrances. Though poor Louisa was the chief sufferer, he seemed far more

anxious to shield Eoline from the inclemencies of th
atmosphere.

"Never mind me," she would say—"I am a child of
the elements. My name is Eoline, and when the winds
play around me, I feel, indeed, like an eolian lyre."

"Eoline—Eoline," repeated the young man, "what a
charming name. How appropriate, how peculiar."

"I was named after the eolian harp," she said, forgetting for the moment, that she was addressing a stranger.
"It was my mother's passion—and well do I remember
hearing one playing in her window the night of her death.
So mournfully, wildly and sweet—I never, never shall
forget it."

"You inherit, then, your love of music," cried the young
man, with animation. "In that respect we are congenial,
for I have breathed an atmosphere of harmony from my
infancy. My parents are both musicians, and I was
taught to play upon the organ before I could reach an
octave."

"She is our music teacher," said Bessie Bell, who running back for her bonnet, that she had dropped far behind,
overheard the remark, and was proud to proclaim the relative position of Eoline towards herself.

Eoline colored high. To be introduced to this very
aristocratic looking young man as a music teacher—she,
the daughter of Mr. Glenmore, of Glenmore Place—struck
her painfully. She tried to repress her swelling pride, but
it would rise, and gave to her countenance an air of haugh-
iness and reserve.

"Indeed!" exclaimed the young man, as Bessie was
bounding along. "I thought her one of your school
companions, whom you had been crowning Queen of
May."

"We made her Queen, because she is so pretty, and because we love her so much," said the child.

The young man looked as if he sympath.zed in their opinion, though he said nothing.

Eoline, whose thoughts were carried back to her deserted home, her banishing father, and Horace Cleveland, walked on in silence, with a cloud resting on her sunny face. She felt uneasy in the prospect of Miss Manly's displeasure, in bringing a stranger to the gates of the seminary; or rather, of its manifestation in such a manner as to make her ashamed of the relation she bore to the institution. She was grateful to his politeness—it was more than politeness—it was kindness, for he had offered his arm to the drooping Louisa, the latter part of the way, and sustained her weary footsteps.

Uncle Ben trudged on before with the children, his red silk handkerchief tied over the top of his hat, and his coat collar turned up above his ears. The young romps were completely jaded and sobered when they arrived at the seminary. The rain had ceased, but it only made their muddy and forlorn appearance more conspicuous. Their shoes were filled with sand, for they had rushed along without choosing a path, and their dresses heavy and saturated with the rain.

Miss Manly stood in the folding doors, with uplifted hands.

"Take off your shoes," she cried, not *loud*, but *deep*, "leave them in the portico. Don't bring all this mud into the house. What a spectacle! Never ask for another holiday. It is always the end of such follies. Wring the water out of the bottom of your dresses before you enter. Hang your wet bonnets on the railing."

She really seemed half-distracted at the thought of the mud and confusion around her, for her love of neatness was second only to her love of authority. But the rueful countenances of the children, which began to have a blue tinge the moment they ceased to exercise—the shivers which ran through their drenched frames, excited her compassion.

"Run," she cried, "yes, you *may* run up stairs, this time, and change your wet clothes, directly. I will have some warm drink prepared. Never mind the tracks.

Never before had they rushed by Miss Manly in such a style. They scampered up stairs in their wet stockings, like a covey of partridges, leaving Miss Manly gazing on the advancing figure of the stranger, who was conducting the two young ladies up the gravel walk. Louisa could scarcely drag one weary foot after the other, and her face was hueless as marble. Eoline turned towards the young man, when, after having ascended the steps, they stood in front of Miss Manly, and said—

"This gentleman has been kind enough to shelter us with his umbrella, and assist Miss More, who, even with his aid, has been scarcely able to reach home."

The young stranger made so handsome and reverential a bow to the tall and stately lady, that she extended her hand graciously to receive the card he placed in it.

"Walk in, Mr. St. Leon," said she, glancing at the card, and repeating the name, as if it had an aristocratic sound to her ears—"though according to the rules of my institution, strangers are excluded from its portals, who do not bring letters of introduction, the services you have rendered these young ladies, who are under my especial guardianship, entitle you to my gratitude and consider-ation."

"Thank you, madam," said St. Leon, (we are glad we have discovered his name, as it is very awkward to speak of him as the young man, and the stranger,) "I am in no condition to sit down in a lady's parlor. I will take the liberty of calling to-morrow, and inquiring after the health of these young ladies, who, I fear, will suffer from their long exposure."

Bowing again, while Miss Manly emulated his politeness by bending over him, he departed, though not without
a farewell glance at Eoline.

Louisa had said that Miss Manly was kind in sickness,
and she proved the truth of the remark in her tender
cares of the exhausted girl, whose gentleness and humility
had endeared her to one whose authority she had never
disputed, and whose wishes she always seemed anxious
to anticipate. She almost carried her to her chamber in
her arms, assisted in undressing her, and establishing her
in dry sheets, and then brought her a tumbler of warm
sangaree, and bathed her temples with cologne.

"I said she had no heart," repeated Eoline, to herself.
"I have wronged her. She really looks amiable, ministering with a woman's tenderness to one so meek and fragile.
Her character seems made of stripes, like a dress I saw
her wear the other day—with a thick heavy stripe of
satin, and then one of the thinnest gauze. There is no
softening into each other—the edges are all hard.

Then the thought of St. Leon, the interesting stranger,
and the dazzling glances of his lustrous dark eyes. How
mellow was his voice, and how graceful his motions, how
winning his manners! St. Leon!—it was a charming name,
and suited well its engaging owner. She thought of
Horace Cleveland, and wondered how *he* would have deport-
ed himself in such a scene. She laughed at the idea of
Horace kneeling on the wet ground and holding an umbrella over their heads.

"And yet," thought she, "he looks far more like one
who could shelter and protect from the storm and wind
than this slender, handsome St. Leon. Horace is the oak,
whose boughs play not with the breeze, nor bow before
the tempest. St. Leon, the graceful willow, whose pliant
branches sway in every zephyr. Horace would never
have thought of taking off his hat to screen me from the
76

rain, though, if real danger approached, he might interpose
his body as a rampart.

Louisa was the only sufferer from the rainy walk. Eoline
and the children, like spring flowers, blossomed more beautifully and brightly after their vernal baptism; but poor
Louisa bowed her head like a lily overcharged with dew,
and had not strength to lift it for several days. And now
she was able to understand that though less admired than
Eoline, she was equally beloved. The same hands that
almost smothered the beautiful Eoline with coronation flowers, without twining one garland for *her* pale and then
neglected brow, now ministered to her weakness, and alle-
viated her sufferings.

"Oh, how ungrateful I have been," said she, to Eoline.
"Yesterday, when I saw you enthroned in your regal
bower, the object of such adoring homage, while I was
left forgotten and alone, I sighed, not for the honors and
adulations which were your due, but at the thought that I
was unloved. Oh, it was a cold, icy cold thought, colder
than the rain from which you sought to shelter me so
kindly. I find there are other flowers, as sweet as May-
day blossoms, which the hand of affection may entwine,
and whose fragrance may penetrate the inmost heart. God
is merciful—in giving me a feeble frame, he has also
given me a claim on the sympathy and tenderness of others,
feelings of which love is born. He does not forget us,
even when we forget ourselves."

Happy they, who, by a divine alchemy, can extract the
balm of consolation from the bitter ingredients of human
suffering.

The evening after the holiday, St. Leon called, and was
received by Miss Manly with unusual graciousness. There
was something so deferential in his manners, so winning
in his appearance, he at once disarmed her of the hercu-
ean club of formality, with which she ban shed all stran-

gers from her portals who were not furnished with the
proper credentials. Eoline had not forgotten the enchanting strains wafted over the waters of the creek, and she
longed once more to listen to a voice of more than manly
melody. St. Leon, who seemed to be an enthusiast in
music, the moment he caught a glimpse of the harp, flew
towards it, and exclaimed—

"Ah! this is indeed a treasure! Do you play, madam?"
asked he, adroitly turning to Miss Manly.

"I am not a great practitioner," she replied, smilingly,
"though I flatter myself I am something of a connoisseur.
I do my playing chiefly by proxy. If you are fond of
music, I can promise you that Miss Glenmore will not refuse to administer to your gratification."

"Fond of music!" cried he, enthusiastically, "I adore
it. It was the idol of my boyhood—the passion of my
manhood. Will Miss Glenmore indeed gratify me so
highly?" added he, uncovering the instrument, and drawing it towards her. As he did so, he ran his hand over the
wires, with a practiced touch.

"Certainly," replied she, seating herself with graceful
readiness, "but you will find my compliance arises from
very selfish motives—the hope of reward. Mr. St. Leon,"
continued she, turning to Miss Manly, "is a musician himself, and added an unexpected charm to our holiday pleasures, by the music of a voice which it is only justice to
say I have never heard equalled."

St. Leon colored with delight. Eoline spoke of a
sweet voice in singing, as she would of a magnolia blos
som. It was a beautiful gift of God, and the owner had
no cause for vanity or pride. She knew that she possessed
this gift herself, and she was grateful for it. Her mother,
a lovely, pious woman, used to tell her, when she was a
child, that she must praise God for having given her a
voice to sing His praise ; that the angels sang divine hymns

to their golden harps, and that one day her angel child
would be enrolled in that glorious choir. Eoline never
seated herself at the harp without remembering the words
of the mother, whose spirit-tongue now warbled the melo-
dies of eternity. She never liked to play upon it any but
holy anthems. It seemed sacrilege to her to mingle with
the sacred associations of her childhood, the light and fashionable songs of the day. The instrument which the arch-
angels waked to hosannas of glory, which the minstrel
monarch swept with adoring hand, and which her mother
assimilated to the lyre of the seraphim, was hallowed in
her eyes.

" Will you accompany me in this ?" said she, commencing part of an oratorio.

He immediately began one of the most melodious
seconds, that flowed in under her clear rich soprano, like
a fountain gushing beneath the surface of a stream, and
mingling with its waves. Or, rather, her voice was the
fountain, sending up its bright silvery wreaths to the sun
shine ; his, the waters, murmuring in the deep reservoir
below.

Eoline was charmed; St. Leon inspired. They sang
again and again—and never did voices harmonize so perfectly. They melted into each other as softly and as
richly as the strains of the eolian lyre whose name she
bore. At length she paused and leaned against the harp—
for its chords, so sweet to the ear, are anything but down
to the touch. St. Leon then seated himself at the piano,
and the keys flashed under his flying fingers. Miss Manly
was in ecstasies. Her curls flew from one side to the
other, in her effort to keep time with his rapid movements.

" What a talent you have, Mr. St Leon !" she exclaimed ; " I cannot but regret that you do not make music
your profession—for then I should be tempted to secure
your services as a vocalist "

St. Leon turned round quickly, with a bright smile.

"Supposing it were my profession, would you inaeed desire my services, when you have such a world of music in Miss Glenmore?"

"Miss Glenmore's voice is admirable," she replied, "but with a fine male voice in addition, we could make the most splendid singing classes that were ever heard in a Female Institution. Such a second as yours would make the fortune of any one who is not already lifted above its caprices."

People who know little of music, always talk enthusiastically of *seconds*, thinking it has a scientific sound.

St. Leon rose from the piano, aud eagerly approached Miss Manly.

"Though I cannot say that I have made music my profession, yet if you think my voice can be of any assistance in your Institution, Miss Manly"—here he made one of his peculiarly graceful bows—"believe me, it is at your service, at all times and all hours."

"Indeed, sir," replied Miss Manly, hardly knowing how to understand an offer, which seemed so gratuitous in expression, but delighted with the manner in which it was made—"I never imagined such a thing possible, when I made the suggestion. But if you are indeed willing to become a coadjutor in the charming science of music, may I ask on what terms I can enlist your vocal powers?"

"Oh, it is of no consequence," he answered, with some confusion; "I will leave that entirely to yourself; it can be arranged hereafter. I am something of a traveller, but have no objection to rest a while in your beautiful valley I would rather have some kind of employment than remain a mere idler. If you indeed desire it, I shall consider myself highly honored to be associated with an Insti tution which combines so many rare attractions."

He addressed Miss Manly, but his glance in conclusion,

was directed towards Eoline. Miss Manly did not perceive this—for she had already commenced a bow of ac-
knowledgment, or she would not have felt so much
gratified at the compliment. Eoline listened with surprise
and embarrassment, to an arrangement which would bring
her in such close companionship with a stranger. She
was astonished that Miss Manly, with her iron rules and
inflexible formality, should have courted a proposition she
would have thought foreign to all her ideas of propriety.
But Miss Manly was not that *strange anomaly*, a woman
without a heart, which Eoline had at first supposed her to
be. She had a heart, though covered with a coat of mail.
It might be supposed that a Goliah or a Sampson would
be more likely to pierce through its steel panoply, than
this young, romantic-looking stranger ; but it is certain,
that she had never looked upon mortal man with the same
favor which he, at the first glance, had won. Though her
extraordinary height, and the still more extraordinary airs
of command which she assumed, gave her an appearance
of fuller maturity—she was not more than five-and twenty.
Though passed the vernal equinox of youth, she had not
reached the summer solstice of womanhood. St. Leon
had those dangerous, languishingly brilliant eyes, that
seemed "to love whate'er they looked upon," and when
he fixed those eyes upon her face, making the earnest offer
of his services, she could not help thinking he was inspired
by no common interest in the Principal of the Magnolia
Vale Seminary. She had no mean estimate of her own
attractions. If nature had not endowed her with the
beauty of a Venus, she believed herself possessed of the
majesty of a Juno, the purity of a Diana, and the wisdom
of a Pallas.

"If you will call to-morrow morning, Mr. St. Leon,"
said she, with dignified affability, "at about eleven o'clock,

the hour of recess, I shall be extremely happy to make the
necessary arrangements on this very interesting subject."

St. Leon called, the arrangements were made, and his
name added to the list of instructors in the Magnolia Vale
Seminary. The young misses were highly pleased with
this addition to the faculty, and Eoline felt a charm
thrown around the lessons by the fascinations of his
voice and manner, unknown before. As they were arranged at those hours when Miss Manly could sanction
them by her majestic presence, Eoline was spared those
feelings of embarrassment which might arise from being
associated so intimately with so young and handsome a
man. There was a mystery about him that added to the
interest he inspired. She was certain that he was as unaccustomed to labor for others as herself, and that whatever motives induced him to assume the position which he
now occupied, he was born to affluence and rank. He did
not board in the seminary, but there was always some excuse for bringing him there in the evening, a piece of new
music to practice, a string of Eoline's harp or guitar to
mend, or some new book to read to Miss Manly. He was
a universal favorite, from the dignified principal to the
smallest child in the establishment. As we said before, he
had those mild, expressive eyes, that seemed to rain love
and sunshine on all; and all the sweet and graceful courtesies of life, which Horace Cleveland had slighted from
his boyhood, St. Leon was ever ready to offer. In their
walks, if Louisa's steps flagged from weariness, his arm
was always extended for her support ; when Miss Manly
commenced her brilliant harangues, he gave her the most
respectful attention, yet it was evident that Eoline was
the inspiration of all his actions,—evident to all but Miss
Manly, who still continued strong in her first impression,
that deep and admiring reverence for herself was the
charm that bound him to Magnolia Vale.

There was only one restriction which Miss Manly imposed upon him—and that was, that he should leave his beautiful, silky-eared dog at Montebello. Being an exceedingly democratic quadruped, though belonging to an aristocratic master, he bade defiance to all her rules, and created an anarchy in the school-room that threatened the destruction of her dynasty. Miss Manly was not fond of dogs or cats. Her only pets were peacocks, whose starry-eyed plumage illuminated the inclosure back of the seminary. The bird consecrated to Juno, seemed alone worthy of *her* caresses.

CHAPTER V.

We will return for a while to the deserted Master of Glenmore,—and see what joy and comfort he finds in his now daughterless home. We will look in upon him, about the time that Horace returned from his visit to Magnolia Vale, while lingering Winter still makes the fireside the brightest, happiest spot. He is sitting on the same sofa which Eoline always wheeled up for him in exactly the same spot, his feet are encased in the beautiful embroidered slippers her hand had wrought, he has on his silver gray wrapper, and the green shade softens the splendor of the astral lamp. He sits with his arms folded, gazing at the illuminated hearth.

"Do you want any thing more, master?"

"Nothing."

"Shall I bring Master Willie down before he goes to bed?"

"Yes."

"Gatty closed the door. "How different," thought he, "from the sweet voice of Eoline. The lamp has too great a glare. Eoline knew how to temper its lustre, so that it was as soft as moonlight. The curtains hang awry. Every thing misses the magic of her graceful touch. She was certainly a most loving and affectionate daughter, till her pride rose up and overshadowed all her lovely domestic virtues. Pride!—pride!" repeated the proud father, perfectly unconscious of being under its tyrannical dominion himself, "it was pride that caused the angels to be banished from heaven. It is the curse of many a domestic Eden If she would even now unbend and obey my will, I would forgive her past rebellion and receive her to my arms, for oh! I do feel such a void, such a dreary void!"

He paused with a long, deep sigh, but no light footstep hovered near, no gentle voice inquired,

"Father, what can *I* do to cheer you?" as in hours that were past.

Yes!—light footsteps did come near—a gentle voice did breathe into his ear, but it brought no balm, for its burden was Eoline, sweet sister Ela. Willie came to pay his nightly visit, but the child who mourned for his sister and refused to be comforted, was always sure to say something that struck like a dagger to his father's heart. The beautiful boy

> "Led by his dusky guide,
> Like morning brought by night,"

glides along in his night-dress and stood by his father's knee.

"When is Ela coming back?" was always his first question. In vain had he been forbidden to ask it. In vain had he been told that no one knew when Ela was coming. He thought as his father went abroad every day, that he must hear something of his sister, and still uniformly as the night came on, and Gatty brought him to his father's knee, he would lift his tender, wistful brown eyes to his face, and repeat the burden of his young and yearning heart,

"When is sister Ela coming home?"

This night the question seemed unusually painful to Mr. Glenmore, and he answered impatiently,

"I have told you a hundred times that I know nothing about it. Why *will* you persist in asking?"

"Because I want to see her so bad. I must see her father. I can't live without seeing her."

His beautiful eyes were crystalized with tears. His father could not speak harshly to such a cherub, though he often sent such barbed arrows to his conscience. He took the child in his arms and talked to him of his playthings, of a little pony he was going to buy him, but no matter what subject was introduced, by some association it brought him back to Ela.

"I don't want a pony, unless you send for Ela to see me ride it. When *are* you going to send for her?"

"She does not want to come home. She went away because she does not love us well enough to stay with us, Willie. You must learn to be happy without her."

"But I cannot," repeated the boy, "and I know she *does* love us. And she didn't want to go away, either. I remember how she rained her tears on my neck, and how she sobbed and wept, as if her heart were breaking all to pieces. What for did she cry so hard about going away, if she wanted to leave us?"

Many a one besides Mr. Glenmore has found it hard to confute, with false sophistry, the pure logic of childhood. He remembered himself the filial shower which drenched his bosom, the warm embrace, the clinging arms, the prayerful entreaties of that night of anguish; and he knew he had spoken falsely when he had said that she *wanted* to leave them. But he could not tell this little single-hearted child, that he had banished her because she would not marry Horace Cleveland.

"You must not talk about Eoline any more, Willie," said he, smoothing back his ringlets, without looking him in the face. "I have told you so many times. I repeat it again. If you do not obey me, I shall tell Gatty to put you to bed without bringing you down stairs to see me. Will you mind me, Willie?"

The child slid out of his father's arms, and took hold of Gatty's hand.

"You needn't bring me down stairs at night any more, Gatty," said he, sadly, but resolutely, "I can't help talk

ing about Ela, and I don't want to. She's good, and I
love her. I will talk about her," added the boy, his heart
swelling and heaving with suppressed sobs. "She's my
sister, and I won't forget her."

Again Mr. Glenmore was left alone, alone with his
inflexibility and his pride. He took up a book and endeavored to read, but he had been so accustomed to have
Eoline read aloud to him, that all books seemed insipid,
wanting the charm of her melodious voice.

"Miserable father!" he exclaimed, throwing down his
book, "both my children turn against me. They care not
for me—intent on their own stubborn will. No one cares
for me. Even Cleveland looks coldly on me since my
daughter has left me, as if I could have helped her rejection of his son? What could I do more than discard, banish
her? Willie, young as he is, boldly reproaches me for the
loss of his sister. Even my negroes roll their eye-balls
saucily in my face when they ask me when I've heard
from Miss Eoline. Yet it is her own fault—all her own
fault—though *I* must bear the blame and the reproach.
Such is the justice of the world. It is, 'There goes the
cruel father'—not a word of the obstinate, ungrateful
daughter."

He was interrupted in his meditations by the announce-
ment of a visitor, and Horace Cleveland entered. He
seemed in haste. His mother was unusually ill. They
were to start for Cuba on the morrow. He came to pay
his parting respects.

"I have seen your daughter," he added, abruptly. "She
burdened me with a thousand messages of love to yourself
and Willie."

"She is well, I trust," said Mr. Glenmore, trying to
speak in an indifferent tone, though he started with surprise and pleasure.

"She is well, but she cannot be happy, situated as she

is. Mr. Glenmore, you cannot allow her to remain there. You cannot permit your daughter to labor under a stern task-mistress, when you have educated her so munificently, nurtured her so tenderly ; when the principles to which she has sacrificed the luxuries of home, ought to glorify her in your eyes."

"Really," said Mr. Glenmore, looking with surprise on the animated countenance of the young man, " if you had manifested as much interest in my daughter's behalf, before her departure, she might perhaps have been reconciled to remain. For, let me tell you, young man," continued he, glad to find some channel in which he could pour out his exasperated feelings, " it always did seem very strange to me, that you should look with such coldness and indifference on a girl of Eoline's acknowledged attractions.   One would have supposed that you were doomed to wed poverty and deformity, instead of affluence and beauty,—that you were to be dragged to the scaffold instead of the altar. If I had not said she should marry you," added he, growing warmer and warmer as he expatiated on the subject, and still clinging to the sheet-anchor of his soul, his own iron will—" if I had not passed my *word*, a word that never has been broken, and never shall be, I would like her all the better for her woman's spirit."

" I never have felt myself worthy of your daughter, sir," replied Horace, apparently stung by Mr. Glenmore's bitter taunts. " I acknowledge I have been unjust to her merits. I have lived in a world of my own, from earliest boyhood, very much like the chrysalis in its shell. I could not be forced to affect an interest I did not feel. The heart admits of no dictator. At least mine does not. Your daughter has nobly asserted the independence of hers. I admire, ι honor her for it. She should be crowned with laurels instead of being doomed to banishment; exalted into a heroine, instead of being forced to earn her daily bread."

"Does she appear unhappy?" asked Mr. Glenmore, charmed, in spite of himself, with Horace's warm eulogium.

"She told me she was resigned, if not happy. A spirit like hers would sustain itself in any situation."

"How did she receive you?" asked the father.

"Far more cordially than I deserved. We parted friends, better friends than we met. Friends, I trust, we shall ever remain."

"Friends!" repeated Mr. Glenmore, with a peculiar smile. "When a young man and a young girl talk about being friends all their lives, we know what it means. I see very well that it rests with yourself to shorten the period of my daughter's banishment. If you wish it, you can hasten her return."

"No, sir," hastily interrupted Horace, the blood rushing even to his temples, "she did not disguise the repugnance which induced her to flee. I have no hope that I could ever conquer it. I am destitute of those graces and accomplishments which charm the eye and win the affections of the young and beautiful. Yet with so little to inspire love, I should be boundless in my wishes, endless in my exactions. If I once loved, I should be an enthusiast, and stake my life's happiness on being loved in return. I tremble for what might be the consequences."

"You have *thought* of the subject since your visit to Magnolia Vale, it seems," said Mr. Glenmore, sarcastically.

"I have," replied he, frankly, "and felt, too, as I have never done before; but, as I leave home to-morrow, and it may be long before I return, I shall have ample time to recover the former tone of my mind. In the meantime, I know your parental heart will plead for your daughter's restoration, and will not plead in vain."

"What fools sensible young men can make of themselves!" exclaimed Mr. Glenmore. "I want to know what is the reason you could not make yourself loved, if you tried? With a fine face, a splendid figure, talents of which any man might be proud, a large fortune, and an unble-mished character, you talk as if you were a scarecrow, terrible enough to frighten away all 'the girls in Chris-tendom."

"I spoke only of Eoline's repugnance, sir."

"And that was born of your indifference. The burden of her song was that she could not be an unloved wife, that she could not marry a man who disliked her."

"Disliked her!" repeated Horace. "I never disliked her. I was indifferent, blind, stolid, perhaps. Mr. Glen-more, I cannot remain to discuss this subject farther, to-night. I should be glad to hear you say, before I leave, that you would recall Eoline from banishment. I should go with a lighter heart."

"Did she commission you to plead in her behalf?"

"No, sir," replied the young man, with growing warmth. "All that I have said, is the spontaneous suggestion of my own mind. She asks nothing, claims nothing from you. If you were in sickness and sorrow, she would fly to you on the wings of filial love; but in your day of prosperity and strength, she feels that you need not her ministrations. But you do, sir—I see that you do."

Horace took up his hat and moved towards the door. Mr. Glenmore held out his hand.

"I am not offended with your frankness, Horace. I am glad that you have seen Eoline, and that you seem to like her better than you once did. I suspect she will be tired of her experiment and come back after a while. I will not turn her from my door, but she knows the conditions on which I can receive her as a daughter, and so do you. Farewell!—a pleasant voyage and the speedy restoration of your mother's health."

"They have entered into a conspiracy against me, to-

night," said Mr. Glenmore, when he retired into his chamber and closed the door. I wonder if they will let me
sleep. I suspect even the ghosts will haunt my pillow,
and cry out, 'Eoline, Eoline.' "

Poor man ! his own heart kept echoing the same eloquent cry, and he heard it through the steel armor of his
pride, and he tried to double the panoply and pile up
mountains of defence, but it would be heard, in sunshine
and shadow, by day and by night, that one, sweet, musical
name, "Eoline, Eoline."

In the unusual agitation of his mind, he forgot to extin-
guish his light, but fell asleep with the lamp blazing on
the table. How long he had slept he knew not, but he
awakened with a thrill of horror, at feeling a little cold
hand laid on his, and starting up in bed, he saw a small
white figure standing by him, with his large, pensive eyes
fixed immovably on his face.

" Willie," he exclaimed, " Willie, what are you doing
here ?"

The child moved not. Its eyes remained fixed as the
eyes of the dead. Its cold hand pressed his. Its auburn
ringlets hung listless on its cheeks.

" When is Ela coming back ?" it cried, in a strange, unnatural tone.

For a moment the father trembled with superstitious
terror—so pale and still and corpse-like the child looked,
in the glare of the yellow lamp-light—but he recollected
that Willie was a somnambulist, and had frequently
alarmed the family by his nocturnal rambles. Still it was
the first time he had ever sought *his* bed—the first time
that the voice of that mysterious existence between life
and death had ever sounded in his ears—and when he
heard the name of Eoline issuing from those statue-like
lips in the silence of the night, and the loneliness of his

apartment, he would have scarcely felt more awe had an inhabitant from the tomb addressed him.

"Willie, my child," cried he, "awake. You must not walk about in your sleep in this manner."

"I'm looking for Ela," replied the boy, fixing his still, star-like eyes on the face of his father. "Is she gone to Heaven?"

"Come to bed, Willie," said his father, stretching out his arms and lifting him into bed by his side. "Now shut your eyes and lie still. Don't say any thing more."

The child lay still and silent, but he did not close his eyes. Calm, deep and serene as a moon-lit lake, when not a breath of wind agitates its surface, their dark, brown orbs, mirrored the troubled glances bent upon them. He was as cold as ice, and his cheeks white as alabaster. His father could not tell whether he were asleep or awake—whether in that awful sleep, which fills with chill, shivering sensations, those who wake to behold it; or in the full consciousness of being pillowed on the bosom, whose pride and self-will had so lately repelled that young and innocent head. Thus they lay, looking into each other's faces, while the long wick of the lamp wavered, and made strange shadows on the wall.

"I cannot bear this any longer," thought Mr. Glenmore, laying his hand gently over the eyes, so awful in their serene immobility. He felt the soft lids closing under his touch. After a while the icy limbs grew warm in his embrace, and a calm, uniform breathing stole like music into his ears.

"I will write to Eoline to-morrow," was the father's last resolve, as he fell asleep by his sleeping boy. When he awoke in the morning, Willie was gone. The little somnambulist had stolen back to his couch, unknown to his father and himself; and like the night-vision of the angel-child, the good resolutions of Mr. Glenmore fled

77

with returning sunshine. Remorse is a pale ghost, that
haunts the midnight shades. Pride, a giant, with greaves
of brass and spear of iron, challenging, under the broad
day-beam, the armies of the living God. If night were
the time for action, Eoline had long since been recalled,
but unfortunately her avengers walked in darkness, and in
the light the strong man defied their power.

He had business to transact that day, which led him
about twenty miles from home. The air was clear and
elastic, the sky blue and clear, the horse which bore him
fleet and spirited. Mr. Glenmore's spirits rose, and the lord
of Glenmore Place seemed to occupy a very enviable
niche in the temple of the world. The business detained
him longer than he anticipated, and he concluded to pass
the night with a friend, an old college friend of his, whom
he had not met since their parting on commencement day,
when, from the threshold of manhood, they had looked
out into life and saw nothing but a crowd of indistinct
and glorious images. For years he had seen nothing of
this friend, and knew not until lately that he had become
a resident of a place so near his own. It was not without
emotion that he inquired the way to his dwelling, and
asked if Mr. Wilton were at home. He was ushered into
a handsome parlor, where he awaited the entrance of his
friend.

"This is an awkward position," thought Mr. Glenmore,
"I know not what has befallen him during these long
years of separation. If I inquire after the health of his
wife, she may, like mine, be sleeping the deep sleep that
knows no awakening here. If I ask after his children, he
may have none, or they may be dead, or what is still
worse, worthless. If he pay me the same compliment, I
shall feel something as if I were under the operation of
the tourniquet It is a dangerous thing for friends to meet

after the lapse of years, unless the tongue of the absent
has been made eloquent during the interval."

While waiting for his friend, he was attracted by a beautiful picture on the wall opposite the mantel-piece. It
was a young girl in the garb of a shepherdess, with a crook
in her hand, and a straw hat, encircled with a garland of
roses, on her head. Her eyes were so black and lustrous,
her hair so black, waving and redundant, her cheeks so
radiant with life-roses, and her whole figure so airy and
buoyant, so full of youth and grace, that it gave one a
joyous sensation to gaze upon it.

" That must be his wife or daughter," thought Mr.
Glenmore. " It is almost as beautiful as my own Eoline.
But Eoline has the beauty of the morning. This reminds
me of the midnight's splendor."

A gentleman entered in whose slender form, thin features,
and sallow complexion, he would never have recognized
the handsome person of the youthful graduate. Neither
would the thin, sallow, yet distinguished looking gentleman
have identified the slender, graceful student, in the portly
person and worldly face of the aristocratic man before him.

" Glenmore, I am glad to see you," said Wilton, in a
deep, melancholy voice, how different from the gay, hila-
rious tone of other days. " You and the world have been
on good terms, I perceive."

" And how fares it with you, my friend ?" asked Glen
more, all his best and kindest feelings stirred within him,
as the visions of his youth rose one by one before his eyes.

" You see I am a kind of walking ghost," he replied,
" but I am better now than I was six months ago. Then,
it would hardly have been thought premature to have mea
sured my grave. But walk into our family sitting-room
The air of this cold parlor seems chill and ungenial to
meet an old friend in. Come, let me introduce you to my
wife. You will see my daughter too," added he, in a low

voice, as they threaded the long passage, " or rather what
was once my daughter. You noticed the picture over the
sofa. See if you can trace any resemblance."

A servant at this moment opening the door, Mr. Wilton
checked what he was about to utter, and ushered his friend
into the room where two ladies were seated. The elder of
the two, a very fine-looking, but pale and care-worn lady,
rose to receive him, the wife and mother of the family.
The other did not move nor take any notice of the introduction, but sat like a statue of stone, her large black eyes
riveted on the floor, with an expression of hopeless despondency. In vain did Mr. Glenmore endeavor to trace in
that wild, faded and stony countenance, any resemblance
to the bright, smiling, blooming shepherdess of the parlor.
He looked at his friend, who turned away his head with a
sigh, then resuming the conversation, he led the way back
through the scenes of their youth, and gathered up a thousand reminiscences of their college life. The evening
glided away unconsciously, and the sallow face of Wilton
lighted up with a kind of sunset glow.

" Amelia, my dear," said Mrs. Wilton, to the pale statue
on the sofa, " you had better retire. It is later than you
usually sit up."

" I cannot go alone, mother," she answered, with a hol-
low, melancholy accent. " I'll go, when you are ready,
but not alone. That is, if you are willing to let me wait.
I'll do just as you think best."

Mrs. Wilton rose with a sad countenance, and bidding
Mr. Glenmore good-night, took her daughter's passive hand
and led her from the room. As they passed through the
door, the latter rolled her large, wild eyes back one moment on the stranger's face, and then disappeared. Mr.
Glenmore started. It seemed to him a voice was echoing
through the apartment, as through his own echoing halls,
" Eoline, Eoline."

" My poor, unhappy child !" exclaimed Wilton, clasping his hands together and leaning his forehead upon them. " How my heart bleeds for her. When I think what she once was, and what she now is, I can scarcely believe in her identity."

" What has been the cause of this calamity ?" asked Mr. Glenmore, strangely associating the thought of his blooming Eoline with this wreck of woman's loveliness.

" A loveless, ill-assorted marriage," exclaimed the father, with emphasis. " A marriage that has frozen the fountains of youthful feelings, paralized the spring of youthful ener-gy, and turned her heart to stone."

The ruddy hue of Mr. Glenmore's cheek turned of ashy paleness. Once more the sweet name of Eoline breathed softly in the father's ear.

" Was it a marriage of compulsion ?" asked the con-science-stricken Glenmore.

" Not exactly of compulsion," replied the father; " but if you will not be a weary listener, I will relate to you all the circumstances."

Mr. Glenmore drew his chair still nearer, and his coun-tenance expressed the deep interest he felt.

"I have two sons in college," continued Mr. Wilton, " but this is my only daughter. Were it not for the picture on which I saw you gazing, you might well believe it a father's partiality, when I tell you how fair and beautiful my poor, faded child once was. She had but one fault—a too yielding temper. Ever swayed by the will of others, ever sacrificing her own wishes to those around her, it was impossible to discover whether she had a wish or will of her own. If I said, ' will you do so and so, my Amelia ?' she always answered, ' If you and my mother desire it.' We never controlled her, never intimidated her by the manifestation of an arbitrary will. We endeavored to give tone to her meek and too passive character. We encou

raged her to lean on her own judgment, to think, feel and
act for herself, but she never would do it; never would
select a ribbon or an ornament without the approval of her
mother's taste, or a book or journal, unsanctioned by her
father's judgment. At length about two years ago, a gentleman of unblemished reputation, wealth and standing, paid
his addresses to her. He was of cold, reserved manners,
and somewhat unattractive in appearance, but he appeared
devotedly attached to our Amelia, who hardly lifted her
eyes in his presence, and very seldom spoke. For several
months previous she had been unusually languid, and frequently sunk into long fits of melancholy, which, not being
able to trace to any mental cause, filled us with solicitude
about her health. We hoped the attentions of Mr. Lovell
would be a source of interest and excitement, and therefore
encouraged them. When we appealed to her for decision on this all-important subject, she again and again repeated, 'I will do just as you, my parents, think best. I
have no will but yours.'

" ' But your own happiness, my child, is at stake. It is
for you to decide where your own heart is concerned
Let it speak, and listen to its dictates. Do you love
him?'

" ' I respect and esteem him,' she would answer. ' I am
willing to marry him if you think it best that I should.'

" Yes—*she* was willing—friends were urgent—the gentleman pressing—and we, believing him to be a moral,
sensible and honorable man, having the responsibility of
hoosing for her, thus forced upon us, advised, nay, even
urged her acceptance of his addresses—we were weary of
her indecision. We saw no reasonable objection, and as
her heart did not seem pre-occupied with another, we
trusted he would, in time, rouse it from the constitutional
apathy in which it was steeped. Were we right in so
doing ?"

"Certainly—certainly," answered Mr. Glenmore.— "What else could you do?"

"Well, she married, and her husband carried her to his own home, very far from ours. In a year's time we yearned to see her. We wrote and entreated her to come. She answered that she would if her husband were willing she had no will but his. He was not willing. He was cold, selfish, and self-willed. We had been all tenderness and indulgence. We had anticipated all her wishes. Her husband thought only of the gratification of his own. The poor child fell into a state of perfect stagnation. Her health languished, her spirits sank into the waveless calm of hopeless despondency, and last week he brought her back to remain with us while he is making an European tour. If you were to ask her now if she is happy, she would say, 'I think so, that is, if my husband is willing.' Glenmore, you have a daughter?"

"Yes."

"Has she a will of her own?"

"Yes, and a pretty strong one."

"Thank God for it. Thank God that she can take the responsibility of her destiny out of your hands. I begin to think my poor girl had no heart, but she must have had one, or she would not have felt it freezing and freezing, like the waters of a still lake in a frosty atmosphere. Had she waited till love had ruffled those still waters, she had escaped this living death. If you love your daughter never let her marry a man whom she does not love with all her heart and soul. Make her take the responsibility of her life's future out of your keeping. God knows that our own accountability is a sufficiently fearful trust. I have been a wretched invalid for many a day, but this affliction has added the weight of twenty years to my existence."

"I am sorry for you," said Mr. Glenmore, thoughtfully.

"This is really an extraordinary case. But I see no possible blame that you can attach to yourself. What a
strange world this is! You are made wretched, because
your daughter has been made a passive being in the hands
of others; I, because I cannot bend the stubborn will of
mine, to my own superior judgment. Certainly my trials
are very different from yours."

Here he related to his friend his own domestic history,
dwelling on his baffled hopes, his defeated plans, his
wounded pride and affection. Wilton listened with intense interest. He rose and walked the room, rubbed his
hands together, and fixed upon the speaker his deep-set
and intelligent eyes.

"And you have discarded, banished this glorious girl!"
he exclaimed, when Glenmore paused for breath. "Cast
her from you, because she has dared to be the judge of
her own happiness; dared to assert the supremacy of conscience, honor and truth, over parental authority. You
ought rather to erect an altar to her, and pay homage to
the purity and rectitude of her principles, the noble independence of her spirit. The young man, too! I like him.
I like his proud sincerity, his unbending firmness. What
a pity you fathers tried to force them together. Had you
left them free, they might have been drawn towards each
other by a natural attraction, but the lordly spirit disdains
coercion. Chains are chains, though forged of gold, and
they will excoriate the heart, though covered with roses.
Glenmore, you must recall this daughter of yours. If
you do not, by Heaven, *I* will adopt her for my own!"

"If I had not pledged my word—a word never yet
broken!" exclaimed Mr. Glenmore.

"Away with such sophistry!" cried his friend. "The
word spoken in passion is no more binding than the oath
of a maniac To utter a rash promise is foolish, to

persist in it, when reason and justice condemn it, is criminal."

"If I thought I should not forfeit my character for consistency !" said the father of Eoline.

Wilton's melancholy features relaxed into a smile.

" We are wretched self-deceivers, my friend. Why, you are the most inconsistent man in the universe, at this moment. For eighteen years, you have been sparing neither time nor money, in forming a lovely, intelligent, high-principled human being, and now you have thrown her from you, because she refuses to be a soulless machine, a heartless piece of barter and merchandise. If that is what you call consistency, I must say, you have studied a very different lexicography from what I have."

"I will write to her!" exclaimed Glenmore, with sudden warmth, grasping Wilton's hand in both his. " You *are* right. I thank you for opening my eyes to the real excellencies of her character. I have never known one moment's peace or happiness since she left me. My home has seemed a tomb, my heart a grave. Give me pen, ink and paper, and I will write to her, this very night. Surely, Providence sent me hither, that the sight of your poor frozen child should restore mine to her forfeit-place in my affections."

A portable writing-desk, containing all the requisite materials, was immediately placed before him. Wilton looked on, with benevolent approbation, while he wrote, under the influence of excited feelings, what would have brought back the banished daughter at once, to her father's arms.

" There," said he, pushing the paper towards Wilton " read it, and write *approved* at the bottom of it, if you will."

" Written like a father, a man and a Christian," replied Wilton, laying his hand on his shoulder. "Believe

me, the only true dignity consists in a practical recanta-
tion of the errors of passion and of pride. Your daughter
will love and respect you far more than ever—so will all
good and honest men."

Mr. Glenmore returned home with a lightened heart.
Day after day and week after week, he waited, with an
impatience that baffles description, for tidings from Magnolia Vale. But no letter, overflowing with grateful emotion—no Eoline, flying on the wings of the wind to the
arms now open to receive her, gladdened the sad monotony of Glenmore Place.

"She scorns my offer of reconciliation," he cried, pride
darkening into wrath. "She refuses my forgiveness, and
spurns my humiliation. Well, let her reap as she has
sown. Though she steep her bread of dependence in bitter tears, though her hireling wages be earned by her
heart's best blood, she shall walk on in the thorny path
she herself has chosen. These rejected arms shall close
forever over my wronged and alienated affections. I
might have known—" continued the excited father, "that
will of hers would never bend. The eternal vault of
Heaven would swerve from its stately arch, sooner than
that blue eye soften its bright, yet resolute beam."

At the remembrance of that blue eye, pure and celestial as the Heavens, whose hue it had borrowed, a feeling of tenderness touched the proud father's heart. A
tear glazed his haughty eye. He dashed it angrily away.

"Why should I feel, since she is forever estranged?"
he cried. "Away with this weakness. Wilton may
weep if he will, over his frozen child, and it is well.
Mine has transformed herself into a pillar of fire, which
her own tears may quench, not mine."

Poor Eoline, how little she dreamed of the storm of
passion she had unconsciously excited in the bosom she
believed impassive to parental emotions. The letter of

reconciliation had never reached her. By a strange fatality, it had miscarried, and thus widened the breach it was intended to heal. The dove of peace was not permitted to perform its heavenly mission, and the olive \ranch withered in its beak.

CHAPTER VI.

Eoline had become accustomed to her little severely-furnished apartment. She no longer contrasted it with her beautiful and airy chamber at Glenmore Place, but with the bustle of the school-room and the pompous formality of the dining hall. Miss Manly had supplied her with a rocking-chair of her own, which, if not covered with crimson velvet, was low and comfortable, in comparison with the Windsor machines, with their tall, tomb-stone backs. The dark counterpane was exchanged for one of snowy-white dimity—the little narrow, green window curtains for white flowing ones; even the morose-looking wardrobe relaxed its stern features under a smiling coat of new varnish. Then her mantel-piece and table were always covered with the sweetest and fairest flowers of the season—the floral offerings of her juvenile admirers—so that she seemed surrounded by the redolence of Spring and the glory of Summer. From her windows she could look down upon Magnolia Vale, with its emerald carpet and flowering trees—and the roar of the mill-dam came like a deep bass in nature's anthem to her musing ear. She could catch the silver flash of the waters as they sparkled in the sun—for though the road which led to the spot was long and winding, encircling a wild and woody glen, the vale itself was not far from the seminary. Eoline had really begun to love the retirement of her little apartment, and to associate with it feelings of home and comfort. Here Louisa often passed with her the evening hours—and Eoline always felt nearer Heaven when she left her. Here darling Fanny would come stealing in, after the nine o'clock bell had rung the

(120)

children to bed, half hidden in her mantle of ringlets; and
Selma, with her straight, black hair of Indian polish and
redundance, unloosened and floating, ready to be gathered
under the muslin cap, would peep in with sly and mischievous smile.   Annie Grey—gentle Annie, as she was
called—could not go to sleep without coming to give Eoline
a loving good night.   And bonny Bessie Bell had learned
the way, after the "curfew tolled," to elude Miss Manly's
vigilant ear, and glide tiptoe along the passage to the Bower
of this May Queen, as they called Eoline's bouquet-scented
apartment.   The girls loved dearly to catch her at her
night toilet.   They almost quarreled for the privilege of
combing out the rippling gold of her hair.   Sometimes she
had half-a-dozen *frizeurs* flying about her head at the same
moment—one braiding, another curling, another smoothing
and burnishing the flowing silk with her rosy palm.   Eoline
would laugh, and call them her bower-maidens, and repay
their toil with fond caresses.   At times, she fell asleep un
der the soothing operation, when she was awakened by a
shower of kisses, mingled with rose leaves stolen from her
vases.

This was all very pleasant to the young and affectionate
Eoline, after being confined all day to her monotonous
lessons, and being measured and squared by Miss Manly's
rule and compass; but she was not permitted to enjoy this
sweet abandonment from restraint much longer.

One evening, after having returned from a walk to the
vale, where St. Leon had met her, and borne her burden
of flowers, she passed up to her room, her cheek flushed
from exercise, and perhaps brightened by the reflection of
St. Leon's languishing dark eyes.   She beheld with astonishment a pile of trunks, band-boxes, bags, and bundles
near the door, and entering, saw, with still greater astonishment, a coarse looking child of about twelve, seated
in her rocking-chair, which she was putting in vehement

motion, while she was craunching a large, green apple, whose skin she had strewn upon the floor. She did not rise as Eoline entered, but stared at her with her light, sullen eyes, without pausing in her fierce mastication of the fruit. Seeing how perfectly she seemed at home, and that she had taken full possession of the apartment, Eoline approached her and said, with that grace and politeness which distinguished all her actions,

"You have mistaken the room, I perceive. This is mine. I presume you are a new pupil of Miss Manly's."

"Miss Manly put me here herself," replied the girl, in a grum voice, half choked with the apple she was swallowing.

"Indeed," said Eoline, her face crimsoning with vexation, "perhaps you do not know Miss Manly. I cannot think she intended you to come in here. It must have been a mistake of the servant's."

"No it wan't," cried the new comer. "'Twas a woman as tall as a steeple, that ordered every body about, and told the folks to bring my trunks up to Miss Glenmore's room. Ain't that your name?"

"Miss Glenmore will probably have something to say about this arrangement herself," cried Eoline, unable to conceal her extreme displeasure at this innovation upon her retirement, and her disgust for the coarse and ill-bred companion thus forced upon her. "I will see Miss Manly immediately."

"I don't want to stay with you, gracious knows, if you don't want me to," said the girl, her face turning as red as a peony. "I didn't put myself here. I'd a heap rather stay with the girls, than one of the teachers, though pa asked Miss Manly to let me sleep with one, 'cause I have the nightmare so bad. I wish I was to home, that I do. I don't want to stay here to be snubbed. Pa's as rich as any body, and has got as many niggers, too. He won't let me be imposed on, either. If he hadn't gone, I'd go back this minute, and so—"

Here she had worked herself up to such a pitch of wounded and indignant feeling, that she began to cry like a big baby, and sobbed out,

"I won't stay here. I'll make pa carry me home. I'm as good as any body, and I'll let folks know it."

Eoline, without attempting to reply to this outbreak of vulgarity and pride, flew down stairs, and encountered Miss Manly in the front passage, conversing in the most gracious manner with St. Leon, who had been presenting her a bouquet of wild flowers. He looked up with surprise at the excitement of Eoline's manner, and at the crimson spot that burned in the roses of her cheeks.

"I should like to speak one moment with you, Miss Manly," said she, "if you are not too much engaged."

"Certainly, Miss Glenmore," replied the principal, "if Mr. St. Leon will excuse me."

Of course Mr. St. Leon excused her, with one of his reverential bows, and a glance of intense anxiety towards Eoline. Miss Manly led the way to the parlor, her eyes looking like a bird of prey's.

"I am certain there has been a mistake," cried Eoline, conscientiously convinced all the time that she was uttering a falsehood; "the servants have put a strange girl in my apartment. I will thank you very much to see that the error is rectified."

"Excuse me, Miss Glenmore," answered Miss Manly, with slight embarrassment, but infinite haughtiness, "I took the liberty, as mistress of this establishment, to put the child there myself. All the dormitories are full. I have a pupil in my own room, and I do not expect my assistants to claim immunities which I do not myself enjoy. As you were absent, I could not inform you of this arrangement. As for asking permission in what manner I might dispose of my own house, I did not think it necessary. I am sorry you are displeased, as it is not possible for me to give counter orders."

"Indeed, Miss Manly," replied Eoline, with grave earnestness, "I cannot consent to this. The apartment is very small, entirely too small for two persons. But even if it were of illimitable extent, I would not share it with a stranger—above all, one so exceedingly vulgar and low-bred as this girl seems to be."

"My former music teacher occupied that same apartment, with one of my pupils," said Miss Manly, with freezing stateliness—"and I never heard any complaint. I must say I think you selfish and disobliging, Miss Glenmore; I always expect my assistants to have the good of the institution more in the heart, than their own personal comfort. There is no sacrifice I would not make to advance its already lofty and spotless reputation. I believe Miss More is actuated by the same high and disinterested motives. She even requested me to place the child in her apartment rather than yours—but her health is so extremely delicate, I did not like her to have any additional charge on her mind."

"I thank you for having some regard for her feelings, if not for mine," exclaimed Eoline, her eyes glistening at this proof of Louisa's self-sacrificing friendship. She began to feel something like the scorpion girt by fire. She could see no way of escape, but by leaving the seminary; and where could she turn, when her father's doors were closed against her? She could not wander abroad, seeking shelter and employment, with the vials of Miss Manly's wrath pouring down upon her devoted head. She was conscious of losing caste with that lady, on account of St. Leon's unrepressed admiration and increasing devotion. She was conscious, too, that Miss Manly had never liked her independence and self-reliance, and was glad of annoying her in a manner most repugnant to her refined and fastidious taste.

"I do not pretend to boast of the meek, Christian temper of Louisa," said she, bitterly. "She is an angel, more fit for Heaven than earth! I wish I were like her—but I never shall be, I fear. If you will give me Fanny or Selma, or Annie, for a companion, Miss Manly, I will not object; but this rude, untaught child, will make my apartment a perfect den of horror."

"I trust the influence of your example will assist in forming her manners. If she has not had the advantages of an early education and refined society, the child is to be pitied, not scorned. However, Miss Glenmore, rather than have the Magnolia Vale Seminary a scene of unlady-like contention, I will go to Miss More and accept her noble and disinterested offer."

Sweeping aside her long ringlets with an imperial motion, she was about to leave the parlor, when Eoline sprang forward and laid her hand on the lock of the door.

"No, madam—let her remain. Louisa shall not sacrifice her tranquillity for mine. I will try to emulate her self-denying and unmurmuring spirit. But when I think of my once loved home—" Eoline could not keep the tears from gushing into her eyes, at the remembrance of all she had sacrificed, and unwilling to give Miss Manly this triumph over her feelings, she hurried into the passage, and avoiding her own apartment, walked out on the green lawn, where the children were playing. Fanny flew forward and put her arms around her.

"Oh! my dear Miss Eoline," she cried, "I have been praying Miss Manly to let me stay with you, and let this new girl take my place; so have half the pupils, but the Colonel will not consent. It is too bad, to put such a coarse, ugly, stray monster with such a dear, sweet, beautiful creature as you are."

78

"I have been asking her, too," said Eoline, holding Fanny's ringlets as a veil before her tearful eyes, " but in vain. So let us say no more about it, darling Fanny. Let us walk among the rose trees, and see if their sweet breath will not soften my bitter feeling. I am ashamed to think how angry I have been."

" I don't wonder you are angry," said Fanny, "just look at the creature! who ever saw such a looking object ?"

Eoline, following the direction of Fanny's scornful glance, beheld Louisa standing in the piazza, with the strange new figure by her side. She seemed to be directing her attention to the romping children, and kindly endeavoring to cheer the sullen and home-sick child. How lonely, how amiable she looked in the eyes of the self-upbraiding Eoline. How swee and dove-like was her smile, how meek and subdued her quiet, gray eye !

"Dear, angel Louisa," exclaimed Eoline, "what an example she sets us; she pities the poor girl, thus brought into a community of strangers, pities her for the very awkwardness we have despised. Fanny, it *is* wrong to laugh at the personal defects of any human being; wrong to look upon them with scorn and derision. Come with me, and you can carry her to the play-ground, and shield her, if necessary, from the ridicule of her companions. *You* are a favorite, and what you do, so will the others."

As they approached, the girl looked sulkily at Eoline from under her thick eye-brows, but without noticing her belligerent expression, she introduced Fanny, and asked if she would not like to accompany her to the play-ground.

" I don't care if I do," said she, glancing sideways at Fanny's ringlets. " What did you say her name was ?"

" Fanny, darling Fanny, we call her, for we all love her so much."

" And what shall I call *your* name ?" asked Fanny.

"Jerusha—Jerusha Spots, is my name. My pa's name

is Jacob Spots—and my mother's Betsy Spots; I was
named after my great aunt, that's an old maid—but she's
got a heap of property, pa says."

Fanny's shoe-string suddenly broke or seemed to, while
the communicative Jerusha unfolded this interesting leaf
of her family history. As soon as Fanny lifted her face,
which was very red, Jerusha put her hand into a big satchel
which was swinging on her arm, and pulling out a large,
green apple, held it right in her face—

" Won't you have an apple ?" said she, " they are mighty
good."

" Thank you," said Fanny, " let us go to the play-
ground."

They started, when Jerusha, who seemed restored to
good-humor, ran back and offered her open satchel to Louisa and Eoline, who politely declined taking advantage
of her generosity. She walked, with long rolling steps,
by the side of the graceful Fanny, to the play-ground,
where she found a ready market for her green apples among
the romping group. Louisa put her arm within Eoline's,
and said—

" I tried to save you from this infliction, dear Eoline. I
am sorry for you."

" Teach me to bear it. Give me a portion of your divine
philosophy."

" Alas! I have very little myself. It is a sad trial, I
acknowledge,—for our quiet rooms seem Edens to us, when
released from the harrowing duties of the day."

" And yet you sought to save me from it at the sacrifice
of your own peace. Ah! Louisa, I have been the child of
indulgence, and *self*, I fear, is ever uppermost in my thoughts
I have heard of people being restored to health, when
languishing on the bed of sickness, by having the pure
stream of life flowing in the veins of another transfused into
their own. Oh! that some of your heavenly spirit could

be transfused into mine, then my soul would be healed of
the leprosy of pride."

"Do not praise me—do not call me heavenly, Eoline. I
cannot bear to hear you. I offered, nay, entreated, to have
this girl as a companion, because I knew it would not be
half so great a trial to me as to yourself. I was born in
the lap of self-denial, and the lessons instilled into me from
earliest childhood, you have been nobly teaching yourself.
Your virtues are all your own—mine those of education."

At the supper table, the new scholar sat with open mouth
and distended eyes, gazing up and down the long table,
like one in a dream. She was placed by the side of Eoline,
being under her immediate wing, who endeavored to put
her more at ease by her kind attentions. She really pitied
her awkwardness, especially as she saw such bright, merry
glances darting upon her from every side. She was evidently as wild and uncultivated an animal as ever was
caught in the deep pine woods of the South.

When Miss Manly, according to custom, rang the little
bell, and called out energetically,

"Young ladies. Xerxes the Great—"

Jerusha actually started from her seat, and exclaimed
aloud,

"Who's that?" looking wildly towards the door, as if
expecting to see some monster walking in.

The Colonel had to ring the bell several times before
order was restored, for when the girls, forgetting all rules,
burst into simultaneous laughter, Jerusha, without knowing
why, laughed more vociferously than all the rest. Indeed,
from having cried a great deal, and gone through a great
many strange feelings, she had become quite hysterical, and
had no control over her risibles.

"Miss Jerusha Spots," cried Miss Manly, with majestic
gravity, "you will become accustomed to our regulations
and learn to respect them. We always overlook and par-

don the errors of inexperience and youth. You will find all our rules comprehended in the compendious aphorism— 'order is heaven's first law, and must be obeyed.' "

Jerusha gazed upon her while she was speaking, with a half-frightened, half-stupid expression, holding her knife and fork suspended in the air, with her elbows squared, in awful defiance of Miss Manly's military drilling. All at once she turned to Eoline, and said,

"Are you the one that teaches playing on the box? Pa says *I* must learn."

"Miss Jerusha," interrupted Miss Manly, looking portentously at the children, ready to explode in a fresh burst of laughter, "no young lady is allowed to speak at table without being addressed first by her teachers. Listen in silence, while we discuss the claims of Xerxes the Great, to the proud epithet which historians have added to his name."

Jerusha listened, and understood as much as if they had conversed in a foreign tongue. As soon as supper was concluded, and she accompanied Eoline to her room, she said she was tired and wanted to go to bed.

"I always go to bed as soon as supper is over at home," she said, beginning to unpack her trunk for her night-clothes. A large, round wooden box appeared on the top, which she eagerly opened.

"Won't you have a ginger-cake?" said she, taking out one in the form of a gridiron and handing it to Eoline.

"No I thank you," replied Eoline, amused, in spite of herself, with her strange companion; "I cannot eat so soon after supper."

"I couldn't eat a bit," said Jerusha, eating the gingerbread with great *goût*—"that tall woman scared me almost to death with her queer talk. Besides, I eat all the time at home. I don't do nothing else. I sometimes get up in the night and eat."

"I don't wonder you have the nightmare then," said Eoline, more and more shocked at the idea of such a cormorant for a room-mate. "You will not be allowed to do it here, and it will be far better for you."

"I wonder who's to hinder me? Ma's going to send me as many cakes as I want, and dried beef and smoked ham, too; that she is."

"*I* shall hinder you," said Eoline, gently, but firmly "As you share my room, you must learn to do as the other young ladies do. It is not at all genteel or refined to eat all the time, and it will make you look very coarse. Don't you want to grow pretty and delicate, like Fanny?"

"Yes! I shouldn't care if I did. But ma says eating will make me look nice and fat. I don't want to be scrawny and have all my bones show."

"I am not scrawny, am I?" asked Eoline, laughing.

"No. I shouldn't care if I looked like you."

"Well, I never eat but three times a day, and if you stay with me, you must try to please me, and obey all Miss Manly's rules. If you are a good girl, I will try to make you happy and assist you in your lessons. I think you will improve very much."

"Do you," cried Jerusha, an expression of delight flashing into her stupid face. "I thought you despised me."

"I hope I do not despise any one," answered the self-rebuked Eoline. "I did not like to have any one in my room, because I prefer being alone, and I am not accustomed to a companion."

"I like you now," said Jerusha, putting on a thick cotton night-cap, which, being unrelieved by any border, made her face look like the full moon of an old fashioned clock. Before she retired she came up with her mouth half full of gingerbread and deposited a loud smack on Eoline's rose-leaf cheek.

"I love you now" said she. "Good-night"

"Good-night," replied poor Eoline, trying to imitate Louisa's Christian graces. "The child seems to have a good heart," thought she. "I *will* try to be patient and forbearing, and perhaps I shall be able to polish her a little. But, oh me! how hard she breathes! I never shall be able to sleep. The nightmare, too, how horrible! Ah! my dear father, you little know what your poor petted child has to endure. Horace Cleveland, when will he return? I wonder if he will ever again visit Magnolia Vale? Strange! even while walking with the fascinating St. Leon, or listening to the entrancing melody of his voice, I sometimes wander in imagination with Horace to the two silent homes of his spirit, and wait for the moving of the deep waters that there roll over his soul. What a magnificent man these two would make, blended in one! Then, indeed, we should see the wild sweep of the eagle, and the brooding tenderness of the dove, the supporting pillar and caressing vine, strength and grace united."

She took up a beautiful bouquet, the gift of St. Leon, and admired the exquisite arrangement of the flowers, the light of the colors, the shade of the leaves. They exhaled a dying sweetness, that penetrated her heart and filled it with the softest and most pensive emotions; again the thought, how strange it would seem in Horace Cleveland to present her with a token like that.

It was very late before Eoline retired to rest. With an unconquerable repugnance to approach so near the unconscious, but energetically breathing Jerusha, she lingered at the window, gazing on the midnight glories of the darkening firmament of June. She had extinguished her light, and sat enveloped in the dim and solemn splendor of the lonely hour. Tears gathered at first slowly into her eyes, then they rolled down her cheeks faster and faster, and at length gushed forth in a real heart-shower, deluging her face and the hands that were clasped upon her knees. She had not wept so long and bitterly since the first night of her banishment. She had not written to her father, for the letter which she had left on the toilet the morning of her departure, the letter full of a daughter's yearning love, and blistered with her tears, had never been answered, and that was equivalent to a ban upon all epistolary intercourse. Yes! she was a banished child, banished forever, doomed to struggle with the hard realities of life, to wrestle still with the iron will and selfish despotism of others. But she did not regret the path she had chosen. Better the prison-house, the rack, the grave itself, than the cold, unloving wedlock, the false hand, the perjury of the soul, from which she had fled.

Lying down on the very edge of the bed, at the imminent risk of being precipitated to the floor if she chanced to sleep with such a heavy bass rolling into her ears, Eoline closed her weary and burning eyes. But she did sleep, and she did not fall, two very miraculous things. The first object which met her wakening vision was Jerusha up and dressed, and seated at an open window. One of the virtuous habits of a country life is early rising, and, as she afterwards told Eoline, she always breakfasted at home by candle-light all the year round, it was not strange that she emulated the birds of Magnolia Vale, who were singing their matin songs. She seemed engaged in a very mysterious operation, of which Eoline had heard, but never before witnessed. She held a large black snuff-box open in her left hand, filled with fine yellow powder, into which she kept dipping a stick resembling a miniature broom, then putting it in her mouth, rubbed her teeth with a lazy but continued friction. She appeared in a kind of ecstatic state, with her eyes closed and her mouth open, filled with the yellow dust that intoxicates before it stupefies.

" Jerusha," exclaimed Eoline, leaning on her elbow,

gazing upon her with a look of horror and disgust, "what are you doing ?"

The child started and rolled her light eyes at Eoline through her short hair, that fell in masses over her forehead.

"I'm just *dipping*," said she, putting her hand over the box, for Eoline had risen and approached her, "where's the harm of that ?"

"I am sorry to see you indulging in so bad, so unlady-like a practice. I certainly never shall allow you to do it in my presence, or my room, and it is expressly forbidden by the rules of the seminary."

"My ma dips," cried Jerusha, boldly, for what child is not emboldened by maternal example, "and aunt Jerusha dips, and a heap of folks that I know—I'd as soon live without eating as dipping."

"You will be obliged to live without it here, Jerusha, it never will be permitted. Do you not wish to be a lady?"

"To be sure I do. Pa says he dont care about my learning books much, just so as I learn manners. That's what he sent me here for, 'cause folks say, Miss Manly teaches the girls how to behave, and makes them smart, too."

"Well! no lady will indulge in such a habit, depend upon it, and the sooner you break yourself of it the happier you will be. The other girls will ridicule you, and Miss Manly expel you, if you persist in it. Give me that box and let me destroy it."

"I've got a heap more in my trunk."

"Give it all to me at once, and then you will be out of the reach of temptation."

"I can't," said Jerusha, beginning to cry, "its nobody's business but mine. It don't hurt nobody, and my ma wouldn't do nothing bad, I know."

"I shall speak to Miss Manly; you will not dare dis-
obey her."

That dreaded name seemed to intimidate the child, at
least after many gentle remonstrances and grave rebukes
on the part of Eoline, she gave up the box, and repro-
duced the bottle which her careful mother had put in the
bottom of her trunk. Eoline encouraged her with warm
praises, and told her she was greater than Xerxes the
Great, whom Miss Manly had talked about the night
before, for *he* had never conquered himself and *she* had.
But poor Jerusha's bad habits were like the Hydra, with
unnumbered heads; as fast as one was destroyed another
rose with equal life and energy. The next thing she
attacked were the beautiful roses, which made an in-door
summer in the little apartment. She began to pick them
to pieces, and chew the leaves like a ruminating animal,
making a very unpleasant sound with her teeth.

"You must not do that," said Eoline, "you must let my
flowers alone. I should not put them in water if I did not
wish to keep them."

"You won't let me do nothing," cried Jerusha, impatiently, taking a pair of scissors from Eoline's work-box,
and cutting her nails over its elegant contents. Eoline
was ready to cry with vexation, but she held down the
swelling flood, and told her to take the Bible and commit a verse to memory to recite at the breakfast-table.

"I will select one for you," said Eoline, kindly.

"No—I want to find one myself, I know how," cried
she, elevating her right shoulder, and looking at Eoline
over it.

At the breakfast-table, when it came her turn to recite,
in a loud, grum voice, that expressed her consciousness
of being able to do as well as any of them in this exercise,
if she did not know who Xerxes the Great was, she re-

peated, "And the Lord said unto Moses and Aaron, saying—"

"I know how to spell Aaron," she whispered to Eoline, after the recitation was concluded, "great A, little a-r-o-n."

"No whispering," cried Miss Manly; "it is a violation of the Chesterfieldian rules of politeness, and is never allowed in the Magnolia Vale Seminary."

Jerusha shook her dull, sandy hair over her eyes, and sat still a few moments, but when a tall, handsome black man, who assisted in waiting on the table, took her plate and asked her what she would be helped to, she electrified every one by calling for bacon and greens. In short, there was no end to Jerusha's *gaucheries*. They were equal in number to the sands of the sea-shore, and the drops of the ocean. In the school-room, Miss Manly found it impossible to preserve the silence and order which were the crowning glories of her institution. The children sat, their hands pressing hard on their mouths, with red and inflated cheeks, stealing side-long glances from their books at the *rara avis* alighted among their flock. When reading, she kept her fore-finger slipping along the line, and she would stop and spell all the hard words, with a loud, determined accent, through her nose. But her exploits on the recitation bench were nothing to what she achieved in the music-room, when Eoline gave her the first lesson in her divine art. She had never before seen a piano, and when she put her short, red fingers on the keys, and felt the little black and white things jumping up and down, she fairly screamed with delight.

"Look, look!" she cried, "they hop just like parched corn. They play Jack and Jill, don't they?"

She had on a large pair of nankin mitts, which terminated in a long point over the back of her hand, but Eoline told her she must take them off, as they impeded the motion of her fingers. She hid her hands behind her for a long time, saying they were so red she was ashamed, but at length she laid the substantial members on the delicate ivory, by the side of Eoline's, as fair as the ivory, and far more beautiful, because they wore the soft blush of life.

"I won't put my hands 'long side of yourn, so there!" cried Jerusha, positively, putting them again behind her, and Eoline was compelled to let her draw on the big, long pointed mitts, before she would touch the keys. Eoline realized for the first time the full weight of man's primeval curse—"By the sweat of thy brow shalt though earn thy bread;" for again and again did she wipe the laboring moisture from her snowy forehead before Jerusha was dismissed from her morning lesson.

Mr. Spots had given Miss Manly a carte-blanche, to be filled as her judgment directed to supply his daughter's wardrobe. He wanted nothing omitted to make her fashionable and genteel, and Miss Manly, for the credit of her establishment, faithfully attended to his instructions. She did, indeed, work a surprising change in the exterior of the young savage, but there was no chemic art which could reach the coarse, hard texture of her vulgar mind. Her nature had become too completely animalized, for immortal longings to be awakened within it. Had Eoline been condemned, as a penance for her sins, to wear around her bosom a girdle of hair cloth, and to sleep upon a bed of iron, she could scarcely have suffered greater torture than she endured in such a room-mate. She resolved to fulfil her engagements with Miss Manly—indeed, she had no other alternative—but if the wide, wide world contained another nome, she determined to seek it before the commencement of a new session.

Without being positively wicked or bad, Jerusha was mischievous and mischief-making. She had an insatiable curiosity to hear every thing; would listen at the door, peep through the key-hole, and every thing she heard and saw she would run and tell Miss Manly. One by one, Eoline found herself curtailed of all her heart pleasures. The stolen visits of her young favorites, after the evening bell, no longer gladdened her room, for Miss Manly, informed of this infringement of her rules, commenced a nightly inspection of the dormitories, and about half-an-hour after the *curfew*, the commanding steps of the Colonel were heard echoing through the long passage, where then reigned the stillness of death. If Eoline left her own and escaped to Louisa's room, Jerusha was sure to follow, saying she was afraid to be alone, and she did not know how to study by herself.

One evening Miss Manly and Uncle Ben took the pupils to Montebello, to hear a celebrated lecturer on Phrenology. It was a favorite science of Miss Manly's, who had been told she had a remarkable head, and the organs of Self-esteem and Firmness, were, indeed, most wonderfully developed. She took Louisa with her, to keep the children in the rear in due order, while *she* marched in the van. Eoline remained at home, notwithstanding Miss Manly's evident displeasure. She longed for the luxury of being alone, and as it was a lovely moonlight night, she went and sat in the piazza, where the lofty shadow of the Tree of Heaven played on the silvery-shining pillars and dewy grass. Soft as the falling dew, the perfect stillness and quietude of the scene descended with balmy influence on Eoline's chafed and weary spirit. She took out her comb and suffered her hair to float back in the night breeze that fanned her aching brow. She had been hard, hard at work all day long, and all the week long, and all the month long. Miss Manly was making great preparations for a public examination and a public concert, and as she had no mercy on herself, she had none on her assistants. She had an iron frame and an iron spirit, which seemed incapable of fatigue, and though when sick ness actually bowed the frame, and confined the sufferer to a sick bed, no one could be kinder or more attentive, she could not conceive it possible that one as young and elastic as Eoline, should bend beneath a burden she deemed very light in comparison to her own. But Eoline, who had been dwelling lately in a narrowing circle of comforts, joys she had really none, and whose labors were constantly increasing, began to wilt under the dreary mono tony of her life. She felt that burning calenture of the soul, which pants for a native atmosphere and a genial home. While thus she sat, with one arm encircling a pillar, her temples bared to the coolness of the hour, and the shadow of a drooping vine upon her brow, St. Leon came across the lawn, and ascended the steps of the piazza.

"Why art thou seated in silence here, light of the dewy night?" exclaimed he, his eyes beaming with pleasure, and sitting down beside her. "And why seems thy spirit sad, oh, blue-eyed daughter of Glenmore?"

"And why dost thou seek me, son of the moonlight hour?" answered she, smiling, in the same Ossianic style, to which she was accustomed from his poetic lips. "I dwell in darkness here—wide over me flies the shadowy mist. Filled with dew are my locks." As she spoke, she attempted to gather them in her hand, and he might well have addressed her, as "the maid with far-wandering hair."

"Do not," he exclaimed, with a deprecatory motion. "You look so wildly romantic, so poetically lovely, I cannot bear that you should break the charm, by imprisoning those beautiful tresses. You speak of dwelling in darkness; but you are covered with the light of Heaven, and the mist turns to silver as it flies over your brow."

"Surely, Mr. St. Leon, you must be a poet as well as musician. At least, you speak in poetry, if you do not write it."

"I *have* written lately," he replied: 'The morning sun has risen upon Memnon, and the lyre of his soul responds in music.'"

"Pray talk to me in prose to-night, Mr. St. Leon, for I feel sadly dull and matter-of-fact; though an eolian harp, the breath of heaven itself could not wake one note of melody now in my weary spirit."

"You *are* weary. I see it, and grieve for it," he cried, changing his high-wrought strain for one of deep feeling. "Miss Glenmore, I know your history. I honor, I adore the noble independence of your character, even more than I admire your matchless beauty and celestial voice."

Eoline started, and the deepest blushes mantled her face.

"How did you learn what I believed known only to my father and myself, and one individual," she added, "most deeply interested?"

"You cannot believe," he answered, "that the daughter of Mr. Glenmore, who had just arisen, a brilliant star on the social horizon that bounded her father's princely mansion, could disappear from the firmament, without exciting the interest and wonder of the world. Believe me, if these walls were not defended by a guardian more formidable than Cerberus, you would be surrounded by admirers more numerous than the leaves of Vallambrosa."

"I do not like to hear you allude to Miss Manly in this manner," said Eoline, gravely, "when you treat her with such studied politeness."

"It is for your sake, Eoline," he answered. "I could kneel for hours at her feet, if by so doing, I could insure, for one moment, the delight of your presence."

"St. Leon, I adore sincerity," Eoline answered with warmth, "as much as I abhor deceit."

"I hope, I pray you do not suspect me of the last?" he cried, with great earnestness.

" Is it not deceit to profess an interest in another you do not feel, to show respect and deference to one whom you do not respect, merely to spend a passing hour with one for whom, perhaps, you really care as little ?"

" Eoline, you are severe, unkind," he exclaimed, rising and pulling the vine-wreaths from the pillar without knowing what he was doing. "I do not deserve this from you. After sacrificing so much, submitting to so much, for the sake of breathing the same air that you breathe, for the mere privilege of being near you, and lightening, if possible, your heavy burden of servitude, I had hoped for more mercy, more justice. Besides, I really do respect Miss Manly."

"I did not mean to be severe or unkind," said Eoline, in a gentle but troubled voice. "I merely meant to be true. You speak of sacrifices you have made for me. Indeed, I am well aware, and have been so from our first interview, that you are not what you seem, that you are departing as much from your natural sphere as I am from mine, in assuming a subordinate position. If it is on my account you have done this, I cannot allow it one moment longer. Instead of lightening my burden of servitude, it will only make it doubly, trebly heavy."

St. Leon's languishing eyes flashed with a dark fire.

" I did not think my presence so oppressive," cried he, in a tone of suppressed passion. " I did not think myself an object of such intense dislike."

" It is not dislike, it is not oppression that I feel," said Eoline, admiring the spirit of St. Leon far more than his boyish grace. " Conscious of the sufferings I myself feel in being in an uncongenial element, I cannot assume the responsibility of those another must endure. Besides, and be not angry that I say it, I would gladly believe that some higher, greater motive had induced you to bow your pride to the yoke you now wear."

"I can imagine no higher motive than the one which now governs every thought, feeling, and action," said St. Leon, his color visibly deepening in the moonlight. Eoline was agitated. So much of her present happiness, and small indeed was the portion, depended upon the nature of her intercourse with St. Leon, that she trembled at the thought of its changing. It is so natural for the young and disengaged heart of woman to feel pleasure in the society and admiring attentions of the other sex, that Eoline had never analyzed the emotions St. Leon inspired. In her father's home, when surrounded by all that was dear and precious to the soul, she would have delighted in mingling her voice with the rich music of his, and listening to his refined and romantic sentiments. How much more, then, in her state of exile, in the cold, ungenial atmosphere Miss Manly diffused around her! When singing with St. Leon, the sweet, impassioned songs of Italy, walking with him in the perfumed shades of Magnolia Vale, or sitting with him in the silver stillness of the moonlight hour, she seemed in her native element—she was at home—she felt happy—she was grateful in her loneliness, for so pleasing and interesting a *friend*. But when he presented himself before her in the aspect of a *lover*, she was startled. The question found her unprepared. Were life all music, and flowers, and moonlight, she would not have asked for a more charming companion, to walk hand in hand with her through its clouds of fragrance, or to float with her over its waves of melody and floods of light. But in the storm and the tempest, the hour of darkness and desolation, where was the heart of strength and the arm of power, where the strong tower in the day of trouble? As these thoughts rolled through her mind, and the lights and shadows flitted over her face, like the flash of the moonbeams and the shade of the vine-leaves, St. Leon stood gazing upon her with an intensity

79

ot emotion, that deprived him of the use of language.
At length she looked up with a very sweet smile, though
a pensive one.

"You shall not again accuse me of being unkind," said
she, "for I will speak to you with the frankness of a sister.
It has been very pleasant for me to look upon you as a
friend, for sadly have I felt the need of one. I am not
insensible to the interest you manifest in my destiny.
Believe me, I am grateful for it. But if you value my
happiness, still address me as a friend. Should you force
me to look upon you in any other light, my position here
would be one of peculiar embarrassment. Promise me
that for the short time we are associated together in this
institution, that you will be to me all that you have ever
been, neither less nor more."

"And then," exclaimed St. Leon, eagerly, "shall I be
rewarded for my forbearance by the privilege of being
more, far more? Oh, Eoline, I am rich—my father is
rolling in affluence. I can place you in the station you
were born to adorn. I can cradle you in the lap of smiling fortune, and lay you upon its downy pillow."

"For worlds I would not deceive you, St. Leon," cried
Eoline, moved by his generous ardor, yet shrinking from
its warmth, "nor would I trifle with your affections. I
cannot answer for the present, I dare not promise for the
future. I do not know my own heart. I do not know
that I have a heart," added she, smiling, and laying her
hand with a grateful emotion on the folds of her white
muslin dress. "I believe I am a very strange young girl.
I sometimes think there is a tissue of asbestos woven
around me, impenetrable to that flame which is said to
illumine the universe. That I have very deep, peculiar,
and solemn feelings with regard to a subject so often
lightly thought of, you must be aware, since you seem
familiar with the circumstances that brought me here. I

believe I have boundless capacities, unfathomable sensibilities which have never yet awakened. Be silent till we part, and I promise you, by my maiden truth, if I feel the movements of the angel troubling the deep waters, I will ingenuously acknowledge it."

Eoline paused with an angelic blush. There was such purity in her countenance, such modesty in her manner, and such dignity and candor in her sentiments, that St. Leon dared not express the enthusiastic emotions this distant hope inspired. He could have prostrated himself at her feet, in the humility of oriental devotion, but he feared to offend the beautiful and vestal simplicity of her character.

"And now," said Eoline, rising, like a true heroine of Ossian, in the midst of her veiling locks, "let me solicit of you a great favor—that is, to leave me. Should Miss Manly return and find you here, she will probably imagine it a preconcerted meeting, as I displeased her by remaining behind. You know I have not too many roses in my path—I would not court the thorns."

"My right hand shall wither ere it willingly plant a thorn in your path, Eoline," replied St. Leon, while the passion she had forbidden him to express in words, added tenfold softness and brilliancy to his dark, expressive eyes.

"It is too late," exclaimed Eoline, in a tone of vexation, resuming her seat in the shadow of the vine.

The Colonel and her retinue were seen marching with measured steps up the gravel walk—Uncle Ben acting as van-guard. The moment she beheld St. Leon, standing by the side of Eoline, and the exceedingly romantic appearance of the young lady herself, her countenance fell far below zero. She actually turned pale, a change that seldom occurred on the surface of *her* face, and cast a withering glance at the twain from her Saturn-like orbs.

"I thought Miss Glenmore remained at home on the plea of solitude," said she, with emphasis.

"And so she did," interrupted St. Leon, "but I intruded upon it, with my perhaps unwelcome presence. I did not know—" he was about to say, with the admitted insincerity of the world, "that he did not know he should not have the honor of her society," when the earnest assertion of Eoline, "that she adored sincerity," and a glance of her truth-beaming eye restrained the words, and the unfinished sentence died on his lips.

"We had better issue a new edition of 'Solitude Sweetened,'" said Miss Manly, sarcastically.

"Come, come!" said Uncle Ben, patting Eoline affectionately on the shoulder. "Little David has worked too hard lately. She shall do just as she pleases, go or stay, and nobody shall molest or make her afraid."

While this scene was passing, the pupils had walked demurely to their dormitories, followed by Louisa, who looked pityingly on Eoline, as she passed.

Eoline, bidding St. Leon a hasty good night, was about to leave the piazza, when the voice of Miss Manly arrested her. The lady had lost her usual self-command, for she was under the influence of that regal passion, to whose influence even the royal virgin of England once bowed.

"Miss Glenmore, I wish to say to you, in the presence of Mr. St. Leon, that he, too, may understand me fully on this subject, that I do not approve of your conduct to-night. It sets a bad example to the young ladies under my guardianship, for whose morals I am personally responsible, while they dwell in Magnolia Vale. I am myself so exceedingly particular in attending to the rules of propriety, that the tongues of the most fastidious must ever be silent. Sorry, indeed, should I be, to have the venom of slander attack the institution, whose unimpeachable reputation is my pride and my glory, through the imprudence of one of my assistants."

The proud Glenmore spirit surged high in the bosom of Eoline at this unexampled attack.

"I came here expecting protection from insult," cried she, with insuppressible emotion, "not to submit to it, Miss Manly. You will do well to supply yourself with another music teacher, for I do assure you I will never give another lesson in your seminary till I receive atonement for the injury of this moment."

She looked involuntarily towards St. Leon, expecting a noble outburst of feeling in vindication of her outraged delicacy. He looked excessively embarrassed. There was a frown upon his brow, and a flush upon his cheek, but instead of uttering the manly determination of also withdrawing, he stammered and declared that he bitterly regretted being the cause of such a misunderstanding, that he would not for the universe have visited Miss Glenmore without the sanction of Miss Manly's presence, had he been aware of its being a violation of her rules.

"I hope," continued he, with one of those graceful bows, which seemed as natural to him as the swaying of the willow's branches, "that I shall be able to restore the harmony I have interrupted, and that Miss Glenmore may never again suffer reproach for my imprudence and presumption."

" Oh! why," thought Eoline, giving him a glance that brought the conscious blood to his cheek, "why does he not boldly and bravely assert his rights and mine? Why does he not express his indignant sense of my wounded feelings, and avenge the insult offered to himself? Why does he not come forward as the champion of my reputation, and oppose with breast of steel, the arrows of calumny and malice. I do believe there is more of manly spirit in my girlish breast than in his."

All this St. Leon read in the kindling light of her coun-

tenance, and he could have writhed in agony at the conviction that he was wanting in that strength and power of
spirit to which she silently and vainly appealed. He could
have bartered a kingdom, were it his, to recall the smooth
words by which he had sought to allay the storm he should
have nobly breasted. He turned away in bitterness of
soul, fearing he had lost a treasure he would willingly
purchase, even if life were to be the immediate sacrifice.

"Niece, niece!" cried Uncle Ben, detaining Eoline,
who again attempted to pass the threshhold, "this will
never do. You ought to be more tender with her. She
is nothing but a young thing, that ought to be petted, instead of scolded. Turn round, little puss, niece did not
mean half what she said, she never does, she's sorry for
it already. What, you won't look at me! You are not
angry with old Uncle Ben, I hope?"

"No, indeed, Uncle Ben, I shall never forget your kindness, never; I thank you for it, even now, but I cannot
cry peace, when there is no peace. Unless I hear an apology from Miss Manly's own lips, I shall consider the
engagement between us forever dissolved. Let me go."

Uncle Ben almost wrung her hand off before he let it go,
when she ran up stairs, before St. Leon had time to address
her again. As she flew along, she heard something rushing
behind her, with clattering steps, like an animal. It was
dark, for the lamp in the passage had gone out, and she
knew not what enemy was in the rear. It seemed too
large and heavy for a cat, too clumsy for a dog. Onward
she ran, through the long, long passage, with the unknown
monster lumbering and panting behind, till she reached
her own door, and fell perfectly breathless against it. A
pair of strong arms grasped her round the neck, and she
was about to utter a wild shriek, when a voice she well
knew, called out,

"What you frightened for? It is nothing but me."

"Jerusha!" exclaimed Eoline, shaking off the unwelcome embrace. "How dare you terrify me so? And where did you come from?"

"I was afraid to come up by myself, and just stopped down there till you were ready—I thought you knew 'twas me."

Louisa came out with her candle, hearing the voice of Eoline. She was alarmed, for the pallid hue of terror still overspread her face.

"They will be my death!" cried she, throwing herself into Louisa's arms, and laughing and crying in the same breath. "Stay and sleep with me to-night; perhaps the last night we shall ever be together. I will make a pallet for Jerusha on the floor. Let me feel your dear, kind arms around me, for my heart is sorely oppressed!"

"I don't want to sleep on the floor, I know," cried Jerusha, poutingly; "'tis too hard."

"Be obliging, Jerusha, said Louisa; "we can make you very comfortable."

"No—let her keep her place, and I will go to your room, Louisa," cried Eoline, "that is, if you do not object."

"If you do, I'll go, too, " exclaimed Jerusha, stoutly. "I ain't going to stay here alone all night, to save nobody's life."

Eoline, with a despairing sigh, sat down on the side of the bed, with Louisa's arm around her. Neither of them spoke for some time. In the meanwhile, Jerusha took possession of the bed, and soon gave audible testimony tha she was asleep. A step, rather less firm than usual, wa heard in the passage. It was Miss Manly on her nocturnal tour. Eoline's heart beat more quickly, when giving a quick rap, she entered and stood before her.

"What is it, now?" thought the young music teacher, "strife or peace?—expiation or fresh insult?"

"Miss Glenmore," said she, trying to speak in a blander

tone than usual, "I am willing to acknowledge that I have spoken without my usual caution and judgment to-night. I am placed in a very peculiar situation, and in my extreme anxiety to avoid even the appearance of evil, I may be led into error, for I do not claim infallibility. As I never encourage the visits of young gentlemen myself, nor allow my pupils to receive them, it did strike me as very impru- dent when I found you had passed the evening alone with Mr. St. Leon, after refusing to accompany us, on the plea of fatigue and a desire for loneliness. I spoke hastily— I regret it—I have said so to Mr. St. Leon—I repeat now the same to you."

There did seem some dignity in this apology, coming from so stiff and proud a woman. It was not without a bitter sense of humiliation that she had compelled herself to make it, but she knew the value of Eoline's services too well to suffer her to leave her, when she expected her to give such brilliancy to her public concerts. Moreover, she had a high sense of justice and truth, and the moment the gust of passion was over, she acquitted Eoline of all premeditation and design. Eoline was as generous as she was high-souled. She took no pleasure in the humiliation of an enemy, and the apparent consciousness of error on their part, was immediately followed by forgiveness on hers. She bowed her head, and said,

"It is enough, Miss Manly!—I ask nothing more!"

And thus the wound was seemingly healed, but a scar remained. Eoline felt hereafter as if she were watched in the presence of St. Leon, whose impassioned feelings for herself became more and more evident. And just in proportion was the manifestation of Miss Manly's jealousy. She struggled with it, she tried to master it, but it had a vitality that would not be destroyed. The greatest of hu- man beings have one vulnerable point. There was one spot in the heel of Achilles, which the waters of the Styx had not bathed,—there was one place in the heart of Miss Manly, which an arrow had pierced. If the goddess-born had their weaknesses, we cannot expect mortals to be exempt.

It wanted now about a month of the Examination, an event which was contemplated with no little anxiety by more than one dweller in Magnolia Vale.

CHAPTER VII.

The approaching Examination was a kind of pivot, on which every thought and action now turned. Miss Manly had a remarkable power of awakening the ambition of her pupils. She had so constantly placed before them heroic and striking examples, that almost all looked forward to the time, when the epithet *Great* would be attached to their names, and immortality their portion. It is true they ridiculed Miss Manly's peculiarities and originalities behind her back; they called her the Colonel, and mimicked her assumption of supreme command; but with all this, they really respected her, and felt the influence of her strong mind on theirs. They saw her exclusive devotion to the cause of education, that she sacrificed her time and her strength to the interests of the school, and that though severe and exacting, she was consistent and true. She never threatened, never scolded. She laid down her rules, fixed, *immutable* rules, and their violation was immediately followed by the known penalty. She might have represented justice, with her scales, weighing every thing, even the *pound of flesh*, with unwavering hand. Were the elements of our being purely intellectual, did not the heart and the affections demand cultivation, did hey not require the kind and genial sunshine, as well as the clear, bracing air, such a system would be admirable; but when children are removed from the endearments of home, when no mother's breast can pillow, no sister's arms entwine, they need the influence of love diffused around them, or their young heart-tendrils will droop for want of support, their budding tenderness wither and die.

But now they were all animated by the spirit of study. Under every spreading tree, in every shaded corner, in little shanties, which they had built themselves with branches and leaves, were seen busy groups intent upon their books, or bending over their slates and pencils. Louisa began to hear recitations soon after the morning bell rang, and finished not till the twilight, and Eoline scarcely breathed out of the walls of the music-room. Close as was the confinement and constant the toil she there endured, she preferred it to the apartment now desecrated by Jerusha, or the parlor, where she was sure to encounter the impassioned glances of St. Leon. They gave her a feeling of unrest, of indecision, which made her unhappy. His love seemed to her more like romance than reality. It gilded her imagination, played upon her heart, and warmed its surface. Whether it would penetrate deeper and deeper, time alone would prove.

Once, after a weary day, she happened to be alone in her chamber, an unusual coincidence, for Jerusha followed her like a shadow. She was pale and languid. Her arms fell listless at her side, and her eyes were turned towards the fading horizon of the West. So deeply was she absorbed in thought, she did not hear even the stately steps of Miss Manly, till they paused at her door.

"Shall I come in?" said she, in a kinder voice than usual.

"I consider it quite a favor," said Eoline, greeting her with as much ceremony as if she were a stranger. It was impossible to be informal with Miss Manly.

"You have confined yourself very much lately, Miss Glenmore. You have been exceedingly faithful to your duties, and the pupils will do great credit to your instructions. You have done more than I could with justice have exacted, but not more than I am willing to be grateful for. Another thing I will take the liberty of saying

I observe, with approbation of your propriety, that you studiously avoid alluring the young gentleman, whom I myself have perhaps imprudently made your associate. We should always be upon our guard with strangers, and there is a certain bound which discretion should not pass."

She paused, but as Eoline was silent, continued—

"You have not been pleased with your room-mate, and I grant, she cannot be the most congenial of companions. The young miss, who has been the sharer of my apartment, leaves to-morrow, for domestic reasons, and I came to tell you that Jerusha can take her place. I will have her things removed from your room to-night."

Eoline clapped her hands together with rapture—a joyous color brightened her cheek.

"Thank you, dear Miss Manly, a thousand, thousand times. Oh! what a favor! what a blessing! I feel like a new being already. But I really grieve to think of the awful infliction it will be to you. You have no conception what she is."

"When the mind is fixed upon one great object," replied Miss Manly, somewhat moved by Eoline's enthusiastic gratitude, "minor things appear comparative trifles. When I assumed the responsibilities of my station, I gave up ease and pleasure. I knew they were incompatible with the stern and self-denying duties of a teacher. I have never shrunk from labor or inconvenience, never hesitated to sacrifice personal comfort to public good. I ook upon myself as a missionary in a great and holy cause, and having taken the cross upon my shoulders, I shall bear it with a firm step and an unshrinking spirit. Those who would lie on beds of down, and pillow on roses, should never think of the onerous and ungrateful vocation to which I have devoted myself with the zeal of a martyr."

Eoline looked upon Miss Manly with respect. There was much in her of the material of which martyrs are made and heroes moulded. She seemed to have forgotten for the moment all her artificial dignity, and expressed herself naturally and energetically, as any strong-minded woman would. She was displaying one of the rich, thick satin stripes of her character. What a pity the flimsy gauze would sometimes appear.

"You have astonishing energy and perseverance," said Eoline. "I have seen you with wonder and admiration sustain a weight of care, sufficient to bow many a strong man to the dust. But if I had my own will, it would be the last vocation I should choose."

"I know it well, Miss Glenmore. You were formed for a different sphere, one to which I doubt not you will shortly return. I have heard of the motives which induced you to quit your father's protection, and it would be doing injustice to your independence and principles, not to say that I approve and honor them."

"Indeed!" exclaimed Eoline, blushing, "I was not aware that you knew anything of my private history. Had I supposed that you would have sympathized in my feelings, I would long since have told you all. I did not expect—I did not know—" she paused, in embarrassment, then added ingenuously, "I do no not think I have done you justice, Miss Manly. You have more feeling and kindness than I have given you credit for. I came here a very proud, inexperienced young girl, born to affluence and indulgence—a perfect novice in the school of discipline and action. I should have found any service hard, and I have no doubt pride has magnified my trials and darkened my judgment. For your present kindness, I thank you. I prize it more for its being unexpected. It reconciles me to a great deal that I was beginning to feel intolerable."

Eoline spoke with earnest grace, and held out ner hand

to Miss Manly, who rose to leave her. The latter was evidently pleased with Eoline's frank and grateful manner, but she was as evidently afraid of committing herself by being too soft and amiable. With one of her own deep, majestic bows she retired, leaving Eoline almost wild with delight. The great stone was about to be rolled away from the sepulchre of her contentment. Jerusha was to be removed. She was free—she was free. Flying to Louisa's room, and catching up a light scarf from the bed, she wreathed it gracefully about her arms, and danced round the astonished girl, like the gay Eoline of Glenmore Place.

"Joy, Louisa, joy," she cried, "come and help me gather laurels to make a crown for Miss Manly's brow; oh! what a good, glorious woman she is. She has taken Jerusha to herself, and we can renew the dear, quiet intercourse so long interrupted. What ungrateful creatures we are! I was sitting moping and almost crying, about to plunge in the slough of despondency, like Bunyan's Pilgrim, when in came Giant Great-heart, and drew me out with a strong, relieving hand. Shame on me, to breathe a word that could sound like disrespect to Miss Manly, when I owe her such a debt of gratitude. She has bound me to her by cords that never can be broken. I am her friend now, henceforth and forever."

Louisa had never seen Eoline in such joyous spirits— and most truly did she sympathize in her joy. They went to the play-ground, where the girls were still lingering, and Eoline challenged Uncle Ben to run with her—a thing she had not done for a long time. Clapping his hands, with boyish glee, he caught up the gauntlet she dropped at his feet, and began the chase. But he might as well have attempted to catch the wild-deer of the forest, as the light-footed and momentarily light-hearted girl. He soon gave up the pursuit in despair—but Eoline had the whole school in chase

of her, and as the enemy lay in ambush, too, Uncle Ben
had his revenge in her captivity.   All were engaged in the
sport but Jerusha, who sat under a tree, in the corner of
the yard, joyless and alone. Eoline, panting from her race,
went to her, and asked her if she were sick.

" No, I ain't sick," said she, sullenly, " I know what makes
you so glad and frisky; I heard you tell Miss Louisa all
about it. But I won't stay with Miss Manly; I'll go home
first.   I ain't agoing to be hauled about from pillar to post,
as if I was nobody—when I'm as good as any body. My
pa is as smart as other folks' pa's, and my ma, too. They
won't see me snubbed."

Eoline was really sorry for the mortification of the child;
but what could she say to comfort her?   She had intended
to repress the exuberance of her joy in her presence, to
avoid wounding her feelings—but the inveterate listener
had defeated her kind intentions.

" I told you I preferred being alone," said she, gently.
" I did not deceive you—and I do feel very glad to have
my room to myself again. But I have always been kind to
you, Jerusha, and tried to make you happy, while with
me—you know I have."

" Yes! that's a fact," cried Jerusha, vehemently, and
beginning to cry at the same time; " you've always been
good to me—and I don't want to go away from you; you've
learned me how to behave, too; and pa says he'd rather
I'd be like you, than any body else—'cause you are so
smart.   He'll be as mad as fire—that he will."

The supper-bell rang, but Jerusha said she did not want
any supper—and she wouldn't eat to save Miss Manly's
life; so they left her under the tree in solitude.   But she
was not allowed to starve—for half-a-dozen of the girls
slipped biscuits in their sleeves, and carried to her, fearing
she would die if she went supperless to bed.   They did not
know that she had her pockets full of cake and cheese, and

that she regaled herself sumptuously under the tree, while
they supposed she was shedding rivers of tears.

Jerusha had not a particle of malice or revenge in her
disposition; and the next night she told Eoline she was
mighty well satisfied, and she liked to be with Miss Manly
a heap better than she expected—that she hadn't scolded
her one bit yet, and she didn't mean she should.

A scene occurred about a week afterward, which left an
impression on Eoline's mind, not to be effaced. They were
all assembled in the music-room to practice some of the
anthems for the Examination. The room was very large—
and lighted with innumerable windows, which were all left
open, as the night was excessively close and sultry. The
air had that pulseless stillness, which shows that the electricity had left the earth, to roll itself in the bosom of the
cloud darkening over head. Eoline looked abroad and
saw with pleasure a dull lead-colored belt girdling the
Heavens, and deadening the deep, clear blue of the horizon.
Across this broadening belt, pale, lambent rays of lightning
were darting, in radiant mockery of its gloom.

"We shall have a thunder-shower, I perceive," said she,
following, with delighted eyes, the dazzling play of the
lightning. "How welcome it will be, after this long
drought! Will it not?" added she, looking up to St. Leon,
who was standing by her side.

"I cannot say that I ever welcome a thunder storm,"
replied St. Leon, with a slight shudder. "From my earliest
recollection, I have had a constitutional dread of electricity.
It deprives me of strength and elasticity. It makes me
nerveless and weak."

"Cannot the mind make the nerves the vassals of its
will?" asked Eoline, the sight of his pallid cheek deepening the hue of her own, "at least in the day of health
and vigor?"

"I have tried to school myself in vain," said St. Leon.

" We cannot fashion ourselves anew nor string with iron chords the spirit wired with silver or with gold. I regret this weakness, if such it may be called, but I cannot conquer it.

" When you sheltered Louisa and myself from that terrible shower," said she, " I thought you quite strong and heroic."

" Ah, that was nothing but rain," he replied. " I should not shrink from all the waters of the deluge, if they came silently down."

" I remember well," replied Eoline, with a sigh, " when I was a little child, my terror of electric power was so great, that I dreaded the approach of summer—all its bloom and beauty and fragrance could not reconcile me to the thunder's awful roll, the lightning's blasting flash. But when I became old enough to listen to *reason*, my fears forsook me ; and they have never returned. I even take a sublime pleasure in gazing on the magnificent fire-works of Heaven ! Look ! how beautiful—how grand !"

" I wish I *could* think and feel as you do," cried St. Leon, " not only on this subject, but on all. In everything you rise superior not only to me, but to the whole world. You were born for *dominion*—I, for *homage*."

" No, St. Leon," she cried, with another unaccountable, yet irrepressible sigh, " I was not born for dominion, nor will I assume it ; I was born to look up—up—high as the eagle's eyrie. It is this upward-reaching spirit that makes me joy in the warring clouds or the rushing winds. They are high and powerful, and I love them."

" Have you no dread of danger ? Do you not think of death ?" asked St. Leon.

" We can die but once," replied Eoline, " and I would far rather be struck suddenly by the bolt of Heaven, and die a pangless death, than waste away in prostrated agonies, or even languish long on the bed of disease. No, I
80

tnink less of dissolution in a moment like this, than in the
loneliness and darkness of the midnight hour."

The entrance of Miss Manly and the pupils interrupted
the conversation. Eoline took her seat at the piano, Miss
Manly hers on the right, while St. Leon stood on the left.
The young choristers were arranged in a semicircle on
either side, exactly as they were to be on the public platform. As they came silently in, the roar of the distant thunder was heard, as a prelude to their opening anthem. To
Eoline it was a grand rolling bass, and she seemed inspired
by the sound. Never had she sung with more power and
sweetness. In one of the anthems, the words seemed singularly appropriate to the scene. They were taken from
one of those awfully sublime Psalms which make the
spirit weak from their overpowering grandeur of expression. It was Eoline's part to sing alone the following
lines—

"He bowed the Heavens also, and came down; and
darkness was under His feet.

"And He rode upon a cherub and did fly; yea, He did
fly upon the wings of the wind."

While Eoline's voice soared like the cherub, who is
represented as bearing Jehovah on its wings, the thunder
came rolling and crashing along, as if the chariot wheels
of Deity were overhead, and the sky was one blaze of
lightning. St. Leon covered his eyes with his hand. He
had a solo which should have followed Eoline's, but he
was voiceless. Eoline raised her eyes, not hearing the
expected notes, and saw his face and lips of ashy paleness.
He looked like a fainting man.

"Mr. St. Leon is ill," said she, lifting her hands from
the keys; "Miss Manly, will you send for a glass of
water?"

Miss Manly, who knew not the cause of his agitation,
and supposed him to be attacked by sudden illness, was

excessively alarmed. She handed him the water with her own hands, and insisted upon his sitting down and not attempting to sing any more. We have noticed before her kindness to all in sickness, and her interest for St. Leon. This combination made her attentions conspicuously assiduous. She dispatched one for cologne, another for camphor, and poured herself some of the fragrant lymph on the waving locks of St. Leon.

"I am ashamed, for causing this interruption," said he looking gratefully at Miss Manly, "and giving you so much trouble. It is a great misfortune of mine."

"Are you subject to these attacks?" inquired Miss Manly, anxiously.

"Always in a thunder-storm or a tempest. It is a constitutional weakness, and, I believe, hereditary."

Eoline glanced at Miss Manly to see the impression this confession had made upon her. She expected to see the pity of this strong and high-minded woman blended with a shade of contempt. But she was mistaken. Her countenance expressed all the tenderness and compassion of which it was capable. Eoline felt for St. Leon, herself— she pitied him, for his agitation seemed perfectly uncontrollable. But she felt humiliated by it, because she had lately associated St. Leon with her most secret thoughts. She could not bear that he should expose this unmanly trepidation to young girls, who have such a keen sense of the weak and effeminate. She heard Fanny whisper to Selma, "He is afraid," and the same sentence was spelled on the fingers of the whole choir.

As the storm continued, and the rising wind added its gusts to the reverberating thunder, the rehearsal was stopped. It could not go on without St. Leon, and he was incapable of proceeding.

"Will it disturb you if I sing?" said Eoline, looking towards St. Leon.

"Oh, no—your voice always seems the voice of an angel. It will be doubly sweet at a moment like this."

Miss Manly had left the hall, to give orders that a room might be prepared for St. Leon. She would not think of his going abroad on such a night.

"I fear you think me unmanly," said he, in a low voice to Eoline; "but believe me, the mind has nothing to do with it. It is altogether physical. Eoline, look down upon me, if you will, but still look upon me. I am strong in one thing—in my love for you."

Eoline was glad that Miss Manly's approach prevented her reply. She condemned herself for the feelings that oppressed her, but she could not help them, any more than St. Leon his physical weakness. When she first met St. Leon, he had appeared in the light of a protector, man's natural and Heaven-appointed office. It is true, he had only sheltered her from the rain, but she remembered him as a help in the hour of need. She imagined herself exposed to the warring elements of such a night as this, with no arm but his to lean upon, no spirit but his to sustain, and she sighed at the prospect. It would be hers to uphold, hers to strengthen. Woman feels that it is her office to watch in sickness and soothe in sorrow—to go down with the sufferer, even into the valley of darkness, without fearing its shadows; but not to be foremost in the battles of life, nor to take the helm when the night is dark, and the billows are roaring, with the master pale and inert at her side.

The rain continued, but the thunder was muttering at a distance. Miss Manly insisted that St. Leon should remain. He would take cold, get sick, his voice would be hoarse at the concert, and then what would they do? St. Leon consented, and again Eoline heard one of the saucy girls whisper very softly to another, that "the Colonel ought to make *Miss* St. Leon some herb tea."

"I am very wicked," said she, to Louisa, when they were alone, for they could be alone now, sometimes, " but I have felt far more vexation than compassion to-night. Do you think a man ought to know the sensation of *fear*, or, knowing ought to yield to it ?"

"St. Leon's nerves were strangely affected," said Louisa, "but, you remember, some very great men have had constitutional weaknesses. Peter the Great, as Miss Manly would say, and Cæsar, too, fainted at the sight of water, so great was their terror."

"Ah, but they conquered it !" exclaimed Eoline, "and became heroes. Their greatest weakness became their crowning glory."

"Perhaps St. Leon will conquer his," said Louisa, "and become a hero, too."

"No," replied Eoline, sadly and thoughtfully ; "I think he had as powerful a motive to-night as could act upon him, but it was in vain. I said I am wicked, because I feel as if I could really admire a man more, who is capable of some great crime nobly repented of, if he have corresponding greatness of character, than one amiably weak and constitutionally timid."

"You should pardon many defects in St. Leon, Eoline, for the exceeding love he bears you. Were I loved, and *so* loved, it seems to me the passion would throw a radiance round the being who thus worshiped. We are all made to differ. 'There is one glory of the sun, and another glory of the moon, and one star differs from another star in glory.'"

"The glory of the sun for me !" exclaimed Eoline, ardently, "even its meridian glory. There is a joy in being loved and worshiped ; but, oh, Louisa, how much deeper, how much holier must be the joy to *feel* love and worship for another !"

St. Leon was really ill and feverish the next day, and

unable to leave his room. Miss Manly did not visit him herself—she thought it the height of impropriety to do so, but, through Uncle Ben, who was a celebrated nurse, she lavished upon him more than needed care. The servants were going in and out with little waiters, mysteriously covered with white napkins, containing delicacies for the invalid. A large stuffed rocking chair was rolled in for his accommodation, and he had as many bouquets sent him as if he were Prima Donna. The children, believing they had wronged him in supposing him afraid, when he was in reality ill, with the reaction peculiar to their age, thought they could not do enough to express their sympathy and regret.

St. Leon was a Creole, the son of a Creole planter, of Louisiana. It is believed that the race from which he sprang is more distinguished for beauty of person, grace of manner, quickness and ardor of feeling, and gentleness of disposition, than for the stern and hardy virtues. It was certainly so with St. Leon. It is said, too, that an exquisite taste for music in men, is accompanied with a fineness of nerve and sensitiveness of temperament, incompatible with a strong will and an unswerving purpose. Whether this be true in general or not, it was true of St. Leon. Even if nature had planted in his mind the germs of a firmer character, the indolence and luxury of his life had never allowed their expansion.

Great qualities are not the hot-bed growth of luxury. They are plants of Heaven's own nurture, and the blasts that shiver the crystal walls of the green-house, destroying the exotics it shelters, only give them a deeper root and stronger tone.

His uncommon delicacy of constitution, which was visible in his pale, transparent complexion, rendered it necessary for him to leave the luxuriant and sickly regions, where his father dwelt, during the sultry months of the year. He spent most of his summers in travelling, and being attracted by the beautiful scenery around Montebello, stopped to linger a few days near its green fields, and beside its still waters. In one of his romantic rambles, he beheld the beautiful Eoline, crowned with the regalia of Spring, a Flora in bloom, a Nightingale in song— the very incarnation of Poetry, Music and Love. Blessings on the rain that gave him an opportunity of approaching her; and blessings on Miss Manly, who opened a door for his admission to the seminary which would bring him in close juxta-position with the object of his intense admiration. As day after day unfolded her noble, intellectual qualities—qualities he never dreamed of finding in so young and fair a girl, his admiration deepened into worship. She seemed to shine above him, a radiant and constantly ascending star, and no Chaldean shepherd ever gazed with more idolatry on the

"Brightest and best of the sons of the morning,"

than the young Creole on the banished daughter of Glenmore. He felt her superiority even painfully, and there were moments when he was tempted to yield to despair; but she had allowed him to hope, she had not rejected him, she had asked for time to analyse her *own* feelings, and study *his* character. He had no rival, and such love us his *must* meet a return.

The night of the thunder-shower, when her sky-lark notes rose clear and rejoicing above the thunder's roar while he, a poor, trembling, stricken dove, was fluttering songless, below; he felt that there was an immeasurable distance between their spirits—a distance the rainbow of hope could scarcely span. It was this conviction acting on his excited nerves, that caused the illness which succeeded. For days he lingered in his room, and Miss Manly began to tremble for his health, as well as for her rehearsals and concerts. At length he came forth, looking more pale and interesting than ever, but declaring himself perfectly well. The languishing softness of his eyes was in keeping with his invalid character—a character which seemed to invest him with new graces. Eoline, conscious she had condemned him too harshly for a weakness he could not conquer, greeted him so kindly that all his wilted hopes revived.

She was looking anxiously into the future. In her altered feelings for Miss Manly, she preferred remaining with her, to seeking a new, perhaps a less desirable home. But there was a long vacation approaching. All the pupils were talking of *home*, of the expected embraces of parents, the joyous welcome of friends. Miss Manly spoke of visiting her Northern relatives during the long holidays; Louisa, of accompanying her. Could she remain alone in that baronial castle, with its long galleries, winding stairs, and empty dormitories? It is true, she had invitations, eagerly reiterated, from all the pupils, Jerusha included, to pass the holidays with them, but she knew not their parents, and the home of the stranger offered no elysium to her yearning heart. She thought of her inflexible father, of Horace Cleveland, of her darling Willie, and—wept.

Poor Eoline !

CHAPTER VIII.

Horace Cleveland returned from Cuba's sea-bound shore, with the remains of his mother, whose last prayer was that she might be buried in her native soil. She had sought health in a foreign clime, and found death among its spicy breezes and tropic flowers. As her son was borne homeward over the tossing billows, with his silent and encoffined companion, he communed in secret with his life's first, great sorrow. Ever reserved and undemonstrative, no one dreamed of the intensity of affection he bore his mother, till he hung over her dying bed. He knew it not himself, for he had never sounded the depths of his own heart. In the pure intellectuality of his existence, he had suffered the fountains of feeling to lie far, far below the surface, imparting neither freshness, beauty, or bloom to the eye; but swollen by the waters of sorrow, the springs gushed and welled up, forming an overflowing Nile, on which the Lotus might float, and the Lily gleam. And even now, as he sat, with folded arms, and calm, thoughtful brow, by the side of the unburied dead, a stranger might have thought him cold and insensible. It is said there are sermons in running brooks, and in the way-side flower, but there is an eloquence in death, all voiceless as it is, that preaches as brook and flower never yet have preached. Strange as it may seem, life, in its fullest, broadest sense, was in this instance born of death. When the strongest earthly tie he had yet known was broken, he felt the immortality of the affections, since they survived the ruins of mind. Reason wandered, judgment grew weak, imagination dim; but love survived the wreck. She clung

(165)

to him, as the sheet-anchor of her heart, while the waves and billows of death washed over her, and he thus learned the unconquerable nature of human love. Strange, too, behind the image of his dead mother, he always beheld the living Eoline. She came upon his memory, a Phœnix, rising from the ashes of death, and brightening its gloom. He remembered his visit to Magnolia Vale, and the alliance of friendship which had succeeded the cold reserve existing between them. When he caught the first glimpse of his father's lordly villa, and immediately turned to the twin-built mansion of Mr. Glenmore, his heart throbbed at the hope of soon meeting there the lately banished Eoline.

Mr. Glenmore came to sympathize with his widowed friend. Horace asked after his daughter as if confident that she was restored to his protection.

"Name her not," exclaimed the father, with a darken-ing brow. "She is nothing to me now and never can be. The door of reconciliation is forever closed, *forever.*"

He was too proud to tell Horace of his slighted overtures, preferring that he should think him the most vindictive and implacable of human beings, rather than that he should know that his offers of reconciliation had been treated with disdain.

Horace, who had been reading law at the University of Gottingen, during his residence in Europe, was now anxious to enter on the active duties of his profession. He longed to throw himself into the battle of life, and test the keenness and strength of the weapons he had been whetting and tempering for the gladiatorial strife of mind. Before seeking the arena he had selected, he resolved to visit Eoline, since he was permitted to do so as a friend, and see if the eagle wings of her spirit had not yet drooped in their unaccustomed flight.

"Perhaps when she learns that I am going to leave my home," thought he, "she may be induced to return, and the father cannot banish her a second time. Implacable as he seems to be, he still loves her, and I see well that this unnatural separation has added more than one furrow to his brow."

"Father is gone away," said little Willie, when Horac called the day before his departure to bid him farewell,' "but *I'm* at home."

Willie had always been fond of Horace. Indeed he was one of those slender, fibrous plants, whose delicate, spreading roots cling to the surrounding soil with closeness and tenacity. Now he had some misgivings about Horace, for, though he did not understand the family compact which had bound him to Eoline, he had heard his father talk, and Mrs. Howe and Gatty talk, and he knew a great deal more than they imagined the child thought of. From all he had gathered he had come to the conviction that if Horace had loved Eoline as he ought, as everybody ought to do, she would never have left him, sisterless, to mourn.

"What for did you let sister Ela go away?" he asked, when Horace took him in his lap, and stroked back his beautiful auburn hair.

"I could not keep her from going," replied Horace, with embarrassment. "I was not even here when she went."

"Yes, but you could, though. I heard father say so. He said you didn't love her, and that was the reason she wouldn't stay. How could you help loving Ela? What's the reason you don't love her?"

Willie fixed his eyes steadily on the face of Horace, that reddened under his gaze. He knew not how to reply to the straight-forward and earnest child, but he said, evasively,

"It is Ela that does not love me. That alters the case very much."

"But you don't answer my question," persisted the boy. "I'll ask it another way. You don't hate Ela, do you?"

"No, indeed. Heaven forbid. Surely you never heard anybody say that I did?"

"Yes—but I have, though. I don't know whether it was father, or Mrs. Howe, or Gatty. Somebody did. But I know it isn't true. I couldn't love you if it was."

"I am going to see Eoline to-morrow, Willie," said Horace, anxious to change the current of Willie's thoughts. "What shall I tell her from you?"

"Tell her to come back with you. Tell her to come back, cried the child, enthusiastically. "Tell her it isn't home without her. Nobody's the same they were before she went away. This is the way father looks all the time." Willie contracted his smooth brow and tried to make a miniature horse-shoe. "The flowers don't look half so sweet, for nobody takes care of them as she did My hair don't curl as pretty, because she isn't her to twist it round her fingers. And I'm not half as good as I was," said little Willie, sorrowfully, and lowering his tone, "for nobody listens to know if God hears my prayers or not. I say them every night, but Mrs. Howe goes to sleep sometimes. Sister Ela carried up my prayers to Heaven herself, for she looked up there to see them go, and held my hands in hers all the time."

Surely never were a sister's praises so innocently, yet so eloquently breathed. Horace felt their glow in his heart, and self-reproach and sorrow were there, too, for had he not, by a coldness and indifference he might forever vainly rue, deprived this beautiful and loving boy of the sister he worshiped?

"I will tell her all you say, and do all I can to persuade her to return for your sake," cried Horace, rising to depart.

"Will you tell her you love her?" said Willie, laying his left cheek on the hand of Horace, and looking beseechingly in his eyes.

"She would be angry if I did," replied he, turning away from the little inquisitor.

"No she would'nt—but don't go yet," said Willie, following him. "Come into the garden and get some flowers for Ela. She loves them so dearly. Then they are her own flowers—and tell her I sent them. She will think them sweet, I know."

He pulled Horace along with him into the garden, and began eagerly gathering the fairest and best. Horace became interested in the task. His mother loved flowers, and he had frequently brought the rich blossoms of the tropic bowers, and laid them on her sick couch. But it was the first time he had ever culled one for Eoline, though the betrothed of his childhood, and there was a charm in the office which he could not explain. They were to be offered in Willie's name, and she should not be made to prize them less by knowing that his hands had assisted to pluck them. Willie would have put the whole garden, and the green-house, too, into a bouquet, if Horace could have carried it, and he mourned when compelled to stop, after having arrived at the limits of human compressibility.

"Tell her I kissed them," cried the boy, pressing them again and again to his rosy lips, while his sweet eyes filled with tears—"and she must kiss them, too."

Thus embalmed, the offering of fraternal love was borne away by Horace, and its fragrance and bloom kept alive by the most devoted attention. As he travelled on horseback, it required some skill to dispose of the bouquet. He could not put it in his valise for it would wither—he did not like to carry it in his hands lest it should make him look too foppish, but it was a sacred offering, and he would

not leave it behind; so winding a wet handkerchief round
the stems, he endured the shame for the sake of the plea
sure he hoped to impart, and every time he stopped he
took care to saturate the linen afresh, and awake the flow
ers to new life. So carefully did he watch them, so ten
derly did he nurse, that he grew to love them, for the care
he bestowed, and instead of one *Picciola*, he had a cluster
to gladden his solitary journey. They were redolent with
memories of Eoline, that noble, beautiful Eoline, whom
his more than Indian stoicism had made an alien from her
home, and on whom he had imposed a lot of toil, perhaps
misery.

It was night when he arrived at Montebello. By going
through the woods, he had condensed a two days' carriage
journey into one. As he entered the hotel he met crowds
of people going out, as if in a great hurry, and he could
hear them say one to another—

"I fear we shall be too late for seats."

While at supper, the landlord, an officiously polite gentleman, remarked—

"I suppose you are going to attend the concert to-
night"

"Where?"

"At the Magnolia Vale Seminary. There will be a great
crowd, and I fear you will find it difficult to get a good
place—that is, if you intend to go. If you are a stranger
in this part of the country, I would advise you by all means
to attend, for they say there never was such music heard
before, as you will have a chance of listening to there."

"Indeed!" said Horace, shrinking at the thought of the
refined and high-bred daughter of Glenmore, being compelled to exhibit herself before a promiscuous and crowded
assembly. "What celebrated musicians are there?"

"Why, there's the young music teacher, a Miss Glenmore, whose father they say is as rich as a Crœsus, and who

turned her out of doors because she wouldn't marry a young
man she didn't like. That's the girl for me. I would
walk forty miles to see such a one, if she was as ugly as
you please—but this young lady is the prettiest creature I
ever saw in my life, and sings like a dozen mocking-birds
put together. All the young men who attended the Examination have been raving about her, and say they pity the
stupid fellow she ran away from."

Horace hastily rose from the table. The words of the
loquacious landlord were daggers to him. He felt as if
he were known, and that the remarks were uttered by
design.

"Then there's the handsome young gentleman that
teaches singing, too," continued the host; "he sings like
a nightingale as well as she. If report speaks true, the
two nightingales will sing in one cage before long."

"Of what gentleman are you speaking?" asked Horace,
a strange pang shooting through his heart.

"His name is St. Leon," replied the landlord. "It is no
doubt he makes believe to be a teacher there, for reasons
best known to himself, but suspected by all. He boards
with us, and he cares no more how much money he spends,
than if it were so much sand. He told me, when he first
came, that he was going to pass the summer in travelling—
but it seems he could not get a step beyond this place.
But, sir, I beg your pardon—I think I have seen your face
before. Did you not stop here in the winter, and inquire
the way to the Seminary! I think you passed the night
here."

Horace answered by a distant bow.

"An acquaintance of Miss Manly's, or perhaps of Miss
Glenmore, herself?"

With another cold, silent bow, Horace sought the door.

"The Colonel is a wonderful woman," continued the
gentleman, facetiously, "we all very proud of her school.

There is not such another this side of the Alleghany. She
made a speech this evening, at the close of her Examination, that, they say, beat all the stump speeches ever heard
in the land of pine woods. If she were a candidate for
Congress, I've no doubt she would be elected by an overwhelming majority. Oh! she's a great woman—our Colonel is."

Horace at last escaped to his room, where he could
shake off the dust of the traveller, and make himself a
fitting guest for Miss Manly's crowded halls. Never had
he felt in such a state of nervous agitation. One moment
he resolved to return at once, without exposing himself
to the hazard of being known as the young man, the "stupid
fellow," from whom the heiress of Glenmore had fled; the
next, he was urged by an irresistible desire to see Eoline,
blushing in maiden beauty, before the gaze of hundreds,
by the side of the handsome and melodious St. Leon. He
wanted to behold this disguised hero, this spendthrift lover,
this rare bird of song, whose magic notes were said to have
captivated the heart that perhaps might have been his, had
he not chilled it with the coldness of polar ice.

He was tempted to throw away the flowers, fearing they
would draw attention to himself—but the remembrance
of Willie's pleading eyes and tearful messages glued them
to his hand. He could not cast them aside. When he
approached the Seminary and saw the crowd around the
building, he gathered confidence in the hope of passing
unnoticed. It looked like an illuminated castle, with its
myriad windows brilliantly lighted, and its lofty towers
leaning against the starry sky. Just as he reached the door
a sudden flood of melody rolling over the throng, drowned
the buzz of mingling voices, and caused such a rush and
pressure inwards, that Horace found himself borne along,
with scarcely any effort of his own. Gaining a window
not far from the platform, he jumped on to its sill, and

drawing back as far as possible in the embrasure, gazed upon a scene which seemed to him more like a dream of the imagination than a living actuality. A very elevated platform ran along the whole breadth of the hall, and was separated from it by a row of classic pillars, which were all decorated for the occasion with garlands of evergreen and flowers. Two flights of steps, covered with green cloth, one on each side, led up to this elevation, and a chandelier suspended above, mingled its lustre with the lamps burning beneath.

Miss Manly sat in the centre on a chair raised so as to resemble a throne or dais, and looked down in her majesty on the throng below. No Queen, surrounded by her court, ever bore a loftier presence or carried herself more royally, than the Principal of the Magnolia Vale Seminary. Certainly no Queen ever felt more proud of her subjects, or reigned with a more absolute dominion over them. She was dressed for the evening with unusual splendor, and held her ivory fan as if it were a sceptre. On each side of her the pupils were arranged in semicircular order, standing, the taller nearer to her, and gradually diminishing in height as they diverged from the great central luminary. Their uniform was white muslin, relieved by sashes of cerulean hue, and almost all were decorated with some favorite flower. There they stood, these young girls, in their white, flowing robes and azure ribbons, with their sweet flowers, all radiant in juvenility and innocence, so bright, so joyous, that it made one's heart ache to look at them and think these morning blos soms of life should ever be exposed to the mildew and the storm, or worse than all, to the cold, bitter frost. In the centre, just in front of Miss Manly, whose lofty position prevented her from being concealed, appeared Eoline, seated at the piano, in the same celestial livery of white and blue. The music leaves unfolded before her, partially

81

concealed her from the gaze of the audience, but this
slight screen did not intercept the view of Horace, who
beheld her with sensations such as woman had never before inspired in his breast.   Never had she seemed so daz-
zlingly fair, so softly, yet resplendently lovely.   He looked
as Adam looked when he beheld the new-made bride of
Eden, beaming on his kindling vision.   He was as one
waking out of a deep sleep, by a flash of conviction, intense as the lightning, and almost as scorching.   When
strong passions have lain dormant for a long time under a
superincumbent weight of intellect, their awakening is the
bound of the giant, strong, exultant and fearful.   Horace
trembled and glowed as the new life came rushing and
flowing in, into every vein—giving him the sense of a new
creation.   It flashed from his eyes—it burned upon his
cheek—he felt it in every fibre of his being.   But the moment that revealed Eoline to him, invested with this new-
born glory, this moment, the warmest, the brightest, soon
proved the darkest of his life.   For on the right hand
stood the minstrel lover, with his pale alabaster face, brilliant eyes, and romantic-waving hair, adorned with every
grace that can captivate the eye of woman.   And all the
time he was gazing, music was gushing forth and filling
the hall and sweeping out into the starry night.   They
were singing an anthem of praise.   *Hosanna* was the burden of the strain—"Hosanna," ascended clear and high,
as the highest warblings of the flute, from the lips of Eoline—"Hosanna," repeated the youthful band, in their
sweet, bird-like contralto—"Hosanna," breathed St. Leon,
in his deep melodious tenor—"Hosanna, Hosanna," re-
sounded the whole choir, in one strong burst of jubilant
harmony, while the keys quivered and sparkled under
Eoline's jewelled fingers.   Horace listened with an interest, an intensity that amounted to agony.   As one by
one, and then all in one, the *Hosannas* swept by him, and

he beheld Eoline the centre of that region of light and
harmony, she seemed lost to him forever—lost by his own
madness.   The words of little Willie rang in his ears—
" How could you help loving Ela ?"—" What did you let
her go away for ?"   " Because I was a fool, dolt, maniac,"
thought he, " and I deserve to be punished, as I am."

There was a breathless silence after the anthem closed,
then a sudden and spontaneous burst of applause.   Once,
twice, thrice the building shook with its thunders.   During
the lull that succeeded, Miss Manly arose.   Her tall figure
at once arrested every eye.

"Hush, hush, the Colonel is going to speak!" ran in a
whisper across the benches.

And truly the Colonel *was* going to make a speech, and
a very sensible one, too.

" We thank the audience," she said, bending graciously
forward, and waving her ivory fan.   " We thank our friends,
for their manifestations of approbation.   We receive them
in the spirit of kindness in which we are certain they
burst forth.   But as the performers are young ladies whose
modesty and delicacy we feel it our duty to guard, as we
would a tender flower, and as they must naturally shrink
from anything like notoriety and acclamation, we would
most respectfully request, that silence, expressive silence,
should hereafter speak their praise."

There was a murmur, when Miss Manly resumed her
seat after a dignified bow, and some boys put their hands
together ready to clap, but the public respected Miss Manly,
and feared her displeasure, and as her pupils had passed a
splendid Examination, they were anxious to conform to
her wishes, and therefore preserved silence.

As St. Leon led Eoline from the instrument, and said
something to her in a low voice, she looked up with a
smile that Horace would have given worlds to call his own.
He wanted to send her the flowers that were withering in

his grasp. They would carry her thoughts back to her
home; they would turn her from the fascinations of the
present moment, perhaps awaken one remembrance of him.
Before he left the hotel he had fastened a slip of paper to
the bouquet, with the simple words—"From Willie, to his
sister Eoline," inscribed upon it. While he was hesitating
by what messenger to send the floral token, little Bessie
Bell, the young fairy, with her blue sash fluttering round
her, came gliding amid the throng, like a gleam of azure
sky breaking through a cloud.

"For Miss Glenmore," said he, bending down, and
placing the flowers in her eagerly extended hand.

Proud of being the bearer of such an offering, to such a
shrine, the little white cloud, with its azure sky-gleam,
floated back to the platform, and seemed to melt away at
Eoline's feet, for it disappeared in the twinkling of an eye.

Eoline received the flowers with a gratified look, supposing them sent as a compliment from some lover of music
in the audience. She had had many similar favors in the
course of the Examination, but there was something in the
fragrance of this, that breathed into her inmost heart.

Horace watched her countenance as she read the inscrip-
tion. The red lightning of sudden emotion darted across
her cheek, then left it of snowy whiteness. She looked
eagerly into the crowd, with a wistful inquiring glance,
that wandered from face to face, growing less and less
hopeful as it wandered, till it fell on the spot where
Horace stood, in the deep embrazure of the window.
Shadows were resting there, but his eyes beaming with
newly enkindled fires, met and arrested that vague and
doubtful glance. Had she recognized him? He could not
tell. But the color came back to her face. No longer the
vanishing lightning but the lingering crimson that dyes
the sunset cloud. She bent her head over the flowers,
and he imagined he saw them sparkling with dew-drops

which were not there a few moments before. Again, she turned towards the window, and this time Horace bowed to her glance. The salutation was immediately acknow- ledged, and a bright smile played on her lips.

The harp was now drawn to the front of the platform by Uncle Ben, who had seemed during the whole evening most superfluously busy, taking up chairs, and putting them down in the same place, going in and out with a hurried and important look, as if he had not one moment to spare.

St. Leon led Eoline forward, and seated her at the grace- ful instrument. Taking the flowers in one hand, and lean- ing lightly on the harp with the other, the handsome Creole stood waiting to accompany her with his rich and mellow voice. To the classic mind, he might recall the young Apollo singing to the impassioned music of Erato's nine- stringed lyre. Horace had seen Eoline at the harp many a time before, but he felt as if it were the first time he had ever experienced her minstrel power. As she raised her hands to sweep the glittering wires, her loose gossamer sleeves fell back, revealing an arm of unrivalled beauty, both as to form and hue. He thought of Ossian's fair- haired maids, of the white-armed daughter of Joscar, and he thought, too, of the angels, and the golden harps of Heaven. His imagination was excited, and beautiful images from the old poets, from ancient mythology and the divine bards, crowded upon his memory. He was transformed into a poet himself. He could write a grand epic poem—of which life should be the subject, man the hero, and the machinery, the hidden springs and wondrous workmanship of the human heart.

The concert was winding to a close; the last anthem was announced. The white-robed choir again arranged themselves in a semi-lunar form, while Eoline and St. Leon took the same position as at the opening of the concert.

Miss Manly stood up to enjoy this last act of a triumphant drama. Eoline, who missed for a moment the voice of St. Leon, looked up and saw him leaning against the piano, with his hand pressed against his side, and his face wearing the pallor of death. Giving her one earnest, thrilling glance, his eyes closed, and he fell back, perfectly insensible.

It would be difficult to describe the scene of confusion that followed. The forward pressure of the crowd impeded every breath of air, and formed an impenetrable barrier round the platform. The frightened children condensed themselves on the other side—Miss Manly, no less alarmed, for once exerting herself in vain to call them to order.

"Stand back!" exclaimed Eoline, in an agony of terror, "keep back, if you would not kill him! He is not dead. Good Heavens!—will nobody help him? Oh, Horace!" she cried, for he had wedged the crowd, he knew not how, and sprang upon the platform, "for God's sake get a glass of water!"

"Here is water! and here!" cried a dozen voices, while Horace knelt and raised the lifeless St. Leon on his arm.

"Carry him to the window!" exclaimed a commanding voice, while another strong pair of arms surrounded the young man, "he will die for want of air."

It was Doctor Hale, the doctor, *par excellence*, of Montebello, whose commands had the authority of Scripture. By the copious application of water, and the current of fresh air admitted to his lungs, St. Leon revived, so as to open his eyes, and give evidence of consciousness—and that was all.

"Yes, madam," said the doctor, in answer to Miss Manly's anxious inquiries, "have a room prepared immediately, where he can remain perfectly quiet. His pulse is faint and flickering. My friends," said the doctor, some-

what authoritatively, to those who pressed round the platform, "we would thank you to retire as silently as possible. Little girls, it is time you were in bed. We shall
have a man's life on our consciences."

The doctor's words had the effect of magic. The illuminated hall was soon vacated, and the streets and dormi
tories filled. St. Leon was borne to his room in the arms
of the doctor and Horace Cleveland. It was a sad and
awful termination of the brilliant evening. Eoline, before she quitted the platform, stooped down and gathered
up poor Willie's fading flowers, which had fallen from the
failing grasp of St. Leon, then mechanically followed the
steps of Miss Manly, steps far less firm and majestic than
usual. Louisa, who fatigued by the exertions of the day,
had early retired from the concert, met them, with her
face as white as her dress. Eoline, oppressed by conflict-
ing emotions, put her arms round her, and burst into
tears.

"Oh, Louisa!—this is dreadful—dreadful! I have been
cruel and unjust!" she cried, scarcely knowing what she
uttered.

The thought of her harsh judgment of St. Leon, the
night of the thunder-shower, filled her with remorseful
pangs, for what a fatal proof he had just given of the fra-
gility of his constitution! The sudden appearance of
Horace, bearing a token from her own deserted home, had
likewise produced a powerful agitation. The excitement
of the preceding scene had made her nerves peculiarly sensitive. One could hardly have recognized the St. Cecili
of the evening, in the pale, trembling girl who sat cling
ing to Louisa, and starting wildly at every sound. Miss
Manly could not sit still. She walked slowly up and
down the long passage, with footsteps that left no sound.
It was the first time hers had ever fallen like down. Every
once in a while Uncle Ben would come stealing on tiptoe,

and whisper that he was a little better, that the doctor thought there was some hope; then putting his finger on his lip, and shaking his head mysteriously, would tiptoe back. It seemed to the two anxious, waiting, weary girls, that the night was all waning away, so long had they sat listening to the muffled sound of carefully closing doors, and whispering voices, whose words they could not gather.

At length Horace Cleveland came within the door. Eoline rose to meet him, without speaking. It was no time for mere formal expressions, and she had no voice to utter them.

"Mr. St. Leon," said Horace, "wishes to see you for a few moments. Doctor Hale thinks him in very great, though perhaps not immediate danger, but such is his own impression. As everything depends upon the quietude of his nerves, the doctor thinks your presence might have a tranquilizing influence; that is, if you can command your own feelings. Are you equal to the scene, Eoline?"

"Alas! I know not," she answered; "I wish he had not asked it."

Miss Manly, who had followed Horace, and heard the request, here spoke, with extreme agitation.

"I think you had better decline going, Miss Glenmore. It can do no possible good, and will excite his nerves, instead of soothing them. Besides, I do not think it consistent with propriety, and, as Miss Glenmore's friend and adviser, I certainly must oppose it."

"If you will accompany her, Miss Manly," said Horace.

"Yes, come with me, dear Miss Manly," interrupted Eoline, "your presence will sanction mine. Oh, it would be cruel, to refuse a sick, perchance a dying man."

"He asked not for *me*—he desires not *me!*" exclaimed Miss Manly, her under lip quivering with repressed emotion. "I should be looked upon as an intruder! No—I cannot go!"

"Louisa, dear Louisa, you will go with me? You can console and comfort, far, far more than I."

"Let me accompany you, Eoline," said Horace, taking her hand, and drawing it round his arm as he spoke. "Let me stand in a brother's place to you in this, and all future trials. Doctor Hale is with him—I think no other friend is necessary. Come, and show the same fortitude you have done on other occasions.—There is, there can be no impropriety in an errand like this. If so, let the angels of mercy be condemned."

Thus sustained, Eoline went with Horace Cleveland to what she supposed was the dying bed of St. Leon. She felt, as she clung to his arm, that it was the arm of a friend and protector, that it had strength to support, and kindness, too. Her spirit grew strong as she leaned upon it. Yet she trembled when she entered the dimly-lighted room where St. Leon lay ; he who so lately stood by her side, music gushing from his lips, and love and passion flashing from his eyes.

"Be composed," said Doctor Hale, kindly, in a low voice, as Horace retired, "I would gladly have spared you this trial, but I could not persuade him to defer the meeting till to-morrow. He thinks it would be too late. Stay but a moment, and promise to return again. *He must not be agitated,*" he added, emphatically.

Eoline approached the bed, but when she saw him lying so pale, and still and death-like, awe settled deep over her excited feelings, and she involuntarily sank upon her knees by his side.

"Eoline," said he feebly extending his hand, "I could not die without seeing you once more."

"You will not die, St. Leon," she murmured, while his dry and feverish hand convulsively clasped hers. "You must not think of death. God will give you back to life."

"For your sake?" asked he faintly.

"For the sake of all who love you, St. Leon."

"You promised me," said he, fixing upon her his dark, languid eyes, that contrasted painfully with his wan face, "you promised me, when the hour of parting came, I should know if I were beloved. Eoline, that hour is come. I cannot lie down in the grave in peace, I cannot surrender my soul to the Great God, who calls it, till you tell me that you love me. I could not live—I cannot die without your love."

"Think not of an erring creature of the dust like me," said Eoline, lifting her weeping eyes to Heaven. "Oh, St. Leon, this is no time for earthly love."

"Tell me that you love me," cried the impassioned Creole. "I will then give my thoughts to God and Heaven. I shall die happy. You tremble, you hesitate," he added, suddenly starting from his pillow, his eyes emitting a wild gleam, like the fires of insanity. "You cannot, dare not curse me, at this moment, by telling me that you love another."

Falling back again upon the pillow, he closed his eyes, and an expression of acute pain contracted his brow. Eoline thought it was the convulsive pang of death, and uttered a faint cry. Doctor Hale approached his patient, and applying his fingers to his fluttering and agitated pulse, looked gravely and earnestly at Eoline, whose countenance expressed as deep suffering as the human heart is capable of feeling. Again and again she tried to speak, but the words seemed glued to her bloodless lips. The doctor laid the hand of St. Leon gently on the bed-cover, then bending down, he raised Eoline from her kneeling position, and drew her to the opposite side of the room.

"Young lady," said he, in a very low and solemn voice,

fixing on her a calm, but piercing eye, "I hope, I believe you are above trifling with the feelings of another at this awful hour. I do not think this young man will live; but I believe his life is far more in your hands than mine. If you can soothe his stormy passions, if you can speak peace to his troubled heart, my skill *may* avail; but I can do nothing in the state of strange agitation he is now in. This is no time for concealment, none for false scruples."

There was a stern emphasis in his low tones, that Eoline felt to her heart's core. Never had she known such a fearful warfare in her bosom. Ten thousand pulses seemed to throb in every vein. To be told that she held perchance in her hands the life of a human being, to know, even if that life were trembling on the verge of death, she was capable of breathing peace to the departing soul, and winging it with joy into eternity—yet refuse to redeem that life, even at the sacrifice of her own happiness; to hesitate to utter those words of peace, to turn a deaf ear to the last prayer of expiring humanity! could she be so cruel, so selfish? Would she not be a murderess, and bathe her soul in the life blood of a fellow mortal, by withholding the remedy which might baffle the power of death? But how dreadful to deceive in that solemn and awful hour! She did not love St. Leon as he yearned to be loved, as she felt capable of loving, as even then she felt she could love another. She could not open her lips and say to the soul, on which the light of an eternal day might be about to dawn, the soul that might carry her words into the presence of a God of Truth—"I love you." There had been moments, many moments during their intercourse, when, carried away by the attraction of his graces, and the fervor of his attachment, she could have given an impulsive affirmative to such an impassioned appeal, though reflection might follow with a cold negation. And now, so deep was her pity, so strong her sympathy, so awful her sense

of responsibility for the happiness, the life of another, she
was wrought up to that high pitch of enthusiasm, which
made her all but willing to immolate herself, rather than
destroy him who hung trembling on her decree. But there
was something held her back with a strength as it were irresistible. It seemed as if powerful arms were around her,
drawing her from the brink of an abyss, as if eyes, which
that very night had flashed upon her with a power unknown
before, revealing in burning characters the hitherto invisible writing traced on the mystic scroll of her heart, were
fixed upon her with scorching intensity; as if voices were
whispering around and about her—" Thou, who hast been
a martyr to truth and integrity, wilt thou falsify thyself
now? For the weak compassion of a moment, wilt thou
sacrifice thy life-long joy? Who knows but by this very
act thou may'st destroy the happiness of another than St.
Leon, as well as thy own?"

"Are you going to let him *die?*" whispered a grave
voice in her ear. She started, and a cold tremor shook
her frame. It seemed to her that she lived years in that
warring moment, and when she heard the tones of Doctor
Hale, so earnest, yet so low, so upbraiding as she thought,
they had a strange, unnatural sound, like the accents of
a friend from whom we have been long parted.

"Can I save him?" she cried, grasping his hand with
unconscious energy. "I am not a physician. Why do you
throw the burden of his life on me? Do you wish to
denounce me as a murderess at the bar of God?" She
spoke wildly—in her excitement she hardly knew what
she uttered.

"This is a strange case—both—very strange," muttered
the doctor. "I hardly know what to make of either of
them. You had better retire," he added, to Eoline, "if you
cannot apply the antidote, your presence must prove a
bane."

He was displeased with her, and his countenance expressed his sentiments more fully than he was aware of. Her agonized cry in the concert-room—"Good Heavens! will nobody help him?" the cry of life, for life so awfully smitten down by her side, and which he mistook for that of a wrung and bleeding heart, was still echoing in his ears. He could not understand the extraordinary agitation she now exhibited, or reconcile it with her reluctance to soothe his apparently expiring patient, by the utterance of feelings she had unconsciously exhibited in the first moment of his danger. Turning coldly from her, he again approached St. Leon, whose appealing eyes were riveted on Eoline with an expression she seemed no longer able to resist. Hurrying forward, she knelt, so that her face was concealed in the folds of the sheet, and exclaimed,

"Live, St. Leon, and live for me."

"That will do, that will do," said the doctor, in a much softened tone. Bless you, young lady—now you may go. My anodyne may take effect after this. Not another word, my patient; not another syllable for your life. There, young gentleman, I commit her to your care," added he, almost carrying Eoline to the door, near which Horace Cleveland awaited her coming. He had too much delicacy to intrude upon a scene he considered sacred, not doubting it was for an affianced lover that Eoline trembled and wept.

"Your father and brother are well," said he, as they passed along through the dimly-lighted passage. "I saw them a day or two before I left home. You received the flowers which Willie sent you—did you not?"

"I did," she answered, "but my father—sent he no message to his banished daughter?"

Horace could not repeat the cruel words he had heard her father utter, neither could he frame a falsehood.

"He feels your absence—I see, I know he does—but he is too proud to acknowledge it."

"Oh! that I had never left him!" exclaimed Eoline, with a burst of feeling she tried in vain to repress.

"Would to Heaven you never had!" cried Horace, with n emphasis of which he was not aware.

They did not speak again, but walked on in silence to the door of the sitting-room. He felt her leaning more heavily on his arm, and when they entered the apartment, where a brighter light flashed upon them, he saw that her complexion was of a deadly pallor. He gave her a glass of water with a trembling hand. As she took it, and lifted it to her lips, she raised her eyes to his, and something in their expression made her shudder.

"I cannot drink it," said she, placing the glass upon the table, and sinking into a chair. "If I were alone," she murmured, passing her hand dreamily over her forehead— "I think I should be well. There is something feels very cold and tight here."

"You are not well, Eoline," said he, sitting down by her, and taking her passive hand in his. "This interview has been too much for you. I regret that I have been the instrument of so much sorrow to you. But do not, I entreat you, yield too readily to your fears. I shall remain with Mr. St. Leon during the night, as well as Doctor Hale. He shall have every care that skill and kindness can bestow. Eoline, most willingly would I redeem his life by the sacrifice of my own—if by so doing I could ecure your happiness—and now go and take care of yourself; let no anxiety which I can relieve rest upon your heart."

Eoline returned the parting pressure of his hand, with one as cold as marble. Taking the lamp, she waited till the last echo of his footsteps died away on the stillness of night, then sought her own room. She did not stop to

speak with Louisa, though she saw a light glimmering under the door, and knew she waited her return. She could
not speak to a human being. She felt the necessity of
being alone—to loosen the feelings so long suppressed,
that were tightening like a metallic girdle round her heart.
She could not sleep—she could not even lie down on her
pillow. The night was sultry and oppressive, and her little chamber seemed too narrow and close for the restless
movements of her spirit. Kneeling down by the open
window, and looking up into the dark blue, moonless
depths of midnight, she sighed and wept under the mysterious burden of life.

At length the deep stillness of the air was stirred, as if
by a thousand invisible wings. The night-wind rose and
moaned through the tall branches of the Tree of Heaven,
that swept against the window-frame, and the dull roar of
the mill-dam murmured gloomily in her ear. The beating
of her own heart sounded like the ticking of the death-
watch, and the shadow of her bed against the cold, white
wall, assumed the long, sharp, formal outline of a coffin.
The full valance, waving to and fro in the rising breeze,
flapped like a funeral pall. Sometimes a lone bird would
breathe forth a mournful, solitary note, in the deep pine
woods, and she imagined it the dying wail of St. Leon.
Then she transported herself in fancy to the brilliant concert-room, the scene of flowers, music and splendor—to
the moment when her wandering eye was arrested by the
magnetic glance darting from the embrasure—that glance
which was indeed the *lightning's flash*. What Promethean
fire had suddenly kindled that cold eye, and given it
such strange fascination? What power had modulated
that deep-toned voice, so that it fell like the music of
Heaven upon her ear?

The morning found Eoline still kneeling by the open
window, her head bowed upon her arms, and her locks

literally heavy with the dews of night. She had fallen
asleep, just at breaking day. Thus Louisa found her,
when she softly unfolded the door, for Miss Manly had
omitted the awakening blast of the horn for St. Leon's
sake. Strangely did Eoline look, in that lowly, drooping
attitude, in her gossamer robes and azure ribbons floating
loosely round her, and pearls glittering like dew-drops in
her hair.

And there was another who had kept vigils through the
remnant of that night. Another—who was draining in
secret the bitter dregs of mortification and grief. Miss
Manly, who had presided with such masculine dignity
during the evening, and who in general seemed inaccessible
to all softer emotions, had saturated her pillow with tears,
such as she had never wept before. We have said that
St. Leon was the first man who had ever touched her
hitherto invulnerable heart. By an inexplicable self-delu-
sion, she had flattered herself that she had awakened a
tender interest in him. It is true, she regarded Eoline
as a powerful rival, but she still looked forward to a day
of final triumph, a day when she would reign in undivided
sovereignty over his affections. Blinded by self-love, she
could not, would not see, what was visible to every percep-
tion but hers. But now the bandage was fallen from her
eyes. All the preposterousness, the magnitude of her folly,
glared upon her at once. She seemed looking at herself
through a solar microscope, and in what she had hitherto
believed pure elements, she beheld serpents writhing,
ana monsters crawling, and everything instinct with unnatural and destructive life. This astonishing self-revelation
was the work of a moment. One simple fact had reflected
the whole. Believing himself dying, his sole thought was
of Eoline, his sole wish to see her once more. He had
forgotten *her* existence, forgotten her who was suffering

pangs of anxiety for him, such as a Roman heroine only could conceal.

But she was a woman of too much good sense, strong sense, to be the slave of any weakness, when it was once fully revealed to herself. She had not studied the example of the great ones of the earth for nothing. There was really no shame in *feeling* human passions, and there was *glory* in conquering them. The lion Queens of England and Sweden were weak and fallible as herself—weaker —for she *would* triumph over her bosom foible—and she *did.*

At the breakfast-table Dr. Hale announced that St. Leon had slept tranquilly the latter part of the night, and that he did not despair of his ultimate recovery.

"It is a very singular case," said the doctor, "very singular, indeed. I should call it an affection of the heart; yet there are symptoms which I have never met with in a disease of that kind. He is a very idiosyncratic young man. He must be kept perfectly composed and still for the present. I think," he added, looking towards Eoline, "that I leave a far better physician behind me than I am myself, one whose prescriptions seem to have a sorcery which I should like to learn."

When Eoline rose from her untasted breakfast, the doctor took her hand and began to count her faint and languid pulse. The marble pallidness of her complexion, the frozen calm of her countenance, the icy coldness of her touch, and the dull, slow beating of her pulse, all continued the same as her hand rested passively in his. There was something about her that puzzled him exceedingly. If she did not love St. Leon, why should she display such excessive sensibility on his account? If she did, why the reluctance to acknowledge the affection, and give the testimony for which he pleaded with such intense agony? She had exhibited no rapture, when he had said there was

a hope of his ultimate recovery. Even Miss Manly's face
was expressive of more joy than hers. While he was pon-
dering on these inconsistencies, still counting professionally
her languid pulsations, Horace Cleveland entered the room.
The languid pulse gave a quick bound, and the slow mov-
ng blood rushed through the veins, and rose instantaneously
o her pallid cheeks.

"Well," thought he, "here is another enigma!"

He knew something of the history of Eoline, for rumor
had spread it with her hundred tongues, and he had also
ascertained that this was the identical young man, whom,
to avoid marrying, she had relinquished the luxuries of a
splendid home. Now, this seemed very unaccountable.
Horace was so fine, so intellectual a young man—

> " Not his the form, not his the eye,
> That youthful maidens wont to fly."

So he had thought the preceding evening—and now,
when he felt the bounding pulse, and saw the glowing hue
caused by his sudden entrance, it seemed more unaccountable still. Indifference could not cause such strong emotion. Dislike nor anger never wore a blush so soft, so deep,
as now transformed the cold pale statue into a living, throbbing, heart-awakened woman. He could only repeat his
first reflection, "that woman was a strange enigma," and
congratulate himself on his homeward way that Mrs. Hale
was one of those transparent-minded and single-hearted
beings that he could read through without any strange
perplexity.

It was impossible that the doctor's injunction of perfect
quietude could be observed that day, for the departure of
so many pupils inevitably caused much bustle and confusion.
The lower passage was lined with trunks and carpet-bags
and bandboxes—the road in front of the lawn darkened
with carriages. One by one the young girls were borne
away Darling Fanny, warm-hearted Selma, gentle Annie,

and blooming Bessie, hung around Eoline with tears in
their eyes, and smiles on their lips. The tears were for
her, the smiles for the homes to which they were bound
Eoline stood in the door watching them as they rolled
away from her sight. She loved all the household pupils,
but dearly did she love these sweet young friends. Even
Jerusha had awakened her interest, for she had *suffered*
and *toiled* for her. Moreover, they were all going *home*,
the forfeit Eden of her own young heart, and it is no
wonder she followed the carriages with tearful eyes, while
the excited travellers threw back kisses as long as they
could catch a glimpse of her figure in the open portals
of the Seminary.

CHAPTER IX.

Several days had passed since the exciting scenes of the concert. St. Leon was able to sit up, bolstered by pillows, in an easy chair; and even Miss Manly, to whom "consideration had, like an angel come," began to think there was no impropriety in ministering to his weakness; Louisa, like a true-hearted sister, associated herself with Eoline in her attentions to the invalid, who felt as if inhaling an atmosphere of Paradise. The words—"Live, St. Leon, and live for me," which had fallen from the pale lips of Eoline, when she thought soul and body were parting, were echoing in his ears by day and by night, in waking and in dreams. He longed to hear her repeat the life-giving sentence, but whenever she approached him, Louisa was with her, in whose presence he could not ask what his sighing heart and expressive eyes continually demanded.

He had another visitor, by day a visitor, by night a nurse, and that was Horace Cleveland, but Horace began to think it was best to go, and so he told Eoline, when, having followed her into the piazza after the hour of supper, he sat down beside her in the soft gloom of dying twilight. How still and lonely seemed that broad, shaded lawn, whose grassy surface had been so long crushed and worn by so many bounding footsteps! How still seemed those long, winding galleries, where no light shadows were reflected, no soft whisper or stifled laugh borne to the ear! But more lonely still seemed the heart of Eoline, when Horace said he should go away by early dawn, when to return, he knew not. There was a support, a protection

(192)

ın his presence, to which she unconsciously clung. He
had asked her to look upon him as a brother, and never
had she so desired to lean upon a brother's arm as at this
moment, when the consciousness of having sealed her
earthly destiny by a few impulsive words, pressed coldly
and heavily on her heart. There was a warmth, a restrained tenderness in the manner of Horace which touched
her more, from its being unexpected; and his eyes—so
full of deep and earnest thought—but which always
seemed so far away, even when looking upon her, now
flashing near, and still nearer, penetrated into the central
depths of her spirit, kindling its latent fires. Silently they
thus sat, in that soft gloom and breathing stillness—these
two beings, whom parental authority had endeavored to
force together, whom their own independent spirits had so
widely sundered, and on whom a secret and powerful
magnetism was now but too late exerting its influence.

"I have felt very unhappy," said Horace, breaking a
silence which began to be too oppressive, " in thinking of
the uncertainty of your destiny. I did think of urging
you strenuously to return to your father, trusting to the
love which I know he feels for an unconditional reconciliation. I did think of soliciting to accompany you, and
assuming the blessed office of peace-maker, however pre-
sumptuous it might seem. But since I have been here,
circumstances have arisen which would make my interfe-
rence more than superfluous. I perceive, Eoline, that
your destiny is fixed, and God grant it may be a happy
one."

He paused in extreme agitation—but Eoline could not
have spoken, had her life depended upon the act.

"I feel," continued he, with still deeper emotion, "that
in this interview, the last one of unrestrained confidence
we may ever enjoy, I must give utterance to feelings that
are wholly irrepressible. They are new and overwhelm

ing, and will not be restrained. Eoline, you deserve an atonement for my past indifference, injustice, stoicism. You deserve an expiation for all the sacrifices you have made—the trials you have endured for me. Now, when it is too late, when I know that you are lost to me for-ever—when a dark abyss seems opening between us, I feel that I love you, with a love purer, deeper, stronger than ever yet warmed the breast of man. Triumph, Eoline, triumph in this confession, wrung from me by throes of passion too mighty to be resisted."

It is impossible to give an idea of the force, the ear-nestness of his manner. He rose and wound one arm round the pillar against which Eoline was seated, and leaned his head upon the cold stone.

" Triumph!" repeated Eoline, in a low voice, "oh, Horace, how little do you know me. Triumph! oh, had I heard those words but one week sooner, they might have filled me with triumphant joy. Now, alas! it is indeed too late."

" One week!" exclaimed Horace, "surely the love which rises as a barrier against mine, is not the growth of one little week."

Eoline had solved in one moment the great problem of her life, the mystery of her own heart. To know that she was beloved by Horace, as the strong in mind and heart alone *can* love, would have created a joy too intense, a triumph, as he called it, too glorious, had it not been chastened and darkened by the conviction that it was *too late!* She felt that it was due to him, to relate the whole history of her acquaintance with St. Leon, her first impres-sions, her after misgivings, settling into a firm belief that he was wanting in those master qualities necessary to in-spire her love—and then the self-sacrifice she had made to impart happiness to his dying hour. And she did do this, while walking with him arm-in-arm, through the hedges of rose-trees that bordered the lawn. She went back still farther, and told him the hopes she had cherished before his return from abroad that she could inspire that affection which would sanction the bonds their parents had imposed, her disappointment at his coldness and reserve, her struggles before leaving home, her awakened interest when he visited her before, and the sudden but complete expansion of her heart during their present intercourse. Under any other circumstances she could not thus have revealed her inner being,—but it is said death is an honest hour, and this which confessed the birth of love, must prove its living grave.

"And now, Horace, I have opened to you my whole heart, only to close it up forever. This disclosure was your right, anything more would be infringing the rights of another. When I uttered the words which sever me from you, I believed them addressed to a dying man, though I said in my soul, I will leave the future in the hands of God. They are as binding as an oath, and have sealed my destiny forever."

"Had you known that I loved you, Eoline, would you then have bid St. Leon live for you?"

"No, I could not then have sacrificed *your* happiness. Had it been placed in my keeping, neither life nor death could have made me faithless to the trust. It was to avoid endangering that more than any other consideration, which led me to resist my father's will. I have always felt I had a right to dispose of my *own*, if by so doing I could redeem another from misery."

"How calmly you talk, how coldly you reason," exclaimed Horace, passionately, "when my whole brain, my whole heart are on fire. I am maddened, Eoline— maddened when I think of my past blindness, my present loss, my future despair."

"The very depth of despair gives calmness," cried Eoline,

in an accent that expressed more than her words. Horace felt his injustice, but every passion was raging in his bosom, and he could not still them. There was another reason for Eoline's calmness. The self-sacrificing spirit is always strong. There is a sustaining power given to those who are willing to sit in darkness that others may have light —to walk on thorns—that others may tread a path of roses.

"There is a way, Eoline," Horace suddenly exclaimed, "I see it as clear as noonday; I will go to St. Leon, and tell him all. He cannot, he ought not to take advantage of your noble, generous impulses. Your happiness ought to be dearer than his own. He could not, would not ask or wish your hand, without your heart. Eoline, let us go together—our only safety, our only trust is in truth."

"You do not know St. Leon," said she, laying her hand on his arm, and arresting his hurrid steps—"we shall *murder* him at once. This very morning Doctor Hale told me that the slightest agitation might prove his death at any moment. Think if he could survive the blow you meditate. You have no conception of the strength, the violence of his love. It is not love—it is idolatry."

"The love which you inspire must be idolatry, Eoline. I feel it but too well."

"Ah!" exclaimed Eoline, "how little we know ourselves. I once thought it would be sweet to be loved, passionately loved, even by those whom I loved not in return—but St. Leon's love has always saddened me by its very excess. Then I thought if the sensibilities of my own heart were awakened, and its capacities known, if I could learn the height and the depth thereof, it would be an earnest of the joys of Heaven. And it is. I have felt as happy, for a *little while* to-night, as human nature is capable of feeling. Through all life its memory will remain. Even in death,

it will not perish—for our affections are immortal—and
God himself is love."

Eoline had not slept for several nights, and for days
her nerves had been in a state of constant tension. She
had had no rest since the fatigue and excitement of the
concert, and she might be said to have lived on air, so
little food had passed her lips. In such a state of the
nervous system it is not strange that her interview with
Horace, so agitating in its nature, should have had something of the influence of opium. She felt unnaturally
spiritualized, exalted, and her language partook of the high
wrought tone of her feelings.

"Yes," she added, "the remembrance of this night will
strengthen me in all coming duties. And so it will you.
You will go out into the world and be a wrestler for its
honors and win its laurels of fame. And I shall hear
of you and be proud. I shall say, 'he is *my* friend, *my*
brother, the friend and brother of my soul.'"

"I care not for honors now, Eoline—I care not for
laurels,—I have had high thoughts, lofty aspirations. In
the solitary musings of my youth, I was always looking
forward to some great future. Meditation, born of ancient
lore, sat a cold-lipped hermit at my side, pointing to the
distant horizon, to the dim and hazy hills. All that was
near and intermediate was overlooked. The future—it
was always the future! and now what is it? A blank!
No, worse than a blank! for disappointment and misery are
written upon it!"

"This is unworthy of yourself, Horace, and of me.
Great minds never despair—they struggle with destiny,
and triumph in the conflict,—it is the weak only who
yield. Let the selfish live for their own happiness. Let
us live for something noble, Horace,—the happiness of
others."

The force, the sublimity of this sentiment, touched a

corresponding chord in the bosom of Horace. Yes! he would live for others, for the good of mankind. He would become the protector of the oppressed, the refuge of the weak, the avenger of the innocent. He would become eloquent, that crime might shrink abashed from his presence, and guilt from before the lightning of his glance. The crowned champion of man's rights, he would defend them with an arm of strength and a heart of steel. The wail of human misery rising from the bosom of the earth, up to the ear of God, should change to notes of joy, as far as his power extended. Then Eoline would hear of him, and though reclining on the bosom of another, she would bless his name and glory in his virtues.

Warmed with a noble emulation, he breathed these resolves into her ear, as they approached the steps of the piazza. She felt proud to have inspired them—proud that she had at last done justice to his exalted character. His protestations of love did not cause so deep a thrill as this almost divine philanthropy. The first humbled while they enraptured her, for they were beyond her merits; the last ennobled himself, and prospectively blest mankind. They now stood upon the threshold, and the shadows of twilight had deepened into the gloom of night.

"Farewell, Horace," said she, while her hand lingered in the farewell clasp of his, "we part here—when to meet again, God only knows! I do not ask, I do not wish," she added, in a faltering voice, "that you should entirely forget me, but think of me only as a sister, and pray for me as such."

Horace held her hand in the strong yet trembling grasp of his, then suddenly dropping it, exclaimed,

"This is not a brother's parting. For the first, for the last time, Eoline," and clasping his arms passionately round her, kissed her pale cheek, and was gone. Gone! what a word that is!—the heavy clod falling on the coffin-lid of hope! Gone! the sad heart echoes, and what an abysmal void is left!

Day by day strength returned to the languid frame of St. Leon. He could leave his room—he could walk through the rose-hedges, leaning on the arm of Eoline and breathe the fresh and balmy air. He was the mos interesting invalid in the world—so grateful, so gentle, so childlike in his dependence and trust. He seemed to have no misgiving for the future. With such a hope as now animated him, health and strength must soon return. He would dwell for hours on the luxuriant beauties of his native clime, of its groves of orange and palmetto bowers, in whose shades the sweet nightingale of the South should find her downy nest. At the close of every soft and glowing description of this future Eden of their hearts, he would implore her to repeat the magic words that had brought him back to life and happiness—and Eoline, with a pallid cheek, but heavenly glance, would utter, in a low, tremulous voice,

"Live, St. Leon, for God—and me."

Miss Manly, who had made preparations to visit her Northern friends during the Summer holidays, and who had been detained by the illness of St. Leon, now asked the opinion of Doctor Hale with regard to his patient.

"He must go with you," said the doctor, decidedly "He is now equal to the journey, and a Northern tour will give a tone to his system which could not be imparted in our debilitating climate. He could not be in better hands than yours and Miss Louisa's—and Uncle Ben is worth a hundred Doctors, myself included. Are you willing that he should accompany you?"

"Certainly," replied Miss Manly, with a glow of pleasure her cold exterior did not betray. "The only barrier to my departure is now removed. But Miss Glenmore," added she, hesitatingly, "I once invited her to join our party to the North, but she declined. Is she now included in this journey ?"

"No," said the doctor, "I am going to take her under my charge. My wife, who is something of an invalid, is going to try the waters of the —— Springs, so celebrated for their pure and bracing qualities. The baths are delicious, the scenery wild and romantic. She is desirous of a companion, and Miss Glenmore is one she will especially delight in. I have arranged all this, and have no doubt I shall obtain the young lady's consent. She told me the other day, with one of those heaven-born smiles of hers, that I was irresistible."

The truth was, the doctor, notwithstanding his perplexity with regard to her, had become deeply interested in the young *enigma.* The remarkable union of strength and sensibility in her character had won his respect and admiration, and her unprotected situation as a discarded daughter, his sympathy and tenderness. Though he hoped much from the invigorating air of the North for the delicate constitution of St. Leon, he feared also. The nature of his disease rendered him liable to a sudden death, and he wished to spare Eoline the trial of witnessing it.

She heard the proposition with so much gratitude and feeling, he blessed himself for having made it.

"Thank you, sir, a thousand times, for your kind consideration," said she, with a joyful sense of relief from a strange embarrassment. "Nothing could be more pleasing, under existing circumstances. For, indeed," she added, with a rising blush, "during Miss Manly's absence I hardly know where to go."

The doctor had far greater difficulty in persuading St Leon to accede to his plans. He strenuously opposed the idea of being parted from Eoline. If she would consent to be united to him, and bear him company, he would be willing to go to the ends of the earth, but it was far better to remain near her and die, than seek life where she was not.

"Come, St. Leon," said the doctor, in that tone of kind authority he knew so well how to assume, "you must not be selfish. I must take your Eoline under my own charge for a time, and bring back her vanishing roses. Were she to accompany you, anxiety on your account would keep her in a state of constant excitement, and she wants rest and recreation. You, too, need rest—and in *her* presence you cannot feel it. No, no—you must not think of making the least opposition. It is all for the best. You will return a renovated being, and claim a bright and blooming bride."

St. Leon at last consented to be guided by the commanding will he had not mental strength to resist, and submitted his passions to the control of reason.

"And now, my dear Louisa," said Eoline to her, the night before her departure, after a long and heart-revealing conversation, "you know all,—all the strength, and all the weakness of my soul. You remember, when I told you in this very room—what love I wish to inspire and what to feel. I have inspired and felt, and must ever feel all I then described; oh! what a strange and wayward destiny! The same being—the cold and impassive being from whom I fled, to save him as well as myself from an unloving wedlock, now seems a twin-born soul, united to mine with clasps strong as iron, and indestructible as gold. But St. Leon has my tenderness, pity, sympathy, and sisterly regard. He shall never know that I am capable of a warmer feeling than he has awakened. If I have erred in uttering more than a true heart sanctions, *he* shall never suffer for my dereliction, from the stern principles of truth and sincerity. Louisa, I believed him dying, and to give peace to his departing soul, I did what I trust a God of Mercy will forgive. I was even vile enough to mourn that the hour of death passed by, that the destroying angel relented when he looked upon his victim. I have resolved that my whole life shall be devoted to expiation for this sin. I would go with him this moment, but the doctor asserts that my presence will retard his restoration, and prove a bane rather than an antidote. To your tender care I commit him. Watch over him as a loving sister, as the guardian angel you were born to be to weak and suffering man. Miss Manly is kind and devoted, but she lacks the soft-ness and gentleness of womanhood, *she* is wanting in what Nature has lavished on *you*."

Louisa wept as she listened to the tender, solemn words of Eoline, and promised all she required.

" And now farewell, my own dear friend," continued Eoline, folding her arms around her. " I shall not see you in the morning. You are going to the embraces of a fond mother and gentle sisters, to the hallowed joys of a native home. You *must* be happy. *I* might have been reconciled to my father and restored to his affection, but it was *too late*. How selfish I am, Louisa—I must go to St. Leon now—and arm myself with fortitude to cheer and console him. To-morrow the task must be yours."

On the morrow the portals and blinds of the Magnolia Vale Seminary were all closed. The kitchen and negro cabins were still occupied, but the stillness of death reigned in the mansion in which so many hearts had lately throbbed.

Eoline, whose feelings had been sorely tried the pre-ceding night, leaned back in the carriage, and under the covering folds of her veil, concealed her sad countenance from the gaze of her new friend. Mrs. Hale was all kind ness, but she was almost a stranger, and Eoline naturally shrunk from any display of sensibility before one who was unacquainted with its source. The doctor had placed her

under his wife's protection, and recommended her as carefully as if she were a patient, but he could not leave his
professional duties to accompany them. At first she felt
very strange and sorrowful, but the sweet influences of
the season, the beautiful scenery through which they rode,
he easy, yet brisk motion of the carriage, and, more than
ll, the natural elasticity of her spirits, contributed to
chase the cloud from her brow. Her grateful apprecia-
tion of the doctor's kindness made her endeavor to prove
a cheering companion to his gentle and charming wife,
and justify his praises.

She was enchanted with the wild beauties of the ——
Springs. The clear, pure mountain air, the icy cold water,
the delicious baths, the Alpine glens and forest bowers—
all infused new life into her languid veins. Then the
stream of existence flowing in and flowing out the whole
time, the new faces, so soon becoming familiar, and the
familiar ones so soon gone, to give place to others;—the
constant changes were animating to one so long confined
to the monotony of a school, where the same figures always
meet the gaze, where one day is an epitome of the next,
and where the constant ringing of the bell imparts a *brazen*
tone to the existence.

Eoline, who believed herself the saddest, most subdued
and resigned of human beings, was astonished to find herself interested in all that surrounded her. The great principle of vitality, fed by new fuel, and burning with new
fire and brightness, triumphed in a great measure over the
depressing influence of past trials. She did not wish to
be borne on the tide of fashionable amusements; she came,
she said, "to be a looker on in Venice." And true to her
resolution she would take her place quietly at Mrs. Hale's
side, resolved to find gratification in witnessing the enjoyment of others. But she was too beautiful, too charming
to be left quiet in the gay scene. There could be no

music without her voice, and she was too unaffectedly obliging to refuse when she could impart pleasure by compliance. She would often say, "I will not dance to-night," but when entreated to make up the one wanting couple in a quadrille, she would yield, not like an automaton, but a real living sylph of the season. Eoline did not wish to be a belle. She had too many causes for deep and anxious thought to desire to be an object of public admiration. The heart that truly loves has no room for vanity or pride. And Eoline not only loved, but was condemned to struggle with emotions which, if no barrier interrupted, she would have gloried in acknowledging. But the distinction which others sought was forced on her—and wherever she moved, she was followed by a crowd of admirers, many of whom she would gladly have transferred to her less attractive companions.

One evening she noticed a tall, thin, sallow gentleman, with a very intelligent and striking countenance, walking in the public hall, with a young, but pale and wildly-mournful looking female clinging to his arm. There was something in her appearance that strangely interested her. Her large and intensely black eyes wandered vaguely over the gay throng, without resting a moment on any particular object, and there was a listlessness in her air which betrayed perfect indifference to the impression she might make on others. The only thing that seemed to interest her was music, and when Eoline, seated at the piano, which was on an elevated platform at the extremity of the hall, drew the crowd around her by the sorcery of her witching voice, the pale, wild-eyed young stranger came nearer and nearer, leaning on the arm of the sallow and intellectual-faced gentleman, and seemed to glue those wild eyes on the beautiful face of the songstress. The gentleman, though apparently of her father's age, seemed scarcely less interested. Every time she looked up, she encountered his fixed and penetrating gaze, as well as the melancholy glance of his strange companion. During the whole evening they seemed to be hovering near her. She was told they were strangers, who had just arrived, and no one with whom she conversed was aware of their names.

At length, the gentleman, taking advantage of a moment when he could obtain access to Eoline, approached, and said,

"Pardon me, Miss Glenmore, for this intrusion. But one of your father's earliest friends takes the liberty of addressing you. Perhaps you may have heard him mention the name of Wilton."

"Often, sir," replied Eoline, with cordial frankness. "But I did not think, you would recognize me from my resemblance to my father. We are not supposed to be alike."

"There is indeed little similitude," said Mr. Wilton, "and I did not imagine when I first beheld you, that I looked upon the daughter of my friend, that daughter I have been so anxious to see. I had no difficulty in knowing Miss Glenmore. I have heard hardly any name but hers since entering the hall. But let me introduce you to my daughter, Mrs. Lovell. Amelia, my dear, this is Miss Glenmore, the young lady whose sweet voice charmed you an hour ago."

Amelia gazed earnestly at Eoline, but suffered her cold hand to remain passive in the soft clasp of Eoline's.

"Is your father with you?" asked Mr. Wilton.

"No, sir," answered Eoline, the blood rushing painfully to her face. "I am under the protection of a lady who will be happy to make your acquaintance. She sits in the opposite corner of the hall. Shall we go to her?"

"How long is it since you have seen your father?"

83

inquired Mr. Wilton, anxiously, as they approached Mrs. Hale.

"It is many months, sir," she replied, with an involuntary sigh.

"He visited me early in the spring," said Mr. Wilton, wondering that the letter of his friend had not softened the heart of the estranged daughter, and carried her back to her father's arms. "He spoke of you, and created in me a strong desire to see a young lady possessed of so firm and independent a character."

She could not judge from his accent whether he spoke in praise or blame. It was evident her history was known. It was more than probable that her father had represented her, as she appeared to him, obstinate, ungrateful, and self-willed, and that Mr. Wilton regarded her in a prejudiced and unfavorable light.

"When a young lady is forced to act independently,' said Eoline, with a conscious blush, "she is very apt to incur the censure of the world. Strength of principle may be mistaken for obstinacy, and self-reliance be branded as self-will."

They had now reached the place where Mrs. Hale was seated, and the ceremony of introduction interrupted the conversation. Amelia seemed glad to sit down by the pleasing and sweet-looking lady who greeted her so kindly, and when Mr. Wilton saw her nestling at her side, as if shrinking from the gay crowd with timidity and terror, he turned to Eoline, and asked her if she were willing to take the arm of her father's friend, and seek the cool air of the piazza a few moments.

Eoline complied, but the hand trembled that rested on his arm. She thought he was going to urge her father's claim to obedience, and the wall she had herself built up against compliance, rose up before her with frowning height.

Neither could she bear to hear Horace Cleveland spoken of as an object of aversion and avoidance.

"I honor your principles, Miss Glenmore," said her new friend, pausing near a pillar, against which he leaned. "I admire the dignity, the loftiness of character you have exhibited, and which I have never seen equalled in one so young. But vindictive feelings against a parent appear so inconsistent with the sensibility and gentleness your countenance expresses, I regret éxtremely seeing you still in a state of estrangement."

"I have never cherished vindictive feelings towards my father, sir," exclaimed Eoline, deeply wounded. "You wrong me greatly. I have always felt for him the tenderness, affection, and respect of a daughter."

"Then why not return to his protecting arms."

"Because, sir, there are conditions which it is now impossible for me to conform to."

"But when he offered you *unconditional* forgiveness— when he wrote in terms which, to a proud man like him, must have been like writing in blood, and entreated you to return; pardon me, but it does seem—"

"Wrote to me, my father write—my father—entreat me to return!" exclaimed she, catching hold of Mr. Wilton's arm, and looking into his face with wild earnestness. "He never wrote to me—never offered forgiveness. Some one has told you falsely."

"But I saw the letter. He wrote it in my house, at my own table, with my own pen and ink. I read every word of it, and it was worthy of a repenting father's heart."

"You read it!" exclaimed Eoline, turning pale as the moonlight. "I never received it—never."

She was so much agitated, that Mr. Wilton, fearing she would attract the notice of the curious and the inquisitive, proposed adjourning to the cabin occupied by Mrs. Hale, an offer which Eoline gladly accepted, finding it impos-

sıble to control her excited feelings. The moment they
arrived at the cabin, she threw herself on the rustic bench
that ran under the stoop, and burst into a passion of
tears.

"Oh! why did I not receive this token of pardoning
love?" she cried. "How blest, how happy I might have
been! Now it is too late."

"No, Eoline—let me thus address the daughter of my
friend. It is not too late. A moment will explain and
reconcile all. Most happy shall I be to assume the office
of peace-maker."

"How cold, how ungrateful he must deem me," she exclaimed, in an agony of emotion, "to slight his proffered
forgiveness, to refuse the pardon that must have been
bought with many a bitter struggle. What an unnatural
monster I must have appeared in his eyes! Oh! my dear
father! how happy we might all have been, had I known
this a little sooner!"

Her promise to St. Leon pressed with a tightening
stricture across her heart. Restored to her father once
more, *his* sanction would be necessary to make that promise binding; for though she might resist the authority
that would force her into an unwilling wedlock, she would
never marry in opposition to a father's will, while occupying a daughter's place in his household. Restoration to
her home, freedom from her impulsive vows, a union with
Horace Cleveland, love, happiness, an earthly Eden—all
beamed in radiant colors on her vision. Then the image
of St. Leon, despairing, dying—with his hand pressed
upon his heart, and his thrilling glance bent on her, just as
she saw him, before he fell insensible at her feet in the
concert-room—glided before her, and filled her with anguish and remorse.

"My dear child," cried Mr. Wilton, sitting by her, and
taking both her hands in his, for she was wringing them

in the conflict of her feelings, "can you not say 'I will arise and go to my father,'—not like the returning prodigal, for you have *not* sinned against Heaven and him, and you *are* worthy to be called his daughter; but in the true spirit of love, obedience and conciliation, and reinstate yourself as the filial angel of his heart and home ?"

"Yes—I will go to my father," she said "and never again would I leave the guardian shades of Glenmore. I will go to my father, and leave all other events in the hands of a directing God. But will he receive me, after my apparent ingratitude and neglect ? Will he not close his doors against me, and suffer me to drift once more on the stormy waves of destiny ?"

"One simple word of explanation is all that is needed. I will write, myself, to-night, and prepare the way for your return. *You* can enclose a letter, if you wish."

"If I wish! Oh! how much have I to write. Yes, I will go in immediately, and pour out my full and grateful heart. How sweet will home seem to the wanderer !—that home from which I thought myself forever exiled! My own sweet Willie—I shall hold him in my arms again—I shall twist my fingers in his shining ringlets, and drink in living fountains of love from his rosy lips. Good Mrs. Howe—faithful Gatty—my garden—my green-house—and the grand, ancestral-looking trees !"

"Then it is not too late," said Mr. Wilton, listening to this burst of natural emotion with delight, "you do love home, yet."

"Love it !" exclaimed Eoline, clasping her hands in the most impassioned manner, and smiling through her tears—"Love it!—ask the exile if he loves his native land! And now," added she, rising, "I must leave you, to write what my heart aches to express. I thank you, I bless you, sir, for telling me what I might never otherwise have known. So many feelings rushed upon me when you first revealed

it, they almost overwhelmed me, and for a little while I
thought I had learned it too late. You will go with me,
and your daughter, too."

"My daughter!" repeated Mr. Wilton, sadly, "I could
almost envy Glenmore the joy in store for him. Nothing
short of a divine miracle will ever restore my poor Amelia
to her primeval brightness. Should you be tempted to
exult in the triumphs of your beauty and charms, think,
that had you consented to the cold union your father urged,
and sacrificed your affections to an unnatural coercion, you
might have been the wreck that she is now, for a more
beautiful and blooming girl never awakened parental
pride than she was before her ill-starred marriage."

How strangely Eoline felt to hear him talk of that *cold
union* which would now realize all her dreams of felicity!
Truly, the human heart is a dark and winding labyrinth,
and Eoline had but lately discovered the silken clue to her
own.

"Your daughter does indeed look very unhappy," she
said, "I grieve for her."

"If she could be roused from this state of apathy,"
said the father, "If she could be made aware of her
own independent existence, I should have some hopes of
her recovery. Even in her brightest hours, she was perfectly passive, never acting from any volition of her own.
So gentle was she, that we never made the pressure of
parental authority heavier than down. After she left us,
an iron will weighed down upon her, with perhaps unconscious force, till it paralized the life of her mind, and
chilled the warmth of her heart. It was the sight of my
poor wilted child, and the mournful consequences of her
mental inertion, that reconciled your father to your
stronger and more independent character."

"I ought to cherish her very tenderly, then," said Eoline,
" since her misfortunes have resulted in blessings to me

I suppose my father did not complain to you of *my* too passive nature."

"No—he seemed to think you were blessed with a will of your own. But console yourself, Eoline—you have acted nobly—and every true and manly heart will say *Amen* to the sentiment I have uttered."

Eoline sat up till past the midnight hour, writing to her father. She wrote sheet after sheet, then tore them in pieces, thinking they did not do justice to her feelings. At last she wrote the simple words—

"Father, dear father, I never received the letter giving me permission to return, or it would have borne me on wings to your feet. I come, ready to devote my future life to your happiness. I have sown in tears, but I shall now reap in joy. Yes, my father, I come, like the dove to the Ark, weary with my wanderings, to fold my wings on your breast. "Your own

EOLINE."

In one of her first letters, which she had torn, she had spoken of St. Leon, but on reflection, she thought it best to wait till her return, and then she intended to give her father a true history of her life since their separation. When St. Leon returned, he must seek her at her paternal home, and obtain her father's sanction to his love. As the son of a rich Louisiana planter, he might find favor in Mr. Glenmore's eyes, since he had released his daughter from the first conditions he had imposed upon her.

Mr. Wilton had made arrangements to follow the letter in a few days, but the illness of his daughter detained him at the Springs.

"I will send you in my carriage," said he, to Eoline, "for I know your yearning desire to be at home."

But Eoline could not leave the poor invalid, who clung to her with an interest she manifested in no other being. She was confined to her bed, and the slightest sound seemed

to agonize her unsheathed nerves, but she would hold
Eoline's hand in hers, and drawing her down close to her
feverish cheek, whisper—

"Sing to me—you are an angel;" then she would add,
still more softly—"that is, if you are willing."

Eoline hung over her sick couch and sung to her, in
a voice sweet and low as the echo of a flute, some of the
holy hymns her mother had taught her in her childhood.
With her glittering hair unbound, for Amelia had loosened
it from confinement, and drawn it as a veil, partially over
her own faded face; her black eyes gleaming mournfully
through the golden meshes, Eoline did resemble one of
those heavenly beings, sent to minister to languishing
humanity. All day, and day after day, she sat by the sufferer, singing to her those low warbling strains which had
such a soothing influence on her excited nerves, and holding her burning hand in hers.

"It has been said by the best medical advisers whom I
have consulted," said Mr. Wilton, who watched with
intense anxiety the effect of Eoline's devotion, "that if
she could become interested in anything, deeply interested,
there would be a gleam of hope. If one electric spark
could be communicated to her palsied mind, she might
perhaps feel the glow of life stealing over her benumbed
faculties. Eoline, I have never seen her manifest the
same interest she does in you, since this leaden dullness
settled on her brain."

"Oh!" thought Eoline, "if I could be the means of
raising this poor, widowed heart to bloom again—of calling back mind and feeling to those wild, lustrous eyes, how
I would bless my God for the gift of existence. I should
feel then that I had not lived in vain."

From this moment she seemed to feel that she had a
peculiar call to devote herself to one, who from the first
had singularly attracted her. She treated her as a little

child—told her fairy tales, the treasured lore of her childhood—described to her, her own beautiful home, its fruits
and its flowers, and dwelt on the happy hours they should
have together in its embowering shades.

Amelia listened, and a smile glimmered on her face.
t was the first that had flitted over it for many a day.

" Tell me about those beautiful things again," said she.

And Eoline, with unwearied lips, repeated the childish
legend, the nursery song, and the charming description
of her native scenes.

Mr. Wilton listened with admiring gratitude, while
Eoline, with patient sweetness, thus beguiled the weary
hours of the poor invalid, apparently forgetful of her own
disappointment and deferred hopes.

" I see, now," said he, " the error we have committed.
Her mother and myself have been too gloomy. Seeing
her in this sad and seemingly hopeless condition, we have
yielded to despondency and gloom. Instead of endeavoring
to rouse and animate her as we should have done, we have
sunk, ourselves, under the blow that crushed her intellect.
You have darted one ray of sunshine into the obscurity.
Heaven grant that it may brighten and brighten into the
perfect day."

This was not said in the hearing of Amelia, who began
to discover a faint interest in what was passing around her.

" Shall I really go with you ?" said she to Eoline.
" Are you *willing* that I should go ?"

" Willing ! I have been begging your father to let you
stay with me. I have a sweet little brother, but no sister ;
and you shall be my own sister, and Willie a darling little
brother to us both."

" And will you sing to me there, too ?" she asked—a
faint color stealing over her wan cheek.

"I will sing the songs you best love to hear, and I will
sing them to a harp with golden strings, such as my

mother used to tell me the angels played upon—and we will gather flowers every day, and make garlands for our hair. Oh! we shall have a merry life, Amelia."

Amelia gave back an answering smile to the sweet smile of Eoline. An electric spark had struck the palsied mass, and life was slowly stealing through it.

" You seem to love music very much," said Eoline; "do you not sing and play yourself?"

"I did," answered Amelia, "but, oh, I have heard *such* music!"

She spoke with more emphasis than usual, and a shade of softness stole over the wild splendor of her eye.

" Where?" asked Eoline.

"In this very place. And when I first heard you sing, I thought it seemed as if I were floating backward in a dream."

" Then you have been here before?"

"Yes! but do not speak of it. My father does not know all."

Amelia put her hand to her head, with an expression of perplexity and pain.

Eoline was certain that there were associations connected with music, to which Amelia's heart still responded, all unstrung as it was. Perhaps they might furnish a key to the mysterious paralysis of her being.

The arrival of the mail at the ——— Springs, which only came once during the week, always created excitement. Incidents in the great world, from which they were so completely shut out, assumed an interest and importance which they did not possess to those who were actors in the busy scene. Mr. Wilton put a packet of letters in the hand of Eoline, and retired to peruse one addressed to himself.

Eoline recognized the hand-writing of St. Leon, and Louisa, and opened the letters with trembling fingers.

The ardent Creole wrote, as he spoke, in a strain of poetic rapture, and every line was glowing with the inspiration of returning health. The future—it was all sunshine. No cloud obscured its noonday effulgence. The pen of fire, which traced these impassioned sentiments, met a surface of snow on the heart of Eoline. She tried to be grateful, she tried to rejoice, and she did rejoice for him, and she was grateful, that warm in youth and love, he was not called to " bid the world farewell." But she felt no answering enthusiasm when he dwelt upon the future, which was mapped out to him as an earthly elysium. St. Leon, blooming in health and radiant in hope, was a very different being to her from St. Leon, languishing on a sick and dying bed, and appealing to her for a gleam of joy to light him through the dark valley. With a suppressed sigh she turned to Louisa's letter, which was a true transcript of her meek and gentle spirit. As it was at least twelve sheets in length, we will not attempt to unfold the whole contents, but extract a passage here and there for those who feel some interest in this unselfish and holy-minded being.

" St. Leon," she wrote, " seems to gather strength every moment from the dewy freshness and mountain elasticity of our Northern atmosphere. His pallid cheek begins to show the living under-current through its transparent whiteness. Miss Manly continues to treat him as an invalid, though he smilingly declares that he is now only an honorary member of the valetudinarian club. Uncle Ben, too, good, kind soul, watches him as if he were a child, and will not allow him to expose himself to the evening air or the noonday sun. I think St. Leon loves to be *petted*, to use a childish expression, better than any man I ever saw. Though he disclaims all *right* to these cherishing and preventing cares, they still please him, and his heart seems overflowing with gratitude. You recollect, dear Eoline, when we were speaking of Miss Manly, in an hour of unreserved confidence, I said I should not be surprised if she had her *weaknesses*, like the rest of her sex. I am certain that this proud, unbending woman—this science-dedicated Minerva, really loves the gentle and romantic St. Leon. She struggles to conceal it, but the weakness exists. I do not think *he* imagines the passion he has inspired, and I sincerely hope, for her sake, he never will. While I love her the better for being capable of a woman's tenderness, I revere her too much not to wish it undiscovered. Pity would be a strange emotion for our commanding Principal to awaken in any bosom. St. Leon is a very interesting traveller, and suffers no beauty of nature, however minute, to pass his artist eye, unpraised by his poet tongue."

"St. Leon—St. Leon !" exclaimed Eoline, "nothing but St. Leon ! Poor, dear Louisa is so eloquent on this one theme ! I wish she would tell me something of her own sweet self."

By-and-bye Louisa came to the moment when she arrived at her own modest and elm-bowered home.

"And now, dear Eoline, I will speak of myself and the holy joy that fills my heart on finding myself once more with the mother and sisters from whom I have been so long parted. Ah! what a blessed thing it is to be loved! I am the present centre of this charming domestic circle, the cynosure of this firmament of peace and love. Can you imagine your humble, retiring Louisa occupying so conspicuous a position? My mother is the perfect model of a lovely, chastened, Christian woman. Resignation sits upon her placid brow, religion beams from her mild, quiet eye, while loving-kindness and tender charity breathe from her gentle lips. Her happiness lies buried in the grave of her husband, but she lives for the happiness of others. My sisters are fair, blooming young girls, very different from your pale-faced drooping friend. But you would hardly know me since I have inhaled my own native air. I have really gained flesh and color, and I could walk twice as far as Magnolia Vale now without being weary. I have done so. The other evening, they call it afternoon here, just before sunset, my sisters and myself, accompanied by Charles Osgood, the son of our present minister, walked to Mossy Pond, one of the most beautiful sheets of water ever crimsoned by the rosy suffusion of the West."

"So," thought Eoline, " dear Louisa is going to weave one little silver thread in the sober web of her life— Charles Osgood! Their minister's son, a minister himself to be, I dare say. I always thought Louisa was born for the wife of a man of God."

"I knew Charles," continued Louisa, " before I went to the south. His father often exchanged with mine, on the Sabbath day, and he frequently accompanied him. I always thought him interesting, good and pious."

" I dare say you did, you sly, demure little Quaker," interrupted Eoline, " never to say one word about this interesting Charles, while I have been pouring out heart and soul into your bosom."

" But," continued the candid letter-writer, " I never saw any one so much improved in all outward and inward graces."

And so Louisa went on ingenuously and modestly and *so humbly*, telling how she walked and talked with Charles, the devout, the ministerial, but still the interesting and most agreeable Charles, not only by the green banks of Mossy Pond, but under the shade of the branching elms, and stood with him in the gloom of twilight by the weeping willow that sighed over her father's grave.

"I never spoke to you of Charles," and Eoline almost imagined she saw a soft blush on the paper, ' because I never dreamed, that I, such as you know I am, could awaken more than a friendly interest in his heart I cannot tell why I shrank from mentioning his name, unless it was this feeling of resigned hopelessness. But it was returning from the grave of my father, when there was just nough light lingering for me to see the mild, holy beam of his eyes as they bent upon me, that he told me he had always loved me, and dared to look forward to the time when I should lighten the burden, and temper the heat of his day of care. I wept—because there is no language but tears, for such feelings as swelled my heart almost to suffocation."

"'You weep, Louisa,'" said he. "'Have I made you unhappy by this confession?'"

"'I weep,'" answered I, "'for my own unworthiness.'"

"And I do feel unworthy, dear Eoline, of the love of so pure, so excellent, so exalted a being; I, who imagined I could never inspire love in any one, to possess the perfect, the undivided affection of one, worthy even of you, my noble, beautiful Eoline! He will seek a portion of his Master's vineyard, warmed by a Southern sun, and fanned by a Southern breeze, so we may meet again when you dwell amid the orange bowers and citron groves that are waiting to embosom you in their fragrant shades."

"Happy, happy Louisa!" cried Eoline, the letter dropping from her hand and tears glistening in her eyes, "thy true humility, thy modest Christian graces, thy meek, self-renouncing spirit are about to receive the greatest reward earth can bestow. And yet in thy blindness, thou hast envied *me*."

Louisa said not one word about physical weakness. She expressed no misgivings for the future. She seemed strong and firm in her new-born happiness. Her greatest trial was the thought of leaving her mother, but her sisters would fill her place, and be more to her than she had ever been. The one next to herself would return with Miss Manly, to take her office in the seminary.

"Farewell," said she in conclusion, "till we meet again in this spiritual intercourse, which is the joy of parted friends. I have described you here, sometimes, as the rose of the South, sometimes as the magnolia of your glorious clime. Eoline, I trust, I know that you will be happy. Surely Heaven would not vouchsafe such a prospect of felicity to *me*, and suffer a heart like *yours* to be chilled by disappointment or darkened by sorrow.

"Your LOUISA.'

Eoline sat with her hands clasped over her knee, still as a statue, for nearly an hour after the perusal of these letters. This was her habit in moments of strong excitement, when she was alone, and no counter current came to mingle with the deep and troubled waters of her soul. At length she rose.

"I have forgotten poor Amelia," she said. "I fear she has pined for my presence."

When she entered her room she found Mr. Wilton sitting by her, with his arms around her, endeavoring to soothe her, for she was in a state of unusual agitation.

"I am glad you are come," said he, in answer to Eoline's inquiring glance, "though I rejoice in witnessing this unwonted sensibility; I have just received the unexpected intelligence of her husband's death. I did not think it would affect her as it seems to have done. It is true the shock is great, but there can be no heart-string broken."

Amelia stretched out her arms to Eoline, who saw that her glazed and unnaturally brilliant eyes were swimming in tears. It was as strange a sight as dew on the burning sands of the desert.

"Weep, Amelia," cried Eoline, taking the father'·'

place by her side, " shed all the tears you have been holding back, lest others should shed them for you."

And she did weep long and freely—wept till Eoline's
cheek and neck were wet as with rain-drops. The father
could not remain to witness this crisis of her malady—for
such it seemed to him. He had so often prayed that he
might see the wasting fire of her eyes quenched in tears,
the oppression of her heart loosened by such a relieving
shower, that he went out hastily and sought the deepest
shades of the grove, where no eye but the One, which
pierces through the densest clouds, could witness his
emotion.

It would be difficult to analyze Amelia's tears. Through
the influence of Eoline, the fearful tension of her nerves
had been relaxed. And now the sudden intelligence of
her husband's death smote on the surface of her heart,
unnaturally hardened, and the long restrained waters gushed
forth. She had never loved him—and they were not
therefore tears of anguish. Perhaps it was the removal
of the iron pressure which had been gradually crushing
and crushing her, producing an insensibility that made
her scarcely conscious of the weight—the heaving off of
an incumbent load, the rolling away of a rock from the
door of the fountain, and giving liberation to the imprisoned waves.

Eoline remained with her long after the paroxysm had
subsided, and drew from the youthful widow the history of
the past, which she had kept so hermetically sealed that
even her parents never suspected the source of her strange
malady.

Amelia slept that night as she had not slept for a long
and weary year. That copious, yet gentle shower of tears,
was like Summer rain on the dry and parched earth. The
revelation too of a bosom secret, which she had been cherishing like some ill-gotten treasure, was an unspeakable

relief to her burdened spirit. Eoline, too, had been whispering to her words of hope and comfort. Eoline had said, with her voice of music and look of love,

"Amelia, you may yet be happy."

"Yes," thought Eoline, while *she* pressed a sleepless pillow, "Louisa will be happy, and Amelia will be happy, and I. Oh! thou God of the lonely night, whose mighty, invisible spirit I feel brooding over the depths of mine, if Thou hast in Thy mystery reserved any unknown joy for me, teach me to wait, patiently to wait, till the day-star shall dawn upon the gloom.

The morning found Amelia so softened, so subdued, so tranquil, that her father embraced her with speechless gratitude.

"We can commence our journey to-morrow," said he, to Eoline, "I long to see my friend. We must rejoice together."

"I wish my mother were with us," cried Amelia, in a soft, natural tone of voice. She seemed for days previous to have forgotten her mother's existence.

"We shall soon be with her," replied her father, "after we have restored Eoline to her father's arms."

"She must meet us at Glenmore Place cried Eoline, "for it will be long before I shall give up Amelia, my new-found friend and adopted sister."

Then Eoline told her plans for the future—how Mr. Wilton was to leave Amelia with her, while he went and brought her mother to form one of their domestic party— and how Amelia was to remain with her till the bright roses of her youth bloomed again upon her cheeks. Mr. Wilton smiled gratefully on the young enthusiast, and blest the Providence which had brought her, a beam of light and comfort, into their darkened pathway.

Towards evening, Eoline, who had several favorite haunts around the springs, and wished to visit them for

the last time, stole out through the broad chestnut trees
behind her cabin, that she might enjoy the pleasure of a
lonely ramble.   There was a fountain not very far from
the way-side, gushing out in the midst of such coolness
and depth of shade, it diffused around the freshness and
verdure of an eternal spring.   Here she loved to sit on
an old gray rock, half covered with moss, and imagine the
green closure one of those silent homes which Horace had
described to her, and like him, she felt waves of deep and
solemn thought rolling in upon her soul.   The fountain
murmuring in the solitude was a pensive yet earnest
teacher of wisdom and godly love, and the soft whisper
of the wind through the trees was an echo to its accents—and far down in her own heart was a deeper echo
still.

In returning, she was obliged to walk a while in the
public road.   She heard the rumbling of carriage-wheels
behind—no unusual sound where life seemed a locomo-
tive engine.   A young silvery voice reached her ears,
that made her blood give a quicker bound in her veins.
She turned round and saw a noble pair of bays, fleaked
with the foam of exercise.   She knew their stately step-
pings well.   She knew, too, the coal-black face gleaming
with ivory, shining down upon her from the coachman's
seat.   There was a large, fine-looking man seated in the
carriage ; she knew him, too ; and that young, silvery
voice—again it thrilled her very soul—

"Ela, sister Ela," it cried.   It was the music of the
opening Heavens to her ears.   The carriage stopped—the
steps were let down, and Eoline sprang in at the same
moment.   Willie jumped into his sister's arms—who,
clasping her precious burden, knelt at her father's feet.
The proud master of Glenmore bent down and folded his
banished daughter in his arms.

CHAPTER X.

A few days after the scene which formed the closing in cident of our last chapter, the party were on their home ward way. Eoline had taken an affectionate farewell of her kind friend, Mrs. Hale, whom she burdened with mes- sages of love and gratitude to the excellent Doctor, and then every thought was directed towards Glenmore. She could have exclaimed, inverting the feelings of the sad exile of Erin.—

> "Now once again in the green sunny bowers,
> Where my father has lived, shall I spend the sweet hours,
> And cover my harp with the wild woven flowers,
> While I sing the wild anthems of *joy and of praise.*"

One unexpected incident in their journey must be re- corded. As they were travelling through the woods, ap- parently far from any habitation, something gave way in the carriage, which obliged them all to descend.

"There must be a dwelling near, for I see a vegetable garden ahead of us," said Mr. Glenmore.

"And I see a chimney peeping through the trees," cried Willie, standing on tip-toe.

As Mr. Wilton's carriage was far behind them, Eoline proposed walking on with Willie to the house, while her father consulted with the coachman about the best means of repairing the injury the carriage had sustained. Lightly Eoline ran on, holding her beautiful little brother by the hand, both glad to exchange the rolling motion of the close carriage for free exercise in the open air.

A large, double log cabin emerged from the trees as they approached. A hospitable-looking bucket, with a nice

(223)

white gourd suspended over it, attracted the eyes of the thirsty Willie. But Eoline was attracted still more strongly by a figure standing in the door, gazing on the approaching strangers. It was a stout coarse-looking girl, in a blue-checked bib apron, with short, sandy hair, that fell over her eyes like a thick, flaxen fringe, holding in her hand a long green pickle, whose truncated end exhibited the print of her incisors.

"La, sus!" she exclaimed, rushing to the gate, to the astonishment and affright of Willie, "if it ain't Miss Eoline. Goodness me! how came you here? I'm mighty glad to see you. Aunt Jerusha!" she cried, running back to the door, and calling out from the top of her lungs— "Aunt Jerusha, come here. Here's Miss Eoline, my music-teacher, that learned me how to play. My ma's sick," she added, "and my pa's out in the cotton field."

"Don't go in, Ela," said Willie, in a low voice, "she's too ugly."

"But you want some water, Willie, and we will be very tired before the carriage is mended."

By this time a very short, fat woman, with a thick cap on the top of her head, and a long pipe in her mouth, came to the door, obedient to Jerusha's summons. She put one hand up over her eyes, for the sun was shining brilliantly, and scanned the figures, near which Jerusha now stood, in a fever of delight.

"Walk in," she cried with a strong nasal twang, "walk in, and make yourselves at home—I'm powerful glad to see you, for I've hearn my niece tell a heap about you, and t'other ladies up at the sinimenary."

Jerusha fairly dragged Eoline into the house, in her impatience, and attempted to take Willie's hand, also, but he resisted her advances with such unconquerable disgust, Eoline feared her feelings would be hurt. She seemed, however, too much excited to notice it much, and the mo-

ment her guests were seated in the split-bottomed chairs,
which adorned the parlor and sitting-room, she ran into
her mother's chamber, to tell her that her music-teacher
was come, with the prettiest little boy she ever sot eyes
on.

Poor Mrs. Jacob Spotts was confined to her bed with
the fever and ague, so she could not rise to do the honors
of hospitality as she would gladly have done.

Jerusha insisted that Eoline should go in and see her
ma, but she declined on the plea of great haste, as she
expected the carriage every moment.

" Go and have something got for the young lady and the
little boy to eat," said aunt Jerusha ; and though Eoline
protested they were not hungry, and could not eat, having
dined very late, a black woman came and spread a table
with ginger-cakes, cheese and pickles, of which she was
compelled to taste, fearing to offend their well-meant,
though oppressive hospitality.

" The tobacco smoke makes me sick, Ela," cried Willie,
" please come away."

" Does it ?" exclaimed Aunt Jerusha, " well, I'll lay down
my old pipe. It's a mighty bad habit, I know. You don't
smoke, honey ?" asked she of Eoline, who shrank with
horror, even from the question. " That's right !—'twould
spoil your pretty skin. You've got a powerful fair skin,
and so's he. I can't make Jerusha keep her bonnet on,
no how in the world, and she gets as black as a nigger.
She did whiten up mightily while she was at the sinimenary, and improved wonderfully. I never did see anybody
larn faster for the time being, in all the days of my life
Sister Spotts is mightily pleased about it, and so we all are.
I'm for having children taught manners, 'fore all other
sorts of larning, and as I'm going to leave my property to
my niece, I mean she shall have a good eddication to go
upon. She's desperate smart—Jerush is."

"No, I ain't, aunt, no such thing," said Jerusha, hanging her head, "it makes me shamed to hear you talk so. If you'd seen the gals at Miss Manly's, how smart they are, you wouldn't think me fit to parch corn for 'em. But I mean to go back and get ahead of 'em yet."

"That's right, Jerusha. Be ambitious, and you cannot fail to improve," cried Eoline, rising to go. She feared to have her father find her there, for she knew how his proud spirit would chafe to hear such a girl as Jerusha address her familiarly as her teacher. "I know the carriage must be ready—we will go and meet it."

But the carriage was already at the door, the soft sand over which it rolled, giving no sound to indicate its approach.

Eoline, taking a hasty but polite leave of Aunt Jerusha, who tried hard to detain her, followed the flying steps of Willie, and bounded into the carriage. But niece Jerusha was not to be put off with a French leave. Unintimidated by the grand and imposing appearance of Mr. Glenmore, she pursued Eoline to the steps, which the footman was folding up, asking her when she was going back to Miss Manly's, telling her she must be sure to come that way, and then her ma would be well, and could see her.

"Drive on," said Mr. Glenmore, in a commanding voice, and the horses started with haughty speed.

"I've got a piano coming!" hallooed Jerusha, after them. "I'm going to practice hard what you learned me. I can most play a tune."

Mr. Glenmore frowned darkly.

"I'm astonished, Eoline," said he "at your allowing uch vulgar familiarity. If such are the associations you have been forming, you have, indeed, disgraced your family forever."

"She called sister her teacher all the time," said Willie, indignantly, "that big, ugly girl. What did she mean?"

"It means," cried Mr. Glenmore, wrathfully, "that the name of Miss Eoline Glenmore will be blazoned all over the country as the teacher of such rough, ill-bred hoosiers as this choice and rare specimen of humanity. That's what it means?"

Eoline was truly distressed at this unfortunate incident, for it gave her father wrong impressions of the beings with whom she had been associated. It disturbed her new-born serenity, and threatened to renew her father's anger against her, at a moment when he seemed over-flowing with parental affection. She did not answer, but looked out of the carriage window, through her fast-gathering tears.

"Don't cry, Ela," said Willie, peeping anxiously in her face, "you couldn't help it."

They rode on silently for a time, for Eoline could not speak, and Mr. Glenmore was occupied in a strong inward strife with his bosom sin.

"Foolish child!" said he at length, putting his arm round Eoline, and drawing her towards him, "when we once reach home, all will be well!"

And so it was well, when the large gate of the avenue swung back on its massy hinges, and the magnificent forest trees stretched out their hundred arms in the breeze, as if to welcome the exile to her home. The little negroes were perched up on the top of the white fence, like so many black crows, grinning their welcome, and Gatty stood upon the marble steps, clapping her hands, her teeth gleaming large and white as the ivory keys of a piano while a little farther back appeared the matronly countenance of Mrs. Howe, beaming with delight.

"Mrs. Howe, Gatty!" cried Willie, putting his cherub face out of the window, "we've got her—we've brought her back, and we'll never let her go any more!"

Eoline was at first so agitated that her father was obliged

to lift her from the carriage, but she was soon flying all over the house, wishing she were a Brierius, that she might embrace the whole household, furniture and all, in her myriad arms. Nothing was said of her strange departure, for this was an interdicted subject. She was greeted as if he had been gone on a long visit, and she began herself to feel that the past might be a dream. By the time Mr. Wilton and Amelia arrived, she was ready to receive them with a composed and smiling countenance.

According to the arrangement made at the Springs, Mr. Wilton departed the next day for his wife, who soon joined, with him, the family party at Glenmore. It was astonishing with what rapidity Amelia recovered the vanished beauty of her youth. Her eyes no longer glared with melancholy brilliancy, but beamed with a soft radiance that reminded Eoline of St. Leon's lustrous orbs. Her thin, pale cheek became round and fair, and a beautiful color played hide-and-go-seek on its surface, as if afraid of remaining all the time, when it had been so long absent.

Eoline beheld her renovating charms with rapture. Hers had been the magic power which had given birth to this new creation, and she looked upon her dawning color and awakening loveliness, as the painter does upon the canvas, living and glowing under his master hand. She had sent for her harp and guitar, and for a while she played and sung without asking for a requital, but gradually she induced Amelia to seat herself at the piano, then to sing some sweet, simple air, till, like a child learning to play, she recalled all the knowledge of music, and all the taste for which she had once been distinguished. Thus occupied in benevolent and hospitable cares, Eoline had not time to brood over her own feelings. Sometimes, when she caught a glimpse of the lordly twin-mansion which had had such an influence on her destiny, she would sigh

and turn away her head, then she would look back with a
smile and a blush, then sigh again, as memory effaced the
illusions of hope.   She had written to St. Leon and Louisa, and the time was drawing near when she might look
for the return of the former.   She had at first intended to
tell her father the history of St. Leon, but lately she decided it would be better to await his arrival, and see what
impression was made by the interesting Creole.

One morning Eoline was reading a journal of the day,
when her eye fell upon a name that quickened every pul-
sation of her being.   There was the record of a thrilling
incident—a child had fallen into a creek, where the waters
were deepest and the current strongest.   The distracted
mother stood upon the bank, calling upon God and man
for aid, while she was forcibly held back from the watery
brink; when the crowd divided, and a young man, throwing his hat and coat upon the bank as he flew along,
plunged in and rescued the drowning boy, though he was
thrice borne down the current himself in the struggle.
" This young man," continued the journal, "has lately
been electrifying the community by a display of eloquence
perfectly unrivalled.   Not the florid and artificial de-
clamation so popular and fashionable, but the eloquence
of deep, concentrated thought, and powerful ratiocination,
warmed and illumined by flashes of the most brilliant
genius.   He is a young member of the bar, and bids fair
to win the highest honors of his profession.   His name is
Horace Cleveland."

Eoline's spirit glowed within her at this testimony to
Horace's worth and fame.   He had been true to his promise.   He was carrying out the noble, philanthropical prin
ciples which he declared should be the guide of his life.
She imagined she beheld him buffeting the angry waves at
the cry of drowning innocence, rising above them, with
pallid cheeks and dripping locks, bearing his rescued trea

sure to the feet of the distracted mother. She imagined, too, she heard him addressing the listening throng; that *she* was borne on that strong tide of eloquence, on whose rushing current so many souls had been drifted by the breath of an overmastering will.

" You seem interested, Eoline," said her father, watching her varying countenance.

"I am glad to see that Horace Cleveland has distinguished himself," she replied, without looking up. " Shall I read you this passage ?"

" I have read it," said he. " I am astonished that you manifest any interest or pride in his success or reputation. I thought it a matter of perfect indifference to you."

" He has my best wishes and highest esteem !" cried she, laying down the paper. " I cannot be unjust to his merits."

" He is expected at home very soon," said Mr. Glenmore. "I should not be surprised if Wilton's daughter secured a treasure mine thought it beneath her ambition to win. His father seems pleased with the idea."

Eoline started, and the color faded from her cheek. Amelia was now very beautiful, and there might be a charm in her passive sweetness and winning gentleness, irresistible to the high-souled Horace Cleveland. But the pang passed away instantaneously. She judged Horace by herself, and believed not only in the steadfastness of his principles, but the duration of his attachment. St. Leon might change, but Horace never.

It was that very evening, when they were gathered round the first autumnal fire of the season, attracted more by its brightness than its warmth, for the air was still genial abroad, a stranger was announced, and St. Leon entered. Eoline advanced to greet him, with an agitation and varying color, that might well have passed for the timid consciousness of love. Her hand trembled in the ardent

pressure of his, and her voice slightly faltered as she introduced him to her father.   She felt that the crisis of her
destiny was at hand.   Mr. Glenmore, seeing a remarkably
handsome and aristocratic looking young gentleman, bearing, too, the well-sounding name of St. Leon, received him
with great urbanity, and began to introduce him to hi
friends.

Mr. Wilton, Mr. St. Leon—Mrs. Lovell, a daughter of
Mr. Wilton.

Amelia, who had risen, sunk back upon her seat, and
averted her head—but St. Leon, who had caught a glimpse
of her countenance as he approached, turned very pale,
and looked at Eoline, with something of that glance of
anguish he had bent upon her in the concert-room.   Eoline
was alarmed, and for one moment all her self-possession
left her.   An invisible bell rang in her ears, and a darkness
came over her sight.

Mr. and Mrs. Wilton looked anxiously at Amelia, who
maintained her singular attitude.   So completely was her
face averted, one could see nothing but the raven tresses
of her glossy hair, with just a glimpse of her marble
cheek.

" You do not seem well, Amelia," said her mother.
" You had better retire with me."

As Mrs. Wilton thus addressed Amelia, Eoline inquired
of St. Leon after Louisa, Miss Manly and Uncle Ben.
She wished to divert his attention from Amelia, while she
quitted the room.   As the youthful widow in her sable
weeds, that set off with a deadly contrast her now colorless
complexion passed out, leaning on her mother's arm, she
gave one glance at St. Leon, and a crimson tide immediately flooded her face and neck.   St. Leon colored, too,
and cast his eyes on the floor.   Mr. Glenmore and his
friend fell into an earnest conversation on some exciting
topic of the day, though the thoughts of the latter often

wandered, thinking of the singular and apparently cause
less agitation of his daughter. St. Leon drew near Eoline.
He gazed upon her with a dark and troubled countenance.

"Cannot I see you alone, Eoline, for a few moments?"
said he, in a low voice. "After such an absence, it is mad-
ess to meet you thus. Are you afraid of the night air?"

"No; but it may be dangerous to you; or is your
health so perfectly established, that you dare to forget
yourself?"

"I am well, perfectly well, now—that is, I was an hour
ago. Any sudden agitation still affects me. Will you
walk with me in the piazza? The moon is just rising."

Eoline hesitated a moment, then led the way to the
portico, where the argent light of the rising moon was
flowing in through the lofty colonnade. They were alone,
they, who had parted as betrothed lovers, and St. Leon,
throwing his arms around her, exclaimed,

"Eoline, I live, and live for you."

"There is another who has prior claims to mine, St.
Leon," said she, withdrawing from his embrace, "and that
you know full well."

"There is none," he cried, passionately, "there can be
none. I have never loved any one but you. I do not
call a boyish fancy love. How came *she* here to poison
your mind and fill it with doubts of my constancy to you?
I never loved her. It was but a passing fancy, and that
was all."

"Let us walk," said Eoline, taking his arm, with a slight
shiver.

"Are you cold, Eoline?"

"No, there is something more chilly than the night-
breeze, and that is, want of faith in those whom we have
once trusted and honored."

"Eoline, can you, do you really doubt my love?"

"No, St. Leon, I know that you love me; but I grieve

to hear you say that you never loved her, who has kept her faith in heart to you, even to the unthroning of her reason."

" She is married," replied St. Leon, bitterly. " That is a strange way of keeping her faith."

" She married according to the will of her parents, be-cause, believing herself forsaken and forgotten, her palsied heart submitted itself passively to the wishes of others. For more than a year she has lived a frozen life, feeling and intellect locked up, and inaccessible to affection or reason, wearing an iron yoke with the meekness of a saint, and the endurance of a martyr. Her friends have never suspected the secret of her heart. It was the night that brought her the tidings that the chains which bound her were broken, for they were chains, and galling ones, that the sealed fountain of her feelings overflowed, and she revealed to me all she had so long concealed from the world. In the very scenes where you wooed and won her young and trusting heart, St. Leon—"

" Good Heavens! Eoline, are you going to make me insane, thus calmly presenting another's claims, as if you intended to throw me from you. What a meeting after months of absence! How cold, how cruel, how madden-ing you are."

Eoline raised her deep, blue eye to his, in which gleams of passion were sparkling, like the flashing of warring weapons. The brightening moonlight enveloped them both. She laid her hand gently on his arm, and in tones, soft and long, she related to him all she knew of Amelia, and all she had revealed of herself. It was a simple story, and may be told in few words. St. Leon had met Amelia more than two years ago at the ———— Springs. She was under the protection of a female friend who, en-grossed herself with the gaities of the scene, took little thought of the young girl just emancipated from the restraints of school, and perfectly "ignorant of" the ways of the world, as well as of the mysteries of her own heart. It was there she met St. Leon, whose charming voice and personal attractions completely fascinated her juvenile imagination. Charmed with her beauty and sim-licity, he did breathe into her ear "many a vow of love and ne'er a true one," for when they parted, he for his Louisianian home, and she for the retirement of hers, he thought of this short episode in his life as a pleasant dream, a boyish fancy, as he had told Eoline;—*she* lived on its remembrances till the powers of her mind seemed consumed, and then it was fed by the life-blood of her heart. It was the hope which Eoline had infused into her spirit that St. Leon would return to her, when made aware of her broken shackles, which had called back the life-blood to her heart, and the love-light to her eye.

"Since I have learned all this, St. Leon," continued Eoline, as they slowly pursued their moonlight walk, now in silver and now in shadow, as they passed the long massy row of pillars that intercepted the night-rays; "I have resolved to restore to her, if possible, the love which *should* be hers, as the price of her sufferings and her faith. I could forgive the levity which tampered with her young affections, unthinking of the ruin it involved—but I could not, would not forgive the coldness, the cruelty, and wanton injustice, which, knowing the consequences, would doom their victim to irremediable woe."

She paused—she felt the quick, nervous shudders run-ning through St. Leon's frame, and she pitied the agony he was enduring.

'You have never loved me, Eoline," he cried, " never. You would have some little mercy, you would find some extenuation for a youthful indiscretion. You would not stab me with such a serene countenance. Even the surgeon when he cuts into the quivering flesh, *looks* the

pity he does not express. Eoline, you have deceived me—
for you never could have loved me."

"I have never deceived you, St. Leon," she replied, with
a quivering lip. "Recall our past intercourse and ask
yourself if I have not been—no" added she with a sigh—
"I have not always been perfectly sincere; but I hav
never made professions which l did not feel. I have always
felt that there was a want of congeniality in our characters, which would one day force itself on your conviction.
You recollect, I doubt not, the evening of the rehearsal,
when the thunder-storm darkened the Heavens, that I told
you I loved the war of elements because it was grand and
powerful; that it was my nature to look up—and so it is.
You felt then—I saw it in your countenance—that there
was a want of sympathy between us. Amelia resembles
you. She is more gentle and yielding than I am. St. Leon,
she is beautiful and good, and loves you with a love 'passing the love of woman.' "

"Yes, I remember that night—I remember it well,"
exclaimed St. Leon, mournfully, "I saw that you despised me—despised the weakness which I could not master."

"No, St. Leon, you wrong me there. I did not despise,
but I pitied—and the man I love must be above my
pity."

She spoke involuntarily, but St. Leon felt her words to
his heart's core. Shaking himself free from the arm that
was locked in his, he leaned back against one of the tall
pillars in an attitude of defiance—

"I ask not your pity—I ask not your love. Soar up to
the highest Heavens if you will, triumph and look down
upon me from your dazzling height. You say it is your
nature to look up—but methinks," he added, in a tone of
bitter sarcasm, "you are prone to look down on all."

"Be as unjust as you please to me, think me cold, proud,

even insolent if you will—but St. Leon, once again, I implore you, be just to yourself, be just to Amelia. I appeal
to your high sense of honor, to the magnanimity now latent
in your bosom, by all that is dear to the heart of man, to
reflect on all I have said to-night. We had better part
now. You are excited, you must be weary from your
journey—and above all, I do not wish you to act from
impulse, but principle. Come to us to-morrow, trying to
forget all that passed at Magnolia Vale. Look upon Amelia
and myself both as friends, for she is still your friend. No
thought of bitterness or resentment mingles with her pure
and gentle feelings. She has never blamed you in words—
but if you had seen her, as I first did, you would have
mourned over the wreck of so much beauty and sweetness.
Will you not come in? The cold mist is stealing over the
valley, and I begin to feel its chillness. You, too, must
remember you have been an invalid."

" No, I cannot go in. Forgive me if I have said anything
passionate or unjust. I feel only too deeply, too bitterly
my own unworthiness. I am but too conscious of the gulf
that separates me from you."

" We shall be better friends than we have ever been
before," said Eoline. "I am grieved if I have given you
pain. If!—I know I have, but I have not done it in wan-
tonness, nor have you suffered alone. Come to us in the
morning. Will you not promise? Then indeed I fear
your are angry."

" I cannot promise, for there is such a whirlwind within—
but believe me, that I am not angry. I feel too crushed,
too wretched, too self-abased to be angry."

" Your best, your truest happiness will be born of that
self abasement, St. Leon," said she, extending her hand in
parting.

St. Leon, as he turned back to gaze upon her, standing
fair and still in the moonlight, saw a tear sparkling in

her eye—and hot scalding drops came blinding into his own.

St. Leon did not come in the morning, nor during the day ; and Eoline trembled at the thought that her persuasions had been unavailing. She could not bear to think of him as a cold, unrepenting deceiver. She had relied on the pliant weakness of his character, to bend to the right, after the first storm of passion had subsided. She watched with painful interest the mutable countenance of Amelia. Every entering step made her start and change color, then she would sink into the sad and dreary abstraction from which she had been so lately roused.

But with the evening St. Leon came, looking very pale and sad, but comparatively calm. Eoline, true to the course she had marked out for herself, treated him with frankness and cordiality. She asked him to sing with her the songs they had sung in Magnolia Vale, subduing her own magnificent voice, that the ear might dwell alone on his. She placed the lights so that they might shine with softened lustre on Amelia, who had drawn back as far as possible from sight, that she might listen, herself unseen. Without being aware of the fact, Eoline selected an air which St. Leon had sung, the first time he had ever met Amelia. She remembered it but too well, and as those sweet, enchanting notes which had sunk so deep on her memory, again stole on her ear, breathing the same pensive, loving words, the crimson tide of emotion ebbed and flowed again and again from her heart to her cheeks, from her cheeks to her heart. The lapse of time was forgotten. She was again in the morning freshness of life, drinking in strains that seemed to her wafted from the world of angels. Forgetting herself, she looked up, and met his sad, earnest gaze. It had upon her the effect of fascination. She did not suffer her eyes to fall, but looked for a moment steadfastly upon him He read in that glance the history of her life, all her suf

85

ferings, and all her love.   Never had he met such a look
from Eoline.   Never had *her* eyes thus melted in the
beams of his.   It was but too true, that Eoline had never
loved him.

Thus passed evening after evening, and thus day after
day he came.   Eoline found a thousand things to do she
had never thought of before, that called her from her
room, so that St. Leon and Amelia were often left together.   She began, too, to have a slight cold, impercep-
tible to others, but which made it an exertion for her to
sing, and Amelia was obliged to supply her place in the
duets with St. Leon.   Indeed, it was astonishing how
many of "the ills which flesh is heir to" fell simulta-
neously to the lot of Eoline.   It wearied her to take long
walks, and sometimes when the trio had started on some
romantic excursion, in the beautiful surroundings of the
twin-villas, she would declare herself overcome with sudden
fatigue, and return, directing them into many a winding
path and shady dell.   St. Leon understood it all, but while
he chafed and struggled, he bent to the influence of her
stronger, nobler will, and his wounded vanity, bleeding
from the consciousness that she not only had the strength,
but the wish to transfer him to another, found healing
and balm in Amelia's undying love.   And still more,
for we would do full justice to his character, all his better feelings had been roused in his interview with Eoline,
when she so eloquently advocated the cause of her injured
friend.   She had appealed to his honor and his magnanimity, and had not appealed in vain.   He resolved to make
himself worthy of her esteem, and when he began to pay
those attentions to Amelia it seemed impossible to avoid,
he thought more of exalting himself in the estimation of
Eoline, than of making Amelia happy.   But St. Leon, as
Louisa had said in her letter, was fond of being *petted*, of
feeling that he was beloved.   Eoline's coldness chilled

him, Amelia's constancy and devotion flattered and soothed
him. Amelia was a true child of earth, a fond, loving, suffering, forgiving woman—Eoline, a daughter of the sun,
enshrined in a radiant sphere of light, far off, inaccessible
to him. We give St. Leon's impressions, not our own.
Eoline was capable of a depth and strength of attachment,
of a generous, self-sacrificing love, which Amelia's passive
nature and morbid sensibility could not fathom. For the
mind and heart do correspond, and when both are strong
and pure, they approach near that arch-angelic nature,
which is said to burn with *Love* before the throne of God
by night and by day—no, not night, for there is no night
to the long day of eternity.

The morning arrived when the Wilton family were to
turn their faces homeward. St. Leon was to accompany
them on horseback. During the bustle of preparation, St.
Leon beheld Eoline a few minutes alone. She did not
avoid the interview, for her mission was accomplished, her
desire fulfilled.

"I told you we should be drawn nearer than ever to each
other," she said with a warmth of manner she had never
before manifested to him. "You now possess my fullest
esteem, my sisterly affection, my heart-felt gratitude. Yes!
gratitude, St. Leon, for having sacrificed your own feelings
for the happiness of another. I have seen your struggles,
and glory in your triumph. You will be happy, for you
have acted rightly, justly. You will be happy, for you
are beloved as your exacting nature requires. Amelia is a
tropic rose, far more fitting to bloom in your orange bowers
than I am. Cherish her tenderly, for she could not bear
neglect. Let her always have the first place in your heart,
but remember, *I* must always claim the second.

" Yes," said St. Leon, as he pressed for the last time
the hand of Eoline, " I now love Amelia for your sake,
but I must ever adore and worship you."

"I owe my happiness to you," whispered Amelia, when she hung round Eoline's neck in parting. "I have no words to thank you, but I bless you, Eoline, and shall forever bless you."

"To your cherishing cares I owe my daughter's restoration from a state far worse than death, to health and happiness," cried Mr. Wilton, and his deep-toned voice faltered with emotion. "In every prayer to Almighty God, we shall remember you."

Mrs. Wilton uttered the same sentiments, while clasping her in a maternal embrace. Thus hallowed by blessings, Eoline ought to have been happy, and she was for awhile, but there soon came a vacuum, which no domestic duties or joys could fill. The barrier to her union with Horace Cleveland was now removed, but were his feelings unchanged? Her father had told her that he was expected at his home, and then he would learn that she was free. But his return was indefinitely postponed, and having learned one lesson of the inconstancy of man, not all her faith in the immutability of his character could prevent the misgivings that entered her heart, and cast a dejected and languid expression over her naturally beaming countenance.

"Well, Eoline," said her father, folding his gray wrapper closely round him, and stretching out his embroidered slippers, "you need fear no more persecution on account of Horace Cleveland. It seems the icy heart you could not thaw is melted at last. I confess I should like to see the *veni vidi vici* lady, who has achieved such a miracle."

"Is he going to be married?" asked she, suppressing all outward emotion, but with a deadly, sinking sensation within.

"I suppose so," replied Mr. Glenmore, sarcastically; "for marriage usually follows love, when fortune favors and friends approve. Mr. Cleveland was anxious to

promote a union between him and the beautiful young
widow, who is left with a splendid jointure, and wrote to
him on the subject. He answered that his affections were
engaged to another, and nothing would induce him to give
his hand without his heart. He did not mention the lady's
name, but some one who had called at Mr. Cleveland's,
who had passed through the town where Horace resides,
told who she was, and says she is a great heiress—a
relative of the child whom he rescued from drowning—
Eoline! what is the matter? You are as pale as ashes."

"It is too warm," said she, drawing her chair back, so
that her father could not see her face. "Go on."

"I have nothing more to say, only this, that I think
you have been the greatest fool in the universe, to throw
away a match unequalled in every respect,—a match that
would have bound two families, unrivalled in wealth and
standing, indissolubly together,—a match, on which I had
set my heart and will, before your eyes beheld the light of
the sun. I have really never given up hope till now. I
always thought the time would come, when you would
both see your folly and repent."

"It is in vain, father!" exclaimed Eoline. She spoke
in such a tone of anguish, that her father was touched.
He thought it was caused by his displeasure, and as he had
promised her unconditional forgiveness for the past, it was
ungentleman-like to break his word. He tried to smooth
out the cloven marks on his brow, and to speak in a
gentler tone.

"I do not wish to make you unhappy, Eoline," said he,
taking the hand that lay upon the arm of the sofa. It
trembled, and was very cold, though she had just com-
plained of the heat. "All my vexation originates in my
love for you. Of course I have some family pride, but it
is on your account."

"All my happiness is now centred in you, dear father,

she cried, pressing his hand with fervor against her heart, that heart so wildly throbbing. "I only ask to live and die with you."

Before she had finished this short sentence, she had wound one arm around his neck, and was weeping unrestrainedly on his breast.

"Come, come, my daughter," said he, soothing her with unwonted tenderness, for he had never seen her wear such a heart-broken look. "I did not mean to be harsh or upbraid you for the past, that past I have promised to forget and forgive. Dry your eyes and sing for me. There is nothing like music to drown unpleasant recollections. Come, let me lead you to the piano."

Eoline followed his motions unresistingly, and he said he had never heard her sing so sweetly and pathetically. Then she flew off into a brilliant bravura, and a bright light came into her eyes, and a crimson spot to her cheek, while her lips wore a scarlet dye. If Doctor Hale had seen her at that moment, he would have persisted in calling her a *young enigma*.

"There is no faith in man," said she, when the midnight found her sitting chilled and ghost-like in the solitude of her chamber, (if it could be called solitude, where Gatty's breathings gave such audible demonstrations of a living presence,) and the expiring lamp was flickering dimly on the wall. "Louisa was right when she said there was but one Being who could satisfy the boundless desires of the human heart. There is One in whom is no variableness or shadow of change. Let me fly to Him for refuge from the wild storm of human passion. Let me anchor my soul on the Rock of eternal ages." It is scarcely metaphorical to say that she wrestled through the night with her own spirit. We will not say she came off conqueror, but she gained at least a truce, and there was an

outward semblance of tranquillity. But even Willie soon
remarked a change in his blooming sister.

"What makes you so white, Ela?" he would say,
passing his hands softly over her pale, oval cheeks, "and
your eyes don't shine as they did. They used to look lik
stars in the sky—now they look like stars down in th
water."

"You will be a poet, Willie," said she smiling and
sighing at the same time. "You were always fond of
metaphors."

"What is a poet?" asked Willie. "Is it a great big
man?"

"It is one who is full of beautiful thoughts," replied
Eoline, "who sees bright images and lovely objects, where
others behold nothing but darkness and deformity. He
creates them, too, out of his own mind, and he sets all
these sweet thoughts to the music of his own lyre."

"Is not God a great poet?" asked the child, reverently.
Then suddenly changing his tone, he added, "Is Horace
Cleveland a poet?"

"I think he has the soul of a poet," replied Eoline;
"but why do you ask?"

"I don't know. Did he tell you he loved you when he
gave you the flowers I sent you?"

"What a strange question, Willie!" cried Eoline, with
a dawning blush.

"I told him to say so," said Willie, as if he were
conscious of having done something very praiseworthy
"Because I told him, too, I would not love him if he di
not love you."

"How could you talk to him in such a manner?"
exclaimed Eoline, more angry than she had ever been
with Willie before. "What could he think? What did
he say?"

"He said you would be angry, and so you be," cried Willie, with a swelling chest.

"It is no matter now," said Eoline, calmly, "he will never think of it again."

"Master Horace got home to-night," said Gatty, the moment she had a chance to speak. This conversation took place in the morning, and Gatty was a privileged being there. "Cæsar said so. (Cæsar, Mr. Cleveland's coachman, was husband to Gatty, and a very devoted one, as most of the colored gentlemen are.) Cæsar say he's monstrous proud of his young master. He say he look like a national prince to what he used to. Cæsar say he guess he come here this very night to see Miss Eoline, my young mistress."

The cunning Gatty manufactured this last piece of news herself, to see what effect it would have on her auditor, and she was quite satisfied that it was not a matter of indifference, when she saw the war of the houses of York and Lancaster revived on Eoline's face. We are not certain that this reflection was Gatty's, but she thought something which meant the same thing. Gatty must have had the gift of prophecy, for Horace Cleveland did call that very night, and found Eoline and her father seated by a comfortable fire, playing a game of chess. Eoline cherished a growing fondness for this game, for she could indulge in long reveries while her father was meditating some awful move, fraught with destruction to her army. He was fond of beating, and as her abstraction rendered the victory more easy, it did not displease him. Mr. Glenmore did not greet Horace quite so cordially as usual. Since he had swerved from his allegiance to his house, he looked upon him as a kind of deserter. But Eoline—it was strange, without one word of explanation, she felt relieved of a crushing burden. The same glance which had electrified her from the embrasure of the window, in the

concert hall, only fraught with deeper power, falsified the
rumor which had reached her father's ear. It was not a
brilliant, passionate glance like St. Leon's, but it darted
like a burning arrow into her heart.

" So," said Mr. Glenmore, making a dashing caracole
with his King's Knight, " so, Horace, they say you are
conquered at last. You have found out you are vulnerable, like other men."

" I do not understand you, sir," said Horace, in a tone
of surprise and embarrassment, giving a glance at Eoline,
as much as to say, " is it possible she has been ungenerous
enough to betray my weakness?"

" Why they say you are going to surrender your liberty
to a young and beautiful heiress, who was captivated by
your heroic exploit on the water. I should like to see her.
She must be a young lady of rare attractions."

" I suppose she is," replied Horace, dryly, " but I have
not seen her yet myself. My father has been questioning
me on this subject. I heard nothing of it before I left the
regions where the unknown lady dwells."

" But you are convicted on your own confession," cried
Eoline's father. " In your letter to your father, you
acknowledged the surrender of your liberty."

" I did not know that *private* letters were matters of
public discussion!" exclaimed Horace, while an expression
of pain and displeasure clouded his brow.

Eoline, who now understood that letter, felt grieved
and disconcerted at her father's want of delicacy towards
him.

" And so you are not going to be married, after all, and
it is a false report!" cried Mr. Glenmore, wheeling round
from the chess-board, and clapping Horace cordially on
the shoulder, without appearing to notice the effect of his
last remark. " I am glad of it—you seem so much like a
boy to me yet," he added, as if to modify the expression

of his joy. "It is difficult to realize the possibility of such an event."

Eoline could not help smiling, thinking how marvelously Horace had degenerated into a boy, since her father's conversation with her on the matrimonial scheme.

From this evening Horace became a constant visitor, and Mr. Glenmore's hopes flourished with new vigor, when one evening they received a mortal blow from the lips of Eoline.

She was in one of her brightest, most sportive moods. She waltzed with Willie till he rolled on the carpet, and every breath was a wood-note, as changeful as the mocking-bird's.

"And now, father," said she, standing behind him as he sat upon the sofa, and putting her arms round his neck, "I have something to tell you—I have a sanction to ask, on which all the happiness of my life depends—I have never yet told you—" here she paused, as if in embarrassment, "that I met a young gentleman at Magnolia Vale who won my undivided affections."

"The devil you did!" exclaimed Mr. Glenmore, starting upon his feet, and forgetting his dignity in his overwhelming astonishment. "Some low-born adventurer; some itinerant musician, I dare say."

"No, sir—in birth, in wealth, in personal and mental endowments, he equals your boasted favorite, Horace Cleveland. You know I inherit something of my father's pride, and I could not love where I did not honor and esteem.

"Eoline, it is in vain—I have borne with your caprices and obstinacy, and forgiven them all, but now when Horace Cleveland is come in our midst, free to choose, when I see so plainly your growing influence over him, when you yourself seem so happy in his presence, as to cheat me :nto the belief that you were learning to love him, when

I was dreaming of seeing my long-cherished wishes at last crowned with fruition—I cannot bear this disappointment —and what is more—*I will not.*"

Mr. Glenmore had talked himself into fever heat, and he fanned himself violently with his handkerchief.

"Father," said Eoline, meekly, "only see him once, and if you *then* will not consent, I promise never to persecute you with my unfortunate attachment—I will go still farther, and pledge my word to wed Horace Cleveland, if he ever honors me by asking your sanction to his vows. You can trust me, father, for you have never yet detected me in a falsehood. But you will, you must approve."

"Remember this promise, Eoline, for by the memory of your mother, I know I shall require its fulfilment. I know the young man lives not whom I could like as a son-in-law, as well as Horace Cleveland. Well, where is this nonpareil, this mysterious, unheard-of personage? And what may be his name?"

"He shall tell you himself," said Eoline, with a hesitating tone, "perhaps you will not like its sound, and it may prejudice you against him."

"John Brown or Peter Stokes, perhaps."

"The name does not make the man, father."

"Well, when is this illustrious stranger to make his appearance?"

"This evening he will call, if you permit it."

"So, you have had clandestine interviews with him already!"

"I have met him when I was walking abroad, but I assure you it was not clandestinely."

"Why have you not told me this sooner?" said he with increasing sternness. "I thought once St. Leon was the happy man, but you turned him off to that little loving simpleton, Amelia, and I was glad of it, for reasons you well know. Though I am confident I should prefer him

to your new prince of darkness.   Why, I ask again, have
you withheld this disclosure so long ?"

" There were obstacles which have only lately been
removed."

" There are obstacles which will *never* be removed.
But never mind—I will see him—I will see him."

There was a ringing of the door-bell, and the sound of
footsteps in the passage.

" He is coming," said Eoline, " I know his step. Now
let me entreat you, father, not to express any disappointment, if you *should* feel it. Do not make any such remarks
as you did a little while ago. It would shock him very
much, for, I assure you, he is a perfect gentleman."

While Eoline went to the door, to ask in the John
Brown or Peter Stokes of her father's imagination, he
seated himself on the sofa, with an air of imposing dignity,
crossed his arms on his chest, and throwing back his head,
fixed his eyes on the ceiling with a look of determined
dislike.

As Eoline left the room she had removed the lamp to a
remote table, and the firelight was burning faint and low.

" She is ashamed that I shall see him," thought he,
noticing the shadows that were settling round. " The
most sensible girls often make the most foolish and ridicu-
lous choice."

He heard the door re-open, and Eoline enter, with one
whose step was firmer and more commanding than hers.
She came near and knelt on the footstool at his feet,
clinging to the arm of her companion, who stood erect, as
man ought to stand in the presence of fellow-man. His
lofty figure did not seem accustomed to the act of genu-
flection. Mr. Glenmore still kept his eyes fixed in a lordly
stare upon the ceiling.

" Father," said Eoline, " all the happiness of my life
hangs trembling on your will."

"Mr. Glenmore," cried the young man, in a low but distinct voice, "all that I hold dear on earth depends upon the decision of this moment."

The eyes of Mr. Glenmore, which had been slowly descending from their astronomical height, suddenly took a precipitous leap on the face of the young man. Holding him at arm's length one moment, he exclaimed—

"Why,—how—what—who's this? Horace Cleveland, by all that's veritable."

"No, father," cried Eoline; "it's John Brown or Peter Stokes, you know."

"You little deceiving gipsy!" Here he caught her in his arms, and gave her a breath-stifling squeeze, then rising, he gave Horace a truly parental, high-pressure embrace. And not satisfied with these demonstrations of satisfaction, he again opened his arms and took them both in, in one fold. "So, you have been trying to make a fool of me, have you?" cried he, rubbing his hands, his face radiant with good humor.

"No, father," replied Eoline, who was now seated between her father and Horace, the centre of as happy a trio as ever sat on a velvet sofa, in front of a bright autumn fire, for it blowed up suddenly, as if participating in the household joy, "You have been so long plotting against us, I thought I would get up one little counter-plot, to wind up the last scene of the last act of the drama."

"Very good—excellent," exclaimed Mr. Glenmore, and growing quite facetious in his joy, he continued—"yes, it would make a capital play from beginning to end. Ha, ha—I remember the first scene as well as if it were but yesterday. Enter a little boy in tunic and trowsers, and sits down on the carpet with a face as long as his arm, making a right-angle of his legs and body. Enter a baby in long clothes, and sits down in his lap."

"I think I could bear the infliction now with a better grace," said Horace.

"I know I must have been a shockingly ugly baby," cried Eoline, laughing, " or Horace would have liked me better."

"And so you really love each other, after all," interrupted the father, "and there is no sham in it? It is a sober, blessed reality, is it?"

"We love each other," exclaimed Horace, taking the hand of Eoline, and clasping it firmly in his own; "we love each other with our whole hearts, minds and souls; we love each other as we always would have done had we been left to our own free will. Were Heaven itself *forced* upon our acceptance, such is the pride of the human heart, we should repel the gift."

"Like the ancient Parthians," said Eoline, "I wounded only in flying."

"All's well that ends well," cried Mr. Glenmore, oracularly. "We fathers may have erred in judgment as to the best way to accomplish our wishes, but you must acknowledge we were right after all."

But it would be impossible to record all the sayings of that memorable evening. Mr. Glenmore was obliged to walk over to Cleveland Villa, so that he and his friend could mingle their rejoicings—and it is not at all probable that Horace and Eoline suffered the conversation to grow dull in his absence.

Not long after there were preparations for a magnificent wedding. The son of Mr. Cleveland, of Cleveland Villa, and the daughter of Mr. Glenmore, of Glenmore Place, were not allowed to marry after a plebeian fashion. Cæsar and Gatty, who were the next happiest people in the world, held consultations on the subject every night.

"I knowed all this time, 'twas nothing but a make-believe," said Cæsar, consequentially—"bout their not

liking each other, just to see what folks would say. As
if there was a white young lady this side of Jerusalem,
wouldn't jump at the chance of my young master."

" Now, Cæsar, you knows nothing at all 'bout the dilli-
cacy of the fair sex," replied Gatty, tossing up her eyes
with a look of lofty experience, " my mistress wan't a
gontu saxifrize herself for nothing. She didn't make
believe, no sich thing. She is beneath such a mean doing
as that ; but she know when the young lady seem sortu
onwilling, the young gentleman think a heap more of her
dignity.

" If that ain't *sham*," exclaimed Cæsar, indignantly,
" I'll eat my head, wool and all. Why didn't you put on
them airs with me, Gatty—say ? Case you knows I was a
gentleman, and wouldn't stand 'em no how. You was a
heap willinger than Cæsar, that's a fact."

Here he laughed with conscious superiority, while he
gave her a saucy punch in the side. Gatty, in return,
slapped him coquettishly on the face, and then they went
on discussing the fair sex in general, and Eoline in particular.

The wedding was indeed a princely festival. One of
those real open-heart, open-door weddings, the Southern
nabob glories in giving to his son or daughter. The twin
mansions were brilliantly illuminated, flashing their festive
radiance far and wide. Even the majestic old oaks stood
blazing with lamps suspended on their branching arms,
sharing in their grand unwithered age, the jubilee of their
lords. Within the bridal hall all was beauty, and splendor,
and hilarity. Eoline, fair as the magnolia of the South,
and blushing as its rose, stood in her white robes, sparkling
with diamonds, the bridal gift of Mr. Cleveland. She
would have preferred the orange blossoms alone, but she
could not refuse the offered decorations of her proud and
magnificent father-in-law.

Gatty was in ecstacies, for she said " any poor and no-account sort of folks could stick on flowers—but it wan't every body that could get diamonds, by a long slip—and Miss Eoline looks just as tho' she was born in 'em."

Messrs. Glenmore and Cleveland made speeches to the bride and bridegroom, which being very long, and as no stenographer was present to take them down, it is impossible to record—but Willie, the cupid of the evening, made a very short one, which produced more manifest effect. Wearied of being admired and caressed, he pressed through the crowd to bid good-night to the beautiful sister-bride.

"Do you love sister Ela now?" said he to Horace, whose countenance certainly expressed no very intense hatred for this fair being at his side.

" You must ask Ela if I do," replied the bridegroom, blushing at the laugh Willie's straight-forward question elicited from those within hearing.

" Have you told her so to night?"

" I think I have, but I may be mistaken. You must ask her."

" You said she would be angry, if you did," said the child—who seemed to have arrived at a very triumphant conclusion of all his doubts—" but she don't look angry one bit. I wish you had told her so at first, then she never would have gone away and left us."

The sister-bride began to look rather disconcerted, and think her little brother more voluble than wise. Certainly if she was incensed at Horace's declaration, she put a very sweet face on her displeasure. There were some who went away from the wedding, saying, " They had heard it was a forced marriage after all, in spite of her running away to get rid of it. But if it were, they were the most deceitful young people they ever saw—for, to look at them, one would think they were really deeply in love with each other."

Horace, at the earnest desire of his father, quitted the town where he had been residing, and which was become quite illustrious by the morning brightness of his renown, and established himself with his young bride in the paternal palace. He resolved, however, to continue in the honorable career he had commenced, and not sit down to eat the bread of indolence. Eoline was a golden link, uniting the two households, and for once the dreams of parental wealth and pride were fully realized.

St. Leon and Amelia, previous to the nuptials of Eoline, after a very private and unostentatious wedding, had departed for his home near the banks of the deep-rolling Mississippi. In consequence of the recent death of her husband, her parents wished to defer the union, but the fear of her relapsing into her former melancholy state, if he were allowed to leave her behind, induced them to give a reluctant consent. St. Leon was aware of the approaching union of Eoline and Horace, and wished to be far away before its consummation. Though he had found strength to resign her himself, he had not courage to remain and think of her as given to the heart of another.

"I should like to see Magnolia Vale once again," said Eoline, just before the May flowers of another Spring unfolded their vernal charms; "I should like to see Uncle Ben, the magnificent Colonel, and the dear affectionate children."

"Let us go," replied Horace, "I, too, should delight in revisiting a spot sacred to the memory of my love."

"You speak as if it were dead, Horace," said Eoline, smiling in the consciousness of its immortal life, "and you were going to weep over its monument."

"Let us go to it, then, as the birth-place of our love, and the scene of its despair. That lawn, with its embowering roses and sheltering trees is the *Vaucluse* of my heart, and embalmed by the recollections of that unforgotten

86

night, when I walked its paths with you, then the affianced bride oi another. Yes, we must visit it once more, and make it a witness of our wedded happiness."

The next morning they started for Magnolia Vale.

Towards the evening of the second day, the carriage stopped at the large gate of the seminary. It was near the sunset hour, and the children were assembled on the play-ground. It seemed as if the day-god had gathered around him more than the usual accompaniments of his departing glory, in honor of their approach. Every hue, from the kingly purple illumined by fiery gold, to the paly saffron, and glittering sea-green, flashed and glowed in the iridescent West. The green carpet of the lawn looked as if sprinkled with burning gold, and the bright foliage of the trees was bronzed here and there with the same rich and gilding hues.

"Is this a reality?" said Eoline, "or does my happy heart throw a sun-bright reflection on every object? Oh, there is dear Uncle Ben. He *is* a reality."

Sure enough, there was his quaint and well-known figure, shooting about the lawn, exactly as she had first beheld him, with a long piece of white paper pinned to his back, the youngest and friskiest of all. And there, too, she distinguished the flaxen ringlets of darling Fanny; the dark, purplish locks of Selma; the soft, chestnut hair of Annie; and the round, rosy face of little Bessie Bell. Jerusha, also, was running for her life, throwing her feet up very high behind, and occasionally falling, with a violent plunge, on her head. As soon as the travelers descended from the carriage, the children paused in their sport, and looked eagerly round. In a moment, Eoline was surrounded by her juvenile friends, and welcomed with as much rapture as if she were a visitant from Heaven. Then the young Misses, recollecting the presence of Horace, drew back and blushed and curtsied with bashful grace. But he, no longer considering them the formidable band whose terrors he dared not face, smiled upon them so cordially and greeted them so frankly, they thought him perfectly captivating. No words could speak the enthusiastic delight of Uncle Ben, in seeing again his inspired little David. He shook her hand so long and hard, she was compelled to call out for mercy; then he capered into the house as if the *talaria* of Mercury were fastened to his heels, to inform his neice of her arrival.

When Eoline entered the doors of the seminary, she beheld the towering form of Miss Manly descending the winding stairs, with her usual dignified and majestic bearing. Yet there was something in her appearance that was strange, and Eoline at first could not define what it was. A second glance discovered the cause of the trans- formation. The two long side curls no longer waved down her cheeks, sweeping against her shoulders, like the untwisting coils of a serpent. They were combed back in a smooth fold, undistinguished in the dark mass that covered her head. There was something softer, more feminine, about her face, and even the white rim of her eye was scarcely visible above the large black iris. She accosted Eoline and Horace with formal but cordial politeness, and expressed herself complimented by a visit as gratifying as it was unexpected.

Eoline missed the meek and gentle Louisa, but she was introduced to a sweet-faced, modest young girl, her junior sister, who told her all about Charles, whom she appeared to consider the model of all human excellence. He had received a call from a town in Southern Virginia, where he was to convey his bride in the autumn.

"And then," exclaimed Eoline, joyously, "we shall meet again, for I would travel from one end of the rain- bow to the other, to see her once more."

She was rejoiced to hear that Louisa's health was so

much invigorated, they had forgotten to think of her as
an invalid. It seems that what she mistook for the
symptoms of a fatal and hereditary malady, was only the
debility resulting from long confinement and unceasing
exertion.

Eoline visited her little chamber, and she could not
help laughing aloud, when Jerusha, as a matter of course,
came lumbering behind her to the scene of her former
achievements.

"We've got a man teacher now," said Jerusha, "who
only comes here in the day-time. But I don't like him
one bit. He keeps my knuckles as red as fire, slapping
them with a stick. I can play a tune though. Don't you
want to hear me?"

Eoline excused herself for the present, thinking if the
gentleman had the art of reddening Jerusha's knuckles, it
was as marvelous and superfluous an act of supererogation
as gilding refined gold and whitening the lily. She was
astonished at the interest that invested every object around
her. Even the grim old wardrobe seemed to welcome its
former mistress from its shadowy corner. It was a massy
link in the great chain of the past, that dark chain on
which her present bright destiny was suspended.

"Perhaps you would prefer a private table," said Miss
Manly, when the well-remembered supper-bell rang, with
prolonged peal, and the rustle of flying dresses was heard
upon the stairs.

"Oh, no," replied Eoline, "I should not feel at home
unless I sat down in the long hall, with your whole household."

Jerusha claimed a seat by Eoline, as a kind of primor-
dial right, but darling Fanny's sweet face sparkled upon
her from the opposite side, and many other radiant countenances beaming with smiles of welcome. Jerusha
seemed anxious to display her progress in the graces, draw-

ing herself up as stiff and erect as a grenadier, pinning her elbows to her sides so close, that her hands hung forward like the paws of a cat sitting on its hind feet. She was evidently on her best behaviour, and kept looking askance at Eoline, to see if she were not admiring her graceful deportment. But Eoline was more interested in observing Miss Manly, who had relaxed much of her iron discipline. She preserved equal order, but with less coldness and formality. The young Misses occasionally spoke to each other in low, gentle tones, without being reproved for violating the rules of Chesterfield. She still kept up her literary banquets, but she no longer confined herself to heroes who had won the honors of the *Great.* She even condescended to bring forward the good and gifted of her own sex, as models for imitation. There was a religious tone also perceptible in her discipline. She often selected subjects from the Divine Records—not only Deborah, sitting under her palm tree, judging the tribes of Israel, but the lovely and self-sacrificing Ruth, following the mother of Mahlon into a foreign land, and the lowly Mary bathing her Saviour's feet with tears, and

> " Wiping them with that golden hair,
> Where once the diamond shone."

Her character had indeed been subjected to a softening influence. She had been made aware of the existence of her own heart, and though she had bought this knowledge with mortification and sorrow, known only to herself, it had given her a key to the hearts of others. Conscious of her own weakness, she became lenient to the errors she had once made a subject of severe discipline. She still wielded with sovereign majesty the sceptre of command, but her authority was tempered with kindness. Her personal habits were not essentially changed, for they had become as it were the drapery of her soul. She waved her head with the same imperial motion, though the curls lav

furled up like banners after a day of battle. She made
long harangues, but there was more wheat and less chaff,
more gold and less dross in the sentiments she uttered. A
South wind seemed to have passed over her spirit, and
winnowed it of its roughest and most repellant particles.

"We must call and see our excellent friend, Doctor
Hale," said Eoline, "I never, never shall forget his kindness."

The doctor seemed delighted to greet the young enigma,
and welcomed her with heart-cheering warmth.

"So, you did not marry my handsome patient, after all,"
said he, in a lowered voice, while Horace was conversing
with Mrs. Hale, at the opposite side of the room. "If
you did not *stoop to conquer*, you fled to be overtaken, it
seems. Well, I think you have made the nobler choice.
I like this young man. All are not men who wear the
form of man. He is one of God's own making. Young
lady, you deserve to be happy, and God grant you may
long enjoy the reward of your virtues, and may it prove
the crown of your rejoicing."

Eoline had always admired and esteemed Doctor Hale,
now she quite adored him for his praises of Horace.

She had consented to remain till after the first of May,
that she might participate in the holiday pleasures which
Miss Manly spontaneously granted, who, even graciously
consented to share them herself, and had an elegant colla-
tion prepared and spread out on the green, under the magnolia's shade, in honor of her guests.

It would be difficult to describe Eoline's feelings, when
she sat once more under those odoriferous boughs, by the
side of Horace Cleveland. Again the hoarse murmurs of
the mill-dam roared with a deep, droning sound in her ears,
and the blue waters twinkled as brightly, and tossed up
their white foam as sportively as when the mellifluous
voice of St. Leon was borne across the stream. She

thought of all the events of the past year, and lifted up her soul in gratitude to Heaven for her present felicity. There was a voice dearer than St. Leon's now breathing in her ear. There was an arm stronger, ready to enfold her, should the stormy winds and beating rains of life dash coldly against her bosom. There was a heart firmer and truer, all her own, on which she could lean for support, secure of its allegiance, though the pillars of the universe were shaken.

While she sat folded in the mantle of dreamy thought, a chaplet of flowers was cast lightly round her brow, and sweet voices, blending together, hailed her as Queen of May.

"You forget that I am married," said Eoline, laughing, "and cannot wear these floral honors now."

"Queens marry like other people," cried Bessie Bell "I am sure—look at Queen Victoria—I wonder if she is not married."

"Suffer me to transfer my diadem of flowers," said Eoline, placing it gracefully on Fanny's sun-bright curls. "I am content with the sovereignty of one kingdom."

"Why is Mr. Cleveland like a King?" asked Uncle Ben, with sudden inspiration. "Can't you guess?" (Uncle Ben was a true Yankee.) "Because a virtuous wife is a crown to her husband. And *he* has a crown of pearls and diamonds worth all the regalia of England."

This was a great speech for Uncle Ben to make, and he looked slyly at Miss Manly, as if he thought he had said something unusually smart. The children, of course began to laugh as soon as he opened his lips, but astonished by the sublimity of his closing remark, they looked exceedingly grave.

Eoline had attended many brilliant parties in honor of her marriage, but never had she enjoyed one so fully and heartily as this charming, rural festival, in the magnolia's

Eden bower. Horace, too, entered into the spirit of the
scene with a graceful gayety that surprised even Eoline,
who had never seen him surrounded by such genial influences. Love, like a warm Southern sun, shining on the
firm rich soil of his character, had prepared it for the
growth of the fairest flowers, as well as the noblest fruit.
His mind resembled one of those beautiful islands of the
tropic seas, formed of the hard and rock-like reef, rising
rugged and cold above the dashing waves of the ocean.
The winds waft the covering earth from the shore, the birds
of the air plant the germs of fertility and beauty, green-
ness and bloom clothe its surface, till Nature rejoices in
its glory, and sets it, a radiant gem, in her emerald crown.

As Uncle Ben waxed merry with his juvenile companions, he ventured to jest with his niece on the probability
of *her* being married before another May-day holiday.

Eoline was alarmed, fearing that was a chord which
could not bear touching; but her fears were groundless.

" No," said Miss Manly, while a shadow flitted momentarily over her brow, caused by the remembrance of St.
Leon—"I have chosen my vocation, and never shall aban-
don it. It has its thorns, but it has its roses, too. Let
others seek happiness in the exercise of domestic virtues,"
here she looked graciously towards Eoline, " I have entered
a broader, and I say it with modesty, a nobler, more exalted
sphere. These children," she added, with that peculiar
wave of her lofty head, which reminded one of a pine-
tree bowing in the wind—" these children are all mine
They are entrusted to my guardian care by that Great
Taskmaster to whom I must one day give an account of
my charge. To use an appropriate metaphor, I consider
myself an humble florist in the garden of my Lord, cul-
tivating for His glory these intellectual and moral flowers
which shall bloom in immortal beauty, when low in dust
shall fade the blossoms of Magnolia Vale."

Miss Manly paused, and bent her head to conceal the unwonted moisture gathering in her eye. A deep and gentle seriousness shaded the blooming countenances around her, for they felt, as she spoke, the truth of their immortal destiny. The sun which had been hidden behind a white, fleecy cloud, now rolled its silver wheel on the clear, blue ether, and a flood of light bathed the bosom of Magnolia Vale.

THE END.